Nightfall at the Billings Fair by Chad Woody.
Digital photograph. 2016.

Moon City Review
2017

Moon City Review is a publication of Moon City Press at Missouri State University and is distributed by the University of Arkansas Press. Exchange subscriptions with literary magazines are encouraged. The editors of *Moon City Review* contract First North American Serial Rights, all rights reverting to the writers upon publication. The views expressed by authors in *Moon City Review* do not necessarily reflect the opinions of its editors, Moon City Press, or Missouri State University.

All other correspondence should be sent to the appropriate editor, using the following information:

Moon City Review
Department of English
Missouri State University
901 South National Avenue
Springfield MO 65897

Submissions are considered at http://mooncitypress.com/mcr/. For more information, please consult www.mooncitypress.com.

Cover designed by Estevan Torres.
Text copyedited by Karen Craigo.

moon city press
springfield missouri

Staff

Table of Contents

Poetry

Fiction

Nonfiction

The Missouri State University Student Literary Competitions

Translation

Contributors' Notes

Travis Mossotti

Narcissus Americana

At the Olympic ceremonies in Los Angeles
they chose to reenact the national epic, westward
expansion, only due to certain staging restrictions
the covered wagons full of unflappable coeds
rolled from west to east, a trivial, barely noticed flaw.
—*Campbell McGrath,* American Noise

Look,
the waitress is new to the menu but she
smoothes things over for the watchers on Sunset,
and when our order comes up she's rehearsing
behind her eyes a scene where she plays
all the parts she'll never land—

this land
has pushed us west for too long, America,
and this boulevard which wastes into the ocean
waits for the concrete to soften and absorb
the nightmare of our self, which sees itself
in every grain,

and holy comes the Hasidic Jew
into view with his curls and wide-brimmed
black hat as he passes below a row
of queen palms muttering a cantilever
prayer to the air that was once the god
in his lungs,

made real with language,
just as the words for asparagus smothered

in peanut sauce and sprinkled with sesame seeds
are made real by the waitress who studies us
as we press them between our chopsticks
at Buddha's Belly,

                  who studies too the flesh
of the palm tree shucker gathering the pruned
fronds into his truck bed—the blue bandanna
he daubs the sweat from his neck with
looks as blue as the ocean must have looked
in the prebirth

            of this country
we find ourselves presently trapped inside,
like a wooden barrel bobbing its way
along the Niagara River, current pulling us
towards some spectacle too late to stop,
and so we brace ourselves

                    for what's to come,
imagining what praise will shower down upon us
if we somehow miraculously survive the fall.

Charles Harper Webb

Nearly Invisible Man

Bastard son of the fully Invisible Man,
he was adopted by a couple not sure they wanted
kids. They named him Nils, stockpiling food
in his crib, sure they'd forget to feed him
occasionally.

                    When teachers at Taft Elementary
failed to hear his "Here," attendance
called home, asking, "Where was Nils today?"
Until they stopped. What did they care?

In high school, he could hide in the girls'
locker room without being seen—
almost. "Look! A ghost," someone
would scream. "No—it's Creepy Nils!"
Slapped by towels that smelled of girl,
he'd make his translucent slink-away.

He failed as traffic cop, but excelled as waiter.
Diners raved, "You barely know he's there."

His wife—nearsighted, and no beauty—
married him because he had a job,
and looked like George Clooney,
for all she knew. Did they have kids?
Maybe. Somewhere.

☾

Three mourners goggle at his corpse:
lips rouged, face pancaked into clarity.
"Who is he, again?" they ask,
their pale heads flickering in no wind.

Marty Carlock

Women Traveling Alone

In the ladies room
    we almost collide
sorry sorry

in that halfsecond glance we recognize ourselves
    drably dressed
    crophaired spectacled flatshod
    towing tiny practical carryons

competent
unhurried
unafraid
    yet

a little bit unsure what
    welcome we will receive.

Andy Jameson

High Plains Drifter

In the new house, unopened boxes were everywhere, even though we'd moved in months ago. They were a minefield we navigated without thinking, tacitly understanding that many would not be unpacked. Perhaps I was resigned to it, Dad's roving. In the span of three years, we'd moved from Rock Hill, South Carolina, to Augusta, Georgia, then made a brief pit stop in Mississippi before ending up in Killeen, the dead center of Texas. Dad's explanations were becoming increasingly hard to accept. At thirteen, even I could see that the "opportunities" he was chasing were an El Dorado, and every promise of gold around the next bend was so much horseshit.

Still, Mom craved some sort of normalcy and expected us to sit down at the table and eat dinner like a family. That was her one rule—the one concession that Dad and I could make for her, just to see to her happiness.

We mumbled grace and Mom asked me about my day. I tried to say something that would show how well I was adjusting to the most recent upheaval, but the words didn't come. That day, like many others, I'd managed not to speak to a single person, except to answer "Here" when roll was called.

"He certainly hasn't inherited the gift of gab," Dad said, as if he was commenting on some hopeless relative back home.

"That's OK, Morris," Mom said. "He'll find his place. Different strokes for different folks."

Dad glared at her and jiggled his legs under the table. His drink seemed like a permanent accessory when he was home now.

Mom began to gather up our plates; she was trying not to meet Dad's now-impassive gaze.

"Making any new friends, sport?"

I hemmed and hawed, mentioned the Merritts. I would often ride the bus back home and go over to the Merritt house until dinner time, mainly because the Merritt brothers were the only kids I knew in the neighborhood. The day we'd moved in, they stood there by the curb draped over their BMX bikes, as we unloaded the U-Haul in the roiling July sun. Neither offered a hand. Later, they would come back to introduce themselves properly, carrying a chocolate pie topped with Cool Whip. Truth be told, I didn't really like them much.

"Those redneck Army brats? You can set your sights higher. Any son of mine can make friends. You just have to apply yourself."

"Look, I'll try," I said.

"That's how I got your mother, isn't it, Mae? Initially, she wouldn't deign to associate with me. But I applied myself. I had gumption and persistence."

"You wore me down," Mom said, not looking up from the sink. "Until I surrendered."

"Good. That's all I ask." It was unclear who exactly he was responding to. Dad slapped his palm flat on the table. Mom glanced up. He took a final swig and then held the glass to his eye and squinted, as if he was peering into a peephole, one that revealed another place altogether, one that was eminently more interesting than a cluttered rental furnished with a skittish woman and a boy who couldn't make a single friend.

The next day, as I waited for the busses, I noticed a girl was staring at me. Her dark eyes never left me for ten minutes. I pretended to ignore her. Finally, she moved closer and leaned her head on my backpack as if she were tired. I felt the weight and jerked back. She giggled.

"Where do you stay?" she asked slowly, uncertain of her English. Somehow, her phrasing seemed apt. I sensed that I was just staying for a little while in Texas.

"I'm going to Harker Heights," I said.

"Harker Heights," she repeated, as if it was a magical land rather than a conglomeration of neighborhoods full of seventies ranch-style houses with dying lawns. The mazelike streets of Harker Heights almost always led to a cul-de-sac; you'd turn your bike around and try to find some landmark to lead you home, which was situated at the end of another cul-de-sac.

"*Mi nombre es Dulce.*" She stretched it out, seeming to savor her own name.

Dulce told me that her family lived near downtown Killeen. I pictured one of the narrow, riotously painted houses that looked like they were about to teeter off their concrete block foundation at any moment. She didn't say much else about her family except that they had come from Mexico City and used to live in a nicer house. Clearly, in moving to Texas, they'd come down in the world, just like my family. Back in Mexico City, Dulce's old house had high outer walls and a little fountain with a courtyard. "You break bottles and lay them on top of the wall to keep the bad people out," she said solemnly. We were both refugees running from something vague and menacing.

Jay and Michael Merritt were twins, but they didn't look anything alike. Fraternal. Jay was stocky and smelled like a fart. Michael had long eyelashes, orange hair, and freckles. They were in ninth grade, the highest grade at our middle school. Jay didn't really want to have much to do with me unless it was to put me in the various holds of the professional wrestlers we admired. He would eviscerate me with Macho Man Randy Savage's Flying Elbow Drop, or choke me half to death with Sergeant Slaughter's Cobra Clutch. Then he would lose interest as I lie on the floor panting. Michael, on the other hand, tolerated me because he was a bit strange and had no other friends. Their mother had a job working for an accounting firm, and their dad was an MP out at Ft. Hood, so they were latchkey kids.

On those afternoons after school, we would roam through the house, with Michael revealing its secrets.

"See this?" He held up what looked to be a smooth black plastic stick, rounded at one end, with a rubber grip on the other. We'd been digging in a closet looking for old Atari cartridges. "What do you think it is?"

I shrugged.

"You ain't got a clue," he said, laughing.

"OK, then, go ahead and tell me."

"It's a baton."

"But what do you do with it?"

"Man, you ask too many questions. You don't know shit."

"You started it." I turned and began to walk out of the room. Michael's need to assert his superiority often rubbed me wrong.

"Hey, all right, don't go. I was just messing with you. Look, you crack skulls with it." He slapped the club in the palm of his hand. "It was my grandfather's. He invented a new kind for the police. See this hole at the end? You spray out tear gas in the face of any scumbag that's hasslin' you. Here's the button you push."

I had to admit this was pretty impressive.

"That's nothing. I'll show you something even freakier."

He swore me to secrecy, and we went into his parents' bedroom. There were clothes all over the floor and the bed was rumpled. The only thing that wasn't a mess was a uniform hanging on the door to the bathroom. It was so immaculate and stiff it looked like it could jump down and walk away by itself. I felt nervous being there, like I was looking at my own parents' room. Michael was rummaging around in the bedside table. Everything stunk of Old Spice and tangerines. Funny how distinct and awful everybody else's houses smell.

"Check this out." He had what looked like another baton in his hand, only it was shorter, metallic, and curved like a bullet at one end. "You don't know what it is so don't even pretend." He clicked a switch at the base, and it hummed.

"OK," I said, my interest piqued.

"It's a vibrator." He licked his lips in an expectant way. "I knew you'd never seen one before."

"Did your grandfather invent it, too?"

"Hell no. Jesus."

"What's it do?"

"Well, it vibrates."

"Thanks," I said.

"OK, you asshole. Women stick it between their legs. In their pussies."

"Your mom?"

"Yeah, sure." Michael shifted on the balls of his feet, suddenly embarrassed. "I mean, it's hers, right?"

"You ever watch? I mean, see her use it?"

At these questions, I seemed to have reached the limits of Michael's patience. "Fuck you." He cocked his head as though he was listening for something and quickly put the vibrator back in its drawer. "Don't be a douche."

It was not until later that Michael Merritt trusted me enough to show me his special hiding place. The cave was little more than a wormy tunnel riddling the nearby scarp above an unfinished lot. It looked like it had been inhabited by bums at some point, because there was a filthy carpet remnant on the floor along with some empty cans of Wolf Chili.

A long beam of light from an opening above shot directly into my eyes, blinding me momentarily. Michael went to a corner and came back with a dog-eared magazine. He held it with both hands underneath like an offering, like it was something sacred.

"You ever see a naked woman?"

I shook my head. The few times I'd accidentally caught my mother dressing didn't count.

The woman on the cover had blond feathered hair in the style of Farrah Fawcett. She smiled broadly. The mystifying word *Oui* floated above her head in red cursive.

"You pronounce it Ooo-ee," Michael said. "It's French. That means it's even dirtier than if it was American. They show full-on beaver shots."

I didn't know what a beaver shot was then but figured that asking any more questions would render me hopeless in Michael's eyes. The pages were slightly damp and hard to peel back without tearing. I carefully thumbed through some advertisements and an article on Formula One racing before I got to the pictures. In the first one, a brunette with smoky, mascara-rimmed eyes leaned forward against a couch. Her smooth, tan ass seemed to glow unnaturally. In several more pictures she coyly shed a gray fur coat from her shoulders and, arms akimbo, taunted me with her sharp pink nipples. Her look seemed to dare me to go further. The next page was Michael's beaver shot, I knew it without asking. She leaned back, her eyes closed dreamily. Her knees were splayed open, her feet just touching each other. Her hand moved towards the fulcrum, the hinge of it all. She opened herself for me, the red slash like a wound.

"Are you excited?" Michael said. "Is your pecker hard?"

That was where Michael's mother puts her vibrator. I tried to imagine Dulce spreading herself like that. Suddenly, I felt very guilty. It was all wrong, yet I couldn't look away.

"Wild, isn't it?" Michael said.

I didn't reply. A centipede began to wiggle near my foot, and I stepped back and used the magazine to whack it.

"Hey, man. Not cool," Michael yelled. "Respect my stuff. R-E-S-P-E-C-T."

After a few minutes, I left. All the way home, I chided myself. How foolish I was, how naive I'd been. I knew that my Dad had dozens of magazines like that in his workshop, and I'd never once thought to look inside one. My hands trembled in anticipation.

At lunch Dulce and I would go off and sit, talking on the swing set of the park that was behind the middle school. Sometimes we played like kids, flinging our bodies like pendulums on the swings, stretching our feet towards the simmering mid-afternoon sun.

"Hold my hand," she said once, and we caught hold of each other, bobbing slightly askew before we found the rhythm. "Now, jump," she said at the apex of our kick. We catapulted out. At some point I let go. We rolled, the dust coating our sweaty skin. She wiped a mustache of dirt from my lip and glanced down.

"You know you are *guapo*," she said. "*Muy guapo*."

"No," I said, but I sensed something flicker in her gaze.

"I wonder ...." She stroked my face, and pulled her hand back quickly as though she had touched an oven. "I wonder if you would ... go with me?"

"Go where?" I laughed at my dumb joke.

She looked confused, hurt. "It's not funny. You don't like me?"

"No, no, no," I said, making it worse. Dulce was starting to cry. "I mean, yes, yes, I do. I was being stupid."

"Serious?"

"Yes, I want to go with you."

After that, we began holding hands while we stood there waiting for the buses. It was all perfectly innocent. Her bus was first and she would wave at me. Her arm moved stiffly back and forth like she was one of those mechanized people in Disney World. She had an almost mournful look as she watched me from the back window.

☾

"Say something," Dad said at dinner. "Anything. You can't go through life with your head in the clouds."

I sat there, formulating a way to get him off my back. Dad continued a monologue filled with the jargon he was so fond of: You had to put yourself out there, to always be "networking," to appear "in demand" so that people respected your time and presence. As if middle school were a pulp-paper-and-assorted-paper-goods supplier convention. "You sell toilet paper," I wanted to say. "That's it."

The things that would make him the proudest were what I needed to keep secret for some reason. I *was* in demand. I had a girlfriend. She thought I was *muy guapo*. There was even another girl at school who was vying for my affection now. Her name was Angie. I had begun to notice that she was following me around, getting in my way. She draped herself in ridiculous poses across the lockers as I passed. If I played basketball at lunch, she always lurked behind the concrete slabs that hemmed in one side of the court. She'd pop her head up now and again like a Whack-A-Mole game at the arcade in the mall.

"Is any of this getting through? Just nod your head," Dad was saying.

"I've been invited to a party," I blurted out, necessity the mother of invention.

Mom brightened. "Well, that's certainly a development."

"It's not those Merritt kids again," Dad said.

"No, it's some other kid from school. He's having ...."—I searched my brain—"... a skating party." In fact, Dulce had told me that she lived a quarter of a mile from a rink.

"Sounds fun," Mom said. "I wish I had a party to go to. I wish I had *anywhere* to go."

"Excuse me." Dad pushed back from the table, his chair scraping stridently across the linoleum. "I'll be in my workshop. Don't wait up."

"Morris," she said, perhaps more sharply than she intended.

He turned back. "What?"

Mom bit her lip and began clearing the table. "Just be careful."

"I'm careful," he said quietly.

Sensing her precariousness, I helped Mom gather the dishes. One of the things we'd lost in this last move was a dishwasher. "Why do we need one," Dad joked to Mom, "when we've got you?"

"You're awfully helpful tonight. What's your angle?" Mom laughed but glanced toward the garage and got quiet. She cut her eyes down to the dishes buried in suds.

"Just doing my part." I thought about those rare times when Dad let me watch him "putter," as he called it. Usually, I just sat in a corner while he measured and sanded boards. He made marks on them with a grease pencil he kept behind his ear but didn't offer to show me what he was doing. He talked about his projects in the abstract, never seeming to actually make anything. Maybe a bookshelf sometimes, but we had no books to put on them. Just those stacks of *Playboy* and *Penthouse*. They were out there in the garage, spines upright and jammed together so tight you couldn't hardly tell what they were. Ever since the cave, I was just biding my time.

"Go on and watch your wrestling," Mom said.

Normally, I wouldn't have thought twice. I would have happily gone off to watch the Junkyard Dog and Nikita Koloff battle it out in a cage match, but I stood there, rooted in the middle of the harvest-orange linoleum floor.

The saw's whine spilled out of the garage. Mom looked intently into the suds; her hands were underneath, doing their secret absolutions. We seemed to be waiting for the same thing.

"It's OK," she said. I couldn't tell if she was talking to me or herself.

The saw went silent, the whir dying slowly. She looked up and we both heard it then, the press of tires rolling down the driveway. The engine of our Suburu coughed the way it always did and then finally revved. Gears ground into first.

"Oh," Mom said, the spell broken. We pretended we hadn't heard anything. I clicked on the TV; she finished drying the dishes.

In the morning, I went to the bathroom and found Dad asleep on the toilet, his pants around his ankles. A gaminess clung to his rumpled suit; he had a cut on his cheek, a runnel of red. Crimson droplets dotted the floor, the sink. I turned and left him there, not bothering to wake him.

When I came home that afternoon, the boxes were all gone. There were no traces of blood in the bathroom. At dinner, Mom beamed at us. "I think we are beginning to get settled in here nicely, don't you think?"

☾

On Friday morning of that week, Mom gave me a ten-dollar bill for the non-existent party. "Your father can swing by and get you on his way home from work." We had only one car now, having sold Mom's temperamental Volkswagen Bug a few moves ago. Another loss, like the dishwasher.

At school, I told Dulce of my plan. "This way we can spend some time together. Alone."

She looked at me, bothered by something. "But why did you lie?"

"It's not a lie," I said. "Just not exactly the whole truth."

"Oh. OK."

I could tell, however, that she was not satisfied with my response. "You like me, right? You want to hang out with me?"

"Sure." She still looked uneasy, as though she was noticing something for the first time. However, that afternoon on the bus, she had forgotten about her concerns. She was so happy not to be leaving me behind for once.

Inside the entrance to the skating rink, we stopped in front of a long glass tank of tropical fish. The syncopated baseline of Queen's "Another One Bites the Dust" rolled towards us like a wave. "Look." Dulce pointed to a delicate-looking fish, dark as ink, with fins jutting everywhere like branches from a tree. "That's crazy."

An Asian man was cleaning the tank. When he saw us, he bowed his head and smiled. Then he began to feed the fish. He took pinches from a jar and sprinkled the shiny flakes into the incandescent tank. I watched the flakes drift about, rising on miniature currents and waves, as the fish bobbed up for a bite and then darted back to the depths of the tank. After a few minutes, the fish seemed pacified, swimming in drunken loops. They were unaware that they were trapped. "Must be careful," the man said, as though talking to himself. "They die. Expensive."

When Dad showed up, he was in one of his moods. He leaned on the horn and drummed his fingers on the wheel.

"You have to go," Dulce said. Halfway to the car, I turned to see her watching me. Her eyes flickered darkly before her expression went blank, and she turned away to walk home. Once, while we were skating, I'd cupped her ass. For a moment, she seemed hurt and confused before pushing my hand away. Later, though, we kissed, nestled in a corner between bleeping and flashing games. She leaned her soft head on my chest afterward.

"Who's that?" Dad said.

"A girl I know."

"A wetback, huh? Well, at least she's pretty."

I knew he was just trying to get a rise but I took the bait anyway. "She's not a wetback. Her name's Dulce."

"I like that. Exotic. Whatever floats your boat, sport."

I stood beside the open car door, as though I could choose not to get in.

"Quit the lollygagging. We got somewhere to go."

"We're not going home for dinner?"

"In a little while. I've got to see someone real quick. It won't be but a second." As soon as I shut the door, Dad began zipping through a warren of back streets. Clearly, he knew where he was going.

"You're the boss." I settled back in my seat.

"You're damn right! Remember that."

A few minutes later, we pulled into the parking lot of the Ideal Motel. A neon sign flickered and popped like a bug zapper. "Just sit tight," Dad said, "and lock the doors. This isn't the best neighborhood."

For a moment, he paused to smooth back his thick wave of ash-blond hair and carefully situate a brand-new black Stetson on his head. I'd never seen him wear a hat before. He was always complaining about the oversized belt buckles men anchored their Levi's with around here, the tacky embroidered shirts they wore.

Dad began to walk down the row of rooms. They all had a full-length window to the right of the door. He stopped, glanced back at me, and knocked on number twenty-four. Someone pulled back the curtain, and I saw a cascade of frizzy hair. The door cracked. Dad put the tip of his finger on the brim of his hat. It was the type of gallant gesture I'd never seen from him before. Suddenly, I realized that he inhabited different roles when he wasn't with us, that he was always selling some other version of himself.

Dad's shit-eating grin wilted fast. A few times he motioned my way and threw his arm up. Finally, the corners of his mouth curled into a scowl that was familiar. I rolled down the window a few inches, trying to catch part of the argument. I couldn't really hear anything because Dad was talking low and the woman's voice was muffled behind the door. Finally, the woman yelled, "Mother*fucker*," and shut the door. Dad was left cradling the Stetson in his hand like a rejected gift he didn't know what to do with now. After a minute, he craned his neck and decorously put the Stetson back on.

"You can't win them all," he said when he got back to the car. We drove home for supper without another word.

A few days later, Dad showed up with the hood of the Subaru covered in spray paint. "Just some punks," he said as we all stood in the driveway and scrutinized the shaky letters MF as though they were hieroglyphics in need of a Rosetta stone.

"Maybe it's someone's initials?" Mom wondered.

Dad watched me uneasily.

"Forget about it, Mom," I said.

A few weeks later, Dad took me to see a matinee of an old spaghetti Western, *High Plains Drifter*. "You want to know how to be tough?" he said. "Well, you are about to see a real man." He bought us a big carton of popcorn and even a Coke just for me. I wondered why he was being so nice; it made me nervous. Maybe he was buying me off for not saying anything about the woman.

But the movie started, and I knew that this was a transcendent experience for him. The popcorn and the drinks were just offerings to the god on the screen. I could see by the look on his face. How he watched the lone man riding at the beginning. Listened rapt to the heavy, animal breathing and clop of hooves. I felt I could almost hear Dad's heart beating too. He could imagine the power of the horse under him as the stranger rode into the desolate town of Lago. And, later, when it all went to shit, and the gunslinger had to do what was necessary, Dad was savoring the stench of cordite as Clint walked through a cloud of smoke.

"Now there's a man," Dad said on the way home. "You saw that, didn't you? You had to feel it. You saw how he handled himself. Didn't take no crap. Just cool as a cucumber." I'd never seen him so genuinely enthusiastic. "But I guess you can't be a drifter anymore, no, sir." He had a far-off look as though he was still out there, the horizon beckoning. "You can't have that kind of freedom. And the thing is— we let it happen."

I was confused, but I kept quiet. I sensed he was trying to impart some lesson that I was only just starting to comprehend.

"They want our soul; they want our balls to display up on a shelf like a trophy and we just offer them up. Never give them the satisfaction."

☾

After playing her games for so long, the other girl, Angie, finally spoke to me. "Hey!" she said, jumping out from around a corner as if she was waiting to ambush me.

I stepped back, surprised.

"Didn't mean to scare you. It's just you're always walking so fast. And your head is down, and you've got this cute line in your brow like you are thinking so hard. So I had to get your attention." She said it all in a rush, every word given equal emphasis.

"I guess I do walk fast," I said.

She seemed more relaxed and intimate now, like we'd been talking every day of the semester, sharing secrets. "You like that Mexican girl, dontcha? I mean, that's like a serious thing? You went to the roller rink and all."

"Wait. How do you know that?"

"Girls talk." Angie flipped her hair, studied her nails, and tried to act blasé.

"Well."

"It's too bad, you know." She pouted; her lip gloss was the color of bubblegum.

"What?"

"If it's really a serious thing."

"I have to go." Something, though, seemed to hold me there a moment or two longer.

"Why don't you like me?" she said. Her mouth was quivering, which suddenly excited me.

It became crystal clear. I saw what I could do. I patted my hips. "Tomorrow. Let's go somewhere by ourselves. Maybe we can talk."

"OK." She hurried away, barely restraining herself from running.

At the buses, Dulce was waiting for me with a sour expression. "Who was that girl you were talking to?"

"Whoa," I said. "What are you, spying on me?"

"It's public." She seemed more exasperated then, perhaps a touch of fear softening the set of her mouth.

"She's just some girl. She's silly."

"*Tonta y fea,*" Dulce said under her breath.

☾

After lunch the next day, I led Angie to an unused stairwell in the back of the school. She kissed like she was well practiced, her tongue flicking into my mouth.

"So you like me *now*."

I fumbled with her jean buttons. "Of course I like you."

"It didn't seem like it before."

"I was just being stupid."

She put her hand protectively over her white panties. "But what about that other girl? The Mexican."

I pulled her hand away and traced the soft trail of fuzz that led to the place I couldn't get out of my head since that day at the cave. I'd learned so much more from my Dad's magazines since. "It doesn't matter. We're here now."

"I've never done anything like this." She giggled nervously, but her body seemed to bely her innocent act.

"I've got something to show you," I said, reaching inside my book bag. I pulled out Michael Merritt's grandfather's baton. I figured Michael wouldn't miss it. He might even appreciate what I had planned for it.

"What are you gonna do with that?" For the first time, she looked doubtful, uncomfortable.

"It's OK. You'll like it." I pushed the baton past the lip of her panties, and gently parted her legs. "Lots of women do."

"You love me, right?" she blurted. "Tell me you love me."

"OK," I said. "I love you."

She whimpered quietly; I pressed my advantage.

When the janitor found us, Angie's panties hung like a lasso around her ankle. She looked like a cornered animal, gazing wildly for a way out. I began making curlicues on the wall with the baton and whistled a tune from *High Plains Drifter*.

"Jesus Christ, what's wrong with you kids!" the janitor said.

My mother was disconsolate. She cried as I sat there silent on the couch after being sent home from school early and suspended for the week. There was talk of expulsion, but that never happened. My father appraised me, a glint of what might have been pride flickering in the corner of his gray eyes. "This is your fault, Morris," Mom screamed. I'd never heard her raise her voice to him before. At the end of the year we'd be back in South Carolina living with my grandparents. "You turn everything you touch to shit."

Dad regarded her coolly. "At least now we know he's not a pansy."

Dulce's heart was broken, too. "Why would you do that with her?" she wailed. "*Incredible.* That ugly, ugly *puta.*"

I shrugged. I didn't really have an answer. "Because she let me."

"Do you think I'm going to do that with you now? Do you think I should let you stick things inside me?"

"Maybe you should."

"You think I'm like her, a slut?" Dulce's luminous eyes were full of fury. I had disabused her about the purity of our love. She couldn't compete with Angie's wet tongue, her docile need.

Sometimes, in the afternoons after school, I'd watch Dulce stare out at me from the back of the bus as she moved away. In that harsh Texas light, her face became an exquisite palimpsest of hatred and desire. She was trapped in a terrible world. But now she knew it.

Michael Meyerhofer

Adjunct

All my friends are buying houses
and rings that won't lime your fingers,

sometimes making the tough choice
between Italy and Amsterdam,

swapping war stories of committees
and escalating taxes and all

I have to share is my concern
that the sink will go dry

before I can rinse off the shaving cream,
and all I know is that their houses

grew from wood that grew over
the graves of prehistoric birds and gold

comes exclusively from the hearts
of supernovas—which makes them

smile since everybody loves
to hear what they already know.

Michael Meyerhofer

The Dying Breed

I donned a dark blue tank top on my way
to the Trump protest because nothing
shuts down a loudmouth bigot like nineteen-
inch arms, but before I could
cross over to the left side of the street,
a gliding fellow in eyeliner called me
a Neanderthal, then this potbellied guy
in a trucker hat asked if I meant to
knock that first guy on his ass and if so
I'd better wear gloves because of the AIDS,
then Trucker Hat looked confused
when I went to stand with the throng
of rail-thin college kids peppered
with black drag queens and the whole
time Eyeliner Guy kept looking over at me
like I was some kind of Manchurian protester,
and even amidst all that noise and naked
Germanic rage, I just kept thinking
about how the TV told me that Neanderthals
invented flutes from the bones
of dead songbirds then died
out so that homo sapiens had to
invent flutes all over again, bamboo
piccolos sailing westward from Byzantium,
migrating from the woods of nameless hunters
to the concert halls of Italy and France,
no longer bone-carved but steel,
capable of bending one shrill breath
into more notes than some can hear,
let alone have the good sense to applaud.

Sarah Broderick

Greetings From the New River Gorge

Because my family lived in the middle of nowhere until I was twelve years old, we drove everywhere. No matter where we needed to go—the post office, a convenience store, a grandparent's house—we had to plan on it taking no less than twenty-five minutes. This meant that my younger sister, Tessa, and I had to find ways to entertain each other every time we hopped in the car.

My sister would barricade herself with puzzle books, favorite stuffed animals, and colored pencils, and I would either read or stare out the window. I would daydream. While at times elaborate, these dreams were often quite simple. I would imagine myself running on the telephone wires beside the car, bolting at great speeds, leaping vast distances, somersaulting, twirling, and pirouetting. Occasionally, this version of myself would smile and wave at the real me down below. Sometimes the real me would have the urge to wave back.

I remember lifting my head from the frayed nylon sling of my seatbelt during one drive on a rare warm day in late October. I was eleven and we were on a family outing. The hills and bends of the road were opening up to an expanse of sky that I'd never seen before.

Having heard about a pick-your-own apple orchard with a petting zoo, my parents had decided to take us on a day trip east to Greenbrier County. This trip was a big deal to my sister and me. They had managed to let the summer pass by without a family vacation or, perhaps, some plan or another had fallen through. Most things did back then due to one constraint or another.

Around this time, my parents stopped touching. When they did accidentally bump one another during a maneuver around the kitchen sink or graze the other's hand when passing the butter, they looked startled and annoyed, helpless.

I had been staring at the backs of their heads, father's brown and curly with tangled neck hairs that needed a trim, mother's blonde and helmeted, bowed over the work in her lap. Then, the branches lifted, and we were crossing a bridge.

The bridge was long and lean and arched across a wooded valley. Red, orange, and yellow trees dappled the brown hillsides. And between large, looming boulders, whitewater rafts and kayaks ducked the speeding, churning current of a river. When we were halfway across, an airplane—a small, four-passenger Cessna—hummed over the far hill's crest, nearly brushing the tops of the trees as it streaked down toward the rapids. The scene reminded me of a postcard, the type my grandparents received from their old, retired friends, and I wondered if this was the most memorable place I had ever been.

"Look at that," my father said from behind the wheel.

I hit Tessa in the arm with my book and pointed.

She stretched in her seatbelt, resting her chin on my shoulder and rubbing the sleep out of her eyes to get a better look over the bridge railing. "Wow," she said.

My father slowed down, allowing the traffic to swerve around us and take the second lane. At the base of the gorge's "V," the small, white plane lifted and doubled back. "Now that's what I call a Sunday drive," he said.

We giggled.

"Shh," my mother said. Because of a highlighter pinned at the corner of her mouth, a bright yellow cigar sitting between her teeth, the sound came out harsh and windy like the whoosh and burn of an ignited pilot light. The highlighter was out whenever she was reading articles, doing her homework, which she did a lot of in those days. She would sometimes forget that it was there and be reminded only after drooling on herself.

"You should take a look at this," he said.

The plane shot over us and veered hard to the left, seeming to balance on one wing, before disappearing behind a rock face. I kept my eye on where it had been. Its soft whirring echoed down the valley through our cracked windows, and I could see myself swooping and soaring high above the ground, hugging the banks of the hills along the thread of the river. I had never been on a plane. To actually fly like a bird, to pass through a cloud, to defy gravity and your own weight, seemed fantastic, magical, even.

Not until we were completely off the bridge did my father allow the car to gain speed again. My mother turned a page and kept reading.

"I used to jump from those things. Man, fifty pounds strapped to my back, and sayonara, baby. See you later."

"You jumped? From planes like that?" Tessa settled her head back down on my shoulder and watched the window for additional flying objects.

"Sure. Choppers, mostly. Sometimes they'd fly us over a jungle, dump our asses …."

My mother scraped the highlighter along the page as if it were sandpaper.

"And it would be black as pitch out, wouldn't know where the hell we were. They didn't care. They'd test us on towers first, line up and leap, to see who was scared shitless and who wasn't."

"Dave," she said. She shuffled the papers in her lap and hovered over them more intently, her short hair falling to the sides of her face like blinders. He paused momentarily, pointed out a historical marker on the edge of the road, and then turned on the radio. My mother had met my father, married him, and never finished her college degree. She had received some scholarship or another, but that hadn't mattered to her then. After they'd had us and he was laid off, she'd enrolled at a branch of the state university and continued to work two part-time jobs—the first managing a Laundromat and the other selling fancy lighters, lighters that could be engraved or made of bone with bird dogs on them, to stores and bars across the county.

We weren't the type of people who had or could afford babysitters, so my sister and I would sit in the hall outside the door to her classes—music, English, and social work—and keep ourselves occupied. If we behaved, were really quiet, my mother would reward us with a trip to the student union pub for slices of pizza. "Go ahead, whatever one you want," she would say. And we would lean up toward the glass in front of the pie trays, the smell of warm dough and tapped beer rising around us, the laughing, smiling students swinging through the doors behind, and decide. Tessa always picked cheese, and I would test out how many toppings, what odd combinations, but no matter what I chose, she never said no. Then, we would pick a table in the front, away from the slouchy groups of young men playing pool, and grin over every bite. We were not supposed to tell my father about these treats. And we didn't for fear that they would be taken away, would disappear altogether.

She yanked the highlighter from her mouth and capped it with the blunt part of her hand. "I'm done," she said. She pushed the mound of articles onto the floor.

He punched an index finger onto a button on the dash. "Good." The radio cycled through the stations until it settled on a soft, bluesy twang. His nail tapped the steering wheel along with the tune. "About that time?" he said privately, to her.

"I don't care," she said.

He ran his fingers through his hair and looked into the rear view mirror, meeting my gaze. "Who's hungry?"

"Me!" Tessa said.

I nodded.

He nodded back and smiled, creasing the corners of his eyes. "All right, then. Your mother and I will start looking for a place to stop."

Still leaning against my shoulder, Tessa poked me in the stomach. "You're always hungry." She giggled and pinched the roll that hung over my seat belt.

"Get off me," I said, pushing her away.

Several miles down the road, a county lane broke off from the highway and meandered through the trees to a rest stop visitor's center, which was little more than a barren field adjacent to the cliff side. Rickety tables, two or three leaning charcoal beds, and a swing set finished off the effect, and a nature trail wound its way through a couple acres of trees to a lookout point and then back. Other families were already there, eating their lunches, staring at a green forest map along the outside of the rest building, or lining up at the portable toilet, and a group of motorcycle riders had set up a tent to sell pulled-pork plates and sweet potato fries.

We parked at the edge of the lot and climbed out.

Over at the tent, a woman handed off three icy cans of Coca-Cola to her daughter and hoisted two heaping plates. The daughter skipped in front of her, two ponytails sprouting off the sides of her head, swinging in time.

"Tessa wants a sandwich," I said.

"No, I don't." She pushed into my side, barely budging me. "Fatty."

My father hefted the cooler and closed the hatch. He hooked the bungee cord back under the rear fender to keep it shut. "You both know we have enough in here for two families."

My mother was already spreading a red-checked, vinyl tablecloth across a picnic table in the far corner of the field.

He headed toward her. "How about behaving yourselves?"

I watched Tessa's bony arms, two sharp angles stiffly moving back and forth with little fists at the ends. She stomped in the gravel, pretending she was madder than she was, and I went up behind. One of her ratty, untied shoelaces tapped against the parking lot, trailing and then twirling around to the front of her toe, and I slammed my foot down on it. Her knee locked, and she crunched onto the rocks, catching herself before landing on her face.

Without a yowl of pain or a flood of tears, Tessa got up and brushed herself off. A few flecks of gravel were embedded into her right elbow and the meat of her hands. She flicked a particularly large chunk from her arm and spit to wipe the blood away. "You're mean," she said.

"So are you."

She shrugged and returned to picking at the pebbles in her skin.

Her jeans, a hand-me-down pair of mine, were dirtier than they'd been, and a small, worn-out hole at the knee had ripped to the size of a gaping mouth. Like her pants, her shirt was too big, the neck angling off her collarbone and her shoulder. She kneeled to tie her shoe. The hair at the back of her head was a tangled nest of knots. It was possible nobody had brushed it for a few days. I reached out to help her, but she shirked away. I watched as she ran toward our parents, settling in on my mother's side of the bench.

As I rounded the table, Tessa hid her hands underneath the wooden lip and stayed quiet, concentrating on picking out the little pieces of dirt as our mother laid out forks and paper plates. A smudgy blot lay across one cheek where Tessa had rubbed her face.

"Slow as mole-asses," my father said as I sat down. He was standing over the grill, careful to make sure all the ash from his Camel landed inside. Just as he took another deep drag, the purring of an engine rose from the direction we'd come.

I lifted myself up partially from my seat to get a better look. The same little, white Cessna glided along the ridge and circled. It seemed to hover without effort, taking the air current up under its wings like some large, elegant bird of prey, a red-tailed hawk or an eagle.

My father formed his mouth into an "O" and produced several smoke rings in succession, three shadowy hoops, as if he were trying to snare the plane or at least give it some obstacles to work with. The rings floated and morphed, finally breaking into wisps as the plane streaked behind. The engine's drone faded and dropped off behind a line of trees.

"I bet there's an airport over there. Right over that hill." He snubbed the butt of his cigarette out and sat down beside me. "One of those small, private-type ones."

My mother settled a lumpy, white mound, a sandwich made of leftover meatloaf, white bread, ketchup, and cheese onto his plate.

"I bet if we took that lane the rest of the way, that's what we'd find." My father often did this—gambled over the random possibility of adventure. He would take roads with grass poking up through tire tracks or that were all mud and ruts just to see where they would end. Sometimes they would lead to the entrance of some grizzled, wild-man's private property, but, generally, they turned out to be well-traveled cow paths, blocked off logging roads, and roads to nothing at all.

My mother handed me my sandwich. She watched as my father unfolded the wax paper from his and bit off a hunk and chewed.

"What?" he said, his mouth full.

"Eat," she said to both of us.

I started to unwrap mine. My sandwich had been squished against the inside of the cooler, upturning one half and leaving the other submerged in melting ice. I pressed the bread back down against the grayish meat and tried to flick off the damp, gooey paste stuck to my fingers. The people in front of us, the mom and little girl from the tent and the girl's dad or whoever he was, were almost done with theirs. After they bit into their sandwiches, you could hear the crunchy bits of sourdough crust specking their plates, and the little girl had a happy clown mouth of barbecue sauce around her lips. The girl threw a sweet potato fry to the ground, trying to lure a squirrel out from under a neighboring table.

"Stop staring at those people," my mother said. I bit and swallowed, the cold lump gradually working its way down my throat and into my stomach.

"I already told them no," my father said.

I took another bite. When I finally had the nerve to look up, she was turning her head back around from the direction where the other family sat. She glanced down toward Tessa, who was swinging her legs and humming to herself. "It's a special day, isn't it? You've been good girls." She nodded, more to herself than anyone in particular, and grabbed for the purse at her side. "They can't be too much." She unzipped her wallet.

My father settled his sandwich onto his plate and sucked the stubborn bits from between his front teeth.

"We could share," I said, a little too enthusiastically.

As he angled his head down toward me, I immediately regretted speaking up. "No, I said." He rapped the pine boards of the table with his fist.

"Why?" my mother said.

"Because."

My mother slammed her wallet back into her purse. A few loose coins flew out and landed in the grass. Closing her eyes, she drew in one long, deep breath and let it out.

Tessa had stopped humming and stared at her plate.

"We're fine, Daddy. We don't need anything else," I said.

My father pushed himself up, almost knocking over our bench, and strode off toward the parking lot. My mother opened her eyes and glanced around the picnic area, but nobody was looking or, if they noticed, cared. The three of us finished in silence as he stood and smoked by the car.

We weren't back on the road long before my father smashed his heel onto the brake and whipped the car around. "I'm going to prove you wrong," he said. "Girls, get ready, we're going on an airplane ride."

"I thought we were going apple-picking," she said.

"We are, eventually," he said.

Then she hit him, right in the back of the skull. "What's wrong with you?" she shouted. "Get me out of here. Get me out!" She rattled the door handle as if she were locked inside and wanted to jump. "You're crazy! You're crazy. You're driving me crazy."

I can still see his face, the way it sunk into itself and darkened, and hers, open and red. Tessa wouldn't look at me. Any other time, he would have screamed right back, leapt out of the car, kicked his boot into the hillside, and ripped up a handful of brown leaves and twigs, scattering them to the ditch along with grunts and curses, flailing his hands until he'd worn himself out.

"But, we're a family," he said.

I remember the sky was very, very blue at that point of the day as if a special color of crayon had melted and spread over its whole surface, the kind of sky that's almost tangible in its extreme, one where you're sure all you have to do is reach out and pull yourself into it. I counted the clouds between the blueness, at least a dozen, as he quietly let go.

She turned her body away from him and leaned against the door. "I'm sorry," she said.

He wiped his face and continued down the highway, lone pieces of gravel plinking within the wheel wells and clunking beneath our feet.

Sam Killmeyer

Postcard to Riley, Kansas, March 22, 1910

Woman in pink leans forward,
     the cheap lithograph print
               offset so the color for lips
    streaks below her nose in a crimson mustache.
The couple beside her bends towards center
     trying to become one creature.
         Something will not have it—
    the moment caught before his lips
press hers. Morning.

Maybe it is afternoon. Light
     is flowing into their tableau. Three
         figures pinched between my fingers,
    discarded among a pile of consignment shop
monochrome photographs. The light
     on their faces has not changed, he still holds
         her gently as he can, she reclines
    back into his body. They are tender,
afraid, arching necks frozen
    in a graceful symmetry
        while the girl in pink stares, unblinking.
    The details are comic now—
frilled collar, too blue suit, saccharine inscription
I want a little loving—

☾

cut off by the broken corner.
The script, *dear friend,*
not unlike the forked, cramped letters
I scratch onto postcards bought
for quarters in garish gift shops,
Hawaiian shirt stamps pushed into the corner.
Here,

her penciled scrawl across wrinkled folds,
Did you have a good time Sunday night
buggy riding? Something said
at a stopover, some bliss had prompted it,
Yes, I am all in. The ride had moved her,
and yet the writer went on, as
we all will, including even
the woman in pink,
You wish, will, must—
graphite on her thumbs, dark
green one-cent stamp,
close, hoping to hear.

Sayuri Ayers

Love Fossil

Our bodies slip into sediment each night,
        hands enfolded like crinoid palms.
    I wait for sleep. All around us darkness
             presses down. Granite teeth
grind against your broad shoulders,
     my breasts. I wonder
   how the last dinosaurs felt, seeing the sun
         blacken above
       volcano's incendiary wheeze.
      As a child, I would trace trilobites scurrying down
quarry's edge—millennia rumbling between
           my fingers, their harried spines.
While you dream, I ease my hands over
     your body, arched brontosaur bone.
   The interchange of my memories to you—
        like flesh to stone.

Daniel Paul

The Difficulties of Loving in Phase Space

There's too much space between us, she says.

I look at the tiny studio apartment that I have just walked into. Our toothbrushes share a mug, and we share an agreement to never discuss the likelihood that we've accidently used the other's brush. I struggle to imagine what *less* space between us would look like.

She presses her palm against mine as if we are separated by prison glass. Do you have any idea how much space is in between us, even when we touch? she says. We delude ourselves into thinking that a surface is smooth. But under a microscope, the plane of your hand is as chaotic as the peaks of a mountain. So, even when we are touching, only a fraction of our skin is really in contact. What feels like closeness is really just a simplistic abstraction that physics students use to make themselves feel better about the real-world futility of their calculations.

I start to say, *Baby, if it is just a theoretical abstraction, then it's the* best *theoretical abstraction I've ever known,* but—as has been the case for much of the past week since she started applying chaos theory to our relationship—I am fairly confused and don't want to make it worse. All I can do is wrap my arms around her, straining to maximize our shared surface area.

Baby, I say, don't we live in a probabilistic universe? Don't we accept abstractions all the time? Can't this be one of those times?

How can an arbitrary assertion of linearity be good enough for you? she shrieks, pushing away from me. I thought you loved me! Or was that all just theoretical, too?

When she first started reading about chaos theory, it was sexy and it was gorgeous. She came home one day, her hair a matted quilt of fractals, and told me that she'd been reading a textbook, and now she wanted to map our sex life in phase space. I didn't understand the math—something about simultaneously graphing the same non-linear equation with different orders of magnitude in order to find patterns—partly because I never got past trig, partly because it is hard to focus on math when a beautiful young woman is scattering her clothes across the apartment, moving towards you. But the idea she had was to try every sexual position we could think of, as erratically and urgently as possible, and see what patterns emerged.

I am nothing if not an advocate of scientific method.

Afterwards, we lay in bed; she pointed out the patterns in her cigarette smoke. She prattled on about chaos theory, and I listened, awed by her beautiful mania. She was so excited about patterns found in the history of cotton prices that it occurred to me she must have been the sort of child who had been content to play with empty boxes for hours on end, and that perhaps our life—which often seemed so unremarkable to me—was another such box.

Equilibrium, she said—smiling, almost unable to get the words out through her giggles—Equilibrium is a fucking joke! Did you know that the only climate model for Earth that would ever reach equilibrium would be a frozen planet? Everything else is flux. Ice or flux.

One night, all we did was touch each other's knees. She said that she wanted to see if our relationship was *scalable*. She said that chaos theoreticians looked at mountains and found that the same patterns and shapes existed at any level of magnification. Ridges and peaks. A whirlpool works the same in a bath tub as it does in the ocean. So if our relationship worked at all, it would work on the level of our knees.

She touched and kissed my knee so deliberately that I forgot for the moment that she had used the word *if.*

It has been a few days since our fight. I come home, terrified to see her in bed, sobbing, holding her knees to her chest—the very knees that I know every millimeter of now. And though I know it is the wrong thing to say—because it is selfish, and because the answer is both yes and no—I cannot help but ask her if she is sad because of something *I* have done.

Shaking her head, irritated, she uses the back of one hand to wipe the water from her eyes in a jagged swipe. Men, she says. You're so … *Newtonian!* You think every effect has a specific cause, and that the cause is determinable and traceable! You think that tears or sadness constitute an aberration from the system rather than demonstrate the instability that is *characteristic* of the system! You think that weather moves from stable to unstable and that's what sunny and rainy days are?

She takes a deep breath and continues, no longer the scorned lover, now the exasperated teacher. If it was something you did, then the initial conditions of our relationship would always have been capable of producing your action. The question isn't what *caused* the system to become turbulent; the question is, is our relationship the kind that collapses under the stress of turbulence (like weather) or the kind that adapts to turbulence and comes to rely on it as an agent of regulation and stability?

I do not know where to begin answering this question. Only that language and theory are tearing us apart and that I am willing to be an anti-intellectual if I can do so from the comfort of her arms. Although I am still wearing my coat, I get into bed next to her. I hold her tightly, with as little space between us as possible.

But I fear I am too late. Her brow is warm against my palm, but her eyes—still red but no longer angry—tell me that she has already settled into the cold equilibrium of loneliness.

L.W. Nicholson

Persimmons on Planet Earth

My mother pointed to the great, luminescent molar, stark against the black mouth of night, crooning, Oh, Ruby. Just look at it. Isn't it beautiful? That's Earth. I lived there once, but it was a long time ago.

Earth did look lovely: so much cleaner than the moon. The Moon was dull-green dust mixed with copper-penny rain, but Earth was pure as new milk.

I wanted to put a label on it, keep it in the fridge.

I cried when my mother said I couldn't.

She warbled in her singsong voice: rubyruby. Kid, you got it bad. The moon is cold and lonely, baby girl. The moon swallows you red and turns you to ash. As soon as I can, as soon as my arms reach high and my legs stretch lean, I'm going to lift myself up off this old moon and touch the white Earth again. Wouldn't it be nice to touch Earth, Ruby?

Yes, I said. It would be nice. I'd dip my fingers into it like cold ice cream and leave a dent like a chicken-pox scar.

I wanted to swallow the Earth.

My mother made me taste everything. She filled my arms with piles of persimmons from the woods, orange as Halloween candy. We took large bites till our mouths puckered and withered, full of piss and vinegar, but we kept on.

We had nothing else to eat.

I wondered that night what it would be like to die, and I knew then death felt like shriveling and turning inside out, like eating a persimmon before it was ripe.

We ate oyster and elk-horn mushrooms and tiny wild garlic custards. We poured hot pickled gooseberries over cold fish and spooned it all into our mouths, balancing ourselves in the middle of the merry-go-'round at the town park. We walked to the edge of the creek, plucked pawpaws until our faces and hands were sticky and shining, wrapping us in new skin.

Everything we ate was goodgoodgood and our days were yellow and pink, but the dirt stuck to the back of my throat after each gulp and the yard was littered with plastic bottles and fish scales delicate as February snow. I wanted what Earth had to offer, its cool, cratered silence. I wanted the soft, white bread slices. I wanted to swim in water as clear as window glass.

When I was eleven, I traded a flamingo rubber stamp and a marble for a pack of surfer stickers. On the back of the toilet, I found my mother's denture box, covered it in surfers catching waves and totally tubular phrases. She was angry enough to kill and clean three chickens with her bare hands before hanging them on the laundry line in front of the house, their feathers sopping and pathetically clumped, their naked bodies the closest thing to porn I'd seen.

I don't have any blue marbles, the boy had said. He held it up in front of one eye, closed the other. It looks just like the Earth, he exclaimed before pocketing it, exploding across the yard in a fury of shouts and dirty elbows.

When I asked her why she switched it all up, why she mixed the names, my mother told me, Rubyruby, I made you love Earth and you're already there. I did you a favor, daffodil. Now you love what you can have instead of what you can't.

You told me you lived there once, I said, pointing to old Earth/ new moon. You said we could touch it.

I did. I did, she choked. Sometimes I still think I'm there, little girl. But you can't come.

I would be so sad if you met me here.

Tara Isabel Zambrano

20 mph

It is another Minnesota morning warmed by Chinook winds, 7:40 a.m. time to drop you to school. Just another day when the sky leaks daylight but the forecast says rain. I brace myself for the "not again" when I answer the phone. A DISH Network representative asks to renew your dead dad's subscription. *He's unable to come to the phone right now,* I say, my fingers spread out on his absence, a left-behind weight.

Eventually, I get dressed, a ghost hiding between the folds. While driving, I go through a mental list of to-do items—change the A/C and car filters, drop the pauses out of conversations, donate his clothes to the Salvation Army, change the pillowcase in your room because I hear you sob every night, probably, when you're finding ways to fall asleep and there's no one to make chocolate milkshakes for you late at night, undo the dark, or show you how to locate a thunderstorm on a radar map.

When the school signs come into view, I slow down to 20 mph, feel that quickening of pulse, if I packed your lunch how your dad used to—two sandwiches, an eight-ounce-chocolate-milk carton, and a pack of banana chips from the bulk he ordered from Amazon. You are playing on your phone when I park next to the curb and look at you: overgrown hair covering the small of your neck, eyes looking beyond the windshield, and you make a fist that will guide you where they teach how to add or subtract your feelings, balance equations, and let your grammar sink and froth in its own errors. I say, *Have a good day,* but no sound comes out. You push your hands in your pocket; walk away, your face burning with questions.

And I drive back, my feet a few centimeters away from the brake pedal as kids rush past, but more so because it's the way of our life—a yellow light inside always ready to go red, and all the distance I cover after returning home is going up and down the stairs while a part of me rattles, willing to break free from the muscles and gravity. When I cast slant glances upward at the same sky devoid of rain, finishing my tea with a side of heartache, I realize that it is past July and the cicadas haven't come this year. The silence drifts across the rooms, and through the bust of the screen door the patio is well lit with the bare neck of the sun. The bed sheets unlearn the language of your dad's body, and I settle into my disquiet as an old man into his slippers. At lunch, I stare into the blue of the TV and, later, practice how I'd smile when I see you at 3 p.m., what I'd talk about: perhaps, homework, and the upcoming dentist's appointment, with a slight concern in my voice.

And it's home again: another pizza takeout and three hours of TV while I fold the laundry, unclog the sink of tight-mouthed condescension, set the soil setting on the washer to Heavy, to start a fresh load that tosses and turns like we do every night. Then I think to write thank-you notes to everyone who helped. Istead, I sit down with you and watch the movie you're watching because you want me to despite the dial of my mind pushed far left to Empty, and a low beam is all we have between us that never gets me past the school driving limit even when the intersection is cleared, the forecast is right as rain, and no warning lights flash asking me to slow down.

Tara Isabel Zambrano

Flawed

Waiting in the lobby, I see an Afghani woman
on *The Wall Street Journal*,
holding a photo of her kidnapped son.
Reminds me I've never returned.

My shrink lectures me about personality disorders.
He hands me two pamphlets, one crackling
with self-love, the other, sanity.

I undress my sins, describe the sensation
of warm sand on my skin,
the lingering smell of burning flesh.
Voices that have set up house inside.

He writes a prescription. Talks about
post-war syndrome with a side
of a constant clicking ball-point pen. I
study his double chin, his doughy neck.

Someday, he'll know things humans are capable of:
hauling hope and despair on the same spine.
How the stubborn soldier in you denies the blame,
pops in small, white pills and calls it peace.

Alita Pirkopf

Rain Forest at the Botanic Gardens

He showed me leaves
of enormous size like those
the soldiers laid down

in monsoon seasons
for sleeping when they could—
terrified as they were

for years of dark nights
and days, in jungles
of machetes, mosquitoes.

He showed me other
huge leaves on trees
with branches men tied

together concealing themselves,
from enemy and rain,
while sleeping with snakes

and orchids, drinking—even now
where the local rain forest
is contained but the former grows

grafted, transplanted,
out of control
in the heads of refugees.

Benjamin Harnett

The Snap

"Now, why don't you collect yourself, and start again," he says. He is looking at me over his reading glasses, with arched eyebrows, which sprout so luxuriously from his brow that I wonder if, somehow, he has been cultivating them to counterbalance the barrenness of his bald pate. He has been looking down at that little pad, you know, where he writes his notes—are they about my state of mind? The words seem to roll out from his pen onto the paper, longhand, in complete sentences, paragraphs. Is he writing a story about me, or recounting a dream, or writing his own name over and over again—I will never know. "Why do you think you felt like striking Mr. Dubelstein?"

I did strike Mr. Dubelstein, I start to protest, not just think about striking him. But of course, that is not the point, not why we're here. It's the thinking that matters, my brain. Mr. Dubelstein, my son's elementary school principal, had just been saying something like, "Now, Mrs. Abbot," the way he pronounced my name with a kind of sneer always bothered me. Bothers me now. "Now Mrs. Abbot, if everyone is special," obviously talking about Robbie, "then no one is special." I'm not sure exactly what he was getting at, other than he couldn't make an exception for my son this time. Mr. Dubelstein never could make an exception. You know the type.

That's when I felt that my knuckle had hit the firm jelly of his eye. He's not a tall man, and I'm not particularly tall. My fist found his eye pretty easily. It hurt my hand, to hit him, a lot. I don't have much of experience, any experience, really, other than this, of punching people. Through the pain, I punched him again, in the neck this time, and then his stomach.

"Jesus Christ!" he shouted. I think he started to blubber like a child.

There was blood on his eye, and he was flailing out at me. I felt the sides of his hands slapping my body, like a child's imagination of a karate chop.

I had really snapped.

To my therapist, I say, "I wanted to strike him because I was tired— tired of everyone pushing along in their own selfish rut, refusing to bend toward compassion, toward sense, toward understanding. I guess I looked at him, listened to him, and thought of all the children who would be warped by this view into becoming just like him. Little men." I realize my therapist is not very tall either.

Actually, I have no therapist. Sometimes I like to sit in a chair at my home, feel the warmth of the sun on me like a cat, and let my mind wander. Surely interrogating yourself is just as good as, or better than, a stranger doing it. Certainly costs less.

Self-help.

I have read, somewhere, that, if the universe is infinite, and there's a lot of reasons it could be, or that our idea of a universe is just one universe in an infinite cluster of them, growing in and out of each other like knobs of cactus, poking their spines forever upward and outward, everything must be repeated over and over again. That what we see here, our life, the very configuration that ties us all together, my hand to Mr. Dubelstein's neck, the miniscule droplets of blood, the nerve impulses that spark pain, is happening somewhere else, again, exactly the same. In fact, happening exactly the same and happening in every possible slight variation in between. At least, that's what I take it to mean.

It's not something I took much stock of, but it did stick with me. I didn't believe it for a second, at least until recently. You see, I have developed a kind of power. You laugh, but don't we all believe we have some inner power, somewhere, that comes out at times. It may be through prayer. You have heard the stories of twins who sense the other's pain, or the wife who got the strength to lift the overturned car off of her babe, or hundred thousand other miracles we call on, without much hope of success, but yet some, do like the way you wish the bus would just come.

My son likes comic books. I used to read them too, as a girl. I'd buy Thor comics from the rack in the drug store, when I was in my teens. I loved the impossible romance of crippled Donald Blake hiding the incredible power of a god, and the contrast between drab Manhattanand the fantastic cornucopia of wonder and magic that was Asgard. Whenever I saw a rainbow, it formed a bridge in my mind.

Things with my son's principal had gone too far. My hands were bruised, and he recovered from his initial shock and struck me back. He hit my shoulder, without any kind of aim, cursing because he had never really hit anyone, to know how much it hurt to inflict pain.

I scratched his face, under my nails were flecks of blood. But my mind had already signaled; somehow, that this had been enough. Then I felt myself convulse, my eyes rolled back a little, and the room filled with a spectrum from red through oranges, yellows, greens, blues, indigo, violet. I felt a shaking in my stomach, sweat, and everything was back to how it had been, Mr. Dubelstein saying again that he couldn't tolerate giving special treatment to any one child, no matter how high his test scores. Didn't I understand?

I blinked a few times. For a moment, as it always is, I wondered if it had happened at all, what I'd envisioned, but looked down and saw bits of blood still on my hands. Mr. Dubelstein was fine, though there was the hint, only, of a bruise, as if he'd received it weeks ago. He winced in unconscious pain.

I felt a wave of remorse shiver through me, like those waves that tumble before an earthquake that only animals can still feel. And then, as if blot out the remorse, I imagined how small and sad his penis must be, from looking at him, and how his wife must hide her flinch every time she saw him naked. And then I felt bad again.

"Are you alright, Mrs. Abbot?" he said.

I said, "Yes," but I know I shook my head.

Dr. Donald Blake found Thor's hammer, disguised as a walking stick, in a cave in Norway and, tapping the stick on the ground, became "The Mighty Thor," transformed from weak, but brilliant doctor into the somewhat simpler-minded but good-hearted and incredibly powerful god. Peter Parker was bitten by a radioactive spider. Superman simply came from another planet, special only in his relation to those around him. I discovered my power, if you can call it my power, while pregnant, as I think many women do.

It's already said by the superstitious that pregnant women have powers. That they can dull your knives. I'll tell you why the knives dull; because it's harder to get to housework, and you find that you let things soak in the sink like a man. Or your husband will take over the duties, fail to do them well, and slyly blame it on you.

I am sure it has something to do with the brain. Because my thoughts were all muddled when it happened. I felt these feelings fall around me like a net. I was at the sink but turned slightly because it was easier than pressing my belly into it. A stray thought made me throw the plate.

Its happening was a surprise to myself. The plate hit the wall and split (and I almost felt that I could see it, though it happened far faster than that), then shattered with a white hiss, the shards spraying out everywhere, skidding across the linoleum. I heard my husband grunt from the other room. I'd never done anything so emotionally charged and it scared me. I must have let out a kind of animal yelp.

And then, as quickly as it had happened, it had not happened. I held the plate in one hand, the wet sponge in the other. In the far room the sound of the TV went on, the hush of golf, the muted claps. My husband grunted (again? For the first time?) and I began to cry. I set the whole plate down into the grey sudsy water, and it went under, like the moon occulted by a confluence of clouds.

I'm sure you've experienced it, too, though, that vision in the mind's eye that flashes so real you can almost feel the heat of it on your palms. I stifled myself and took a deep breath. Perhaps I was going crazy. Obviously I was full of hormones. Later, sweeping the kitchen, seeing the dirt and bits of dust crawl up the long, straight plastic bristles of the broom, I wondered at the filth of modern living, how outside of the house in a field, on the blanketed forest floor, nature cleaned itself, bringing life up out of the bits of life shattered over the giving ground, when the bristles splayed against a sliver of porcelain.

I shivered. Though it could have come from anywhere, from anywhen, I knew it had escaped from a happening that had, somehow, unhappened.

It's strange but to be expected, things that haven't happened impact your life and feelings as much as things that have.

I love my husband. We've been married for so long, it seems, that he's become a part of the landscape, and part of me. So much so that I forget to introduce him. Alan. He's a few years older than me. I think his brother was in my class at school.

One day, some friends and I were taking her parents' car to the mall. I was sitting in back, brooding, when I glanced through the station wagon window and saw Alan on a road crew. It was his summer job from college. He was shirtless, and I could see the sweat on him shine in the sun. They were shoveling asphalt to fill a wide crack in the pavement.

As the car turned I realized I had been staring, and that he was looking straight into me. That look. My teenage self was struck by an epiphany. I was desirable, and I desired him. The story of how we got together is a convoluted one, but I'm not sure it matters. From the moment we locked eyes, I knew we were fated to be together.

Or at least that we would fuck. In my mind I relished the word, and almost understood it.

Alan's always been handsome, then, now.

I used to joke about robbing the cradle, even though he's older than me. He was always good to me, too, though something changed after that first pregnancy.

Robbie came later, a gift, or cosmic recompense—well, if you believe in that kind of stuff.

That evening I thought of something. Imagine going back to the dawn of time, rewinding the tape of life. Some people say it's such an accident that people came about that if you replayed the tape of those billions of years over a billion times, you'd only get us and this once. Perhaps the little uni-cells would never even merge. Perhaps the most intellectual species would be a kind of tree.

We were sitting, apart, me resting one hand on the life growing inside me, while Alan half-turned from us. On the television, in those sad, grainy phosphors, I saw the first lotto ball go up, a shocking, solid white, while pixels jumped and balls jumped, and the forced jollity of the host, a too-tan Ken doll with bigger things in his eyes, my eyes rolled back, and the rainbows came. It had been a five. I held my breath. Five came again.

Fate?

Was the same ball guaranteed to whip itself up each time, or did this power just not stretch so far? Even if the number had changed, would it have been just the pattern on the screen I had twisted around, would the number posted at the convenience store be the same? For a while I tried to probe these mysteries, but life just kept getting in the way. I had a mouth to feed. I found myself turning back the clock on life's little misfortunes, another chance, and not dropping my wallet at the bank, not turning the wrong way in a store and running into someone I didn't want to see.

"Where's your mind?" asked Alan. We were sitting together on the couch. I must not have responded, lost in thought, because Alan turned bodily to me and repeated his question.

Alan is the polar opposite of my imaginary therapist. Not just in that he's tall, rugged, no glasses, a full head of hair. But he looks into you (or not at all) and gives you all of him, it's enough to make you want to tell the truth. Say what, exactly? But it's incredible and impossible.

I still had a faint bruise on my knuckles from striking the principal. I started to tell him about it. "I got into—a disagreement, with that Dubelstein, you know, he really doesn't understand Robbie."

"Robbie needs a little tough love," Alan said. "He's so moody now. He needs to snap out of it."

No, it's my fault, I thought. No reason for it otherwise. Robbie didn't have any trouble with school, maybe it was a bit too boring for him. But I've been distant, too preoccupied with my own precarious standing in the universe. Too preoccupied with myself. I flexed my aching hand.

"What happened to you?" Alan asked, resting his thumb gently against the small bruise on my face. It felt good, this surprising touch, considering how little we did touch now.

"Can you believe it?" I lied. "I tripped, fell yesterday."

I was woozy. I wondered if time was going to walk back and give me another chance at lying, better this time. But it didn't.

There were meetings all week at work. I had to give a presentation on Wednesday and left it to the last minute. Up late Tuesday night, like a college student again. Alan went to bed without me.

You know those late nights, your body isn't used to it anymore, and you wonder how you ever did anything you used to do, go out all night, work the next day. Of course I forgot everything I had printed out. I should have just e-mailed it to myself, but I hadn't been thinking. If it had just been outside the door that I noticed, I'd have blinked myself back to the desk where I left it. Sometimes I wondered if blinking back time had bored holes into my head or if it was just age.

I had the key in my office door when I stopped.

"Shit!"

I stood there, frozen. Then I marched back to the car.

Forty minutes back to the hous: I'd make it just in time for my go at the podium.

The sky was white, but wisps of mist and heavy clouds poked through or loomed overhead. Every horizontal surface weeped with the remnants of the late rain.

Everything was dull but car lights, which pierced yellow or, going the other way sparkled and teased like casino cherries on the drab highway.

Something was wrong.

I felt it tugging on me like someone had tied a long strand around my middle, and it was anchored off in the mist.

Our house is on a cul-de-sac, right where the arc begins to shift back to the highway.

Alan's car was still there.

Running late, I thought.

I put my key in the lock and pushed open the door.

There was just that unmistakable sound, the low moan and one more frequent and higher pitched. Then the rainbows scattered my view, and I was holding the key into the lock again. My heart thumped into my neck. I opened the door again.

Alan's ass was in front of me, a pair of legs, our deep green couch.

I blinked back to the door.

I clawed it open and started toward the pair, something sent me back.

I yelled at the closed door. Heard noises.

Back.

I shrieked.

Back.

I got right up to them, saw her face, a stranger, in real or feigned ecstasy before they tumbled away from me, and the rainbows warped me back.

How many times did I try to come through that door, begin to vomit, slam my fists, yell, cry, hear him cry my name in shock, grunt hers in pleasure, start to stammer an excuse? I tore through myself and always found myself back on the other side, hand bringing key to lock, the doorknob the only solid thing? A hundred? A thousand?

Did days pass? Months? Am I still standing there?

At last I stopped. I felt the sun, which had begun to burn off the clouds, warm, firm, like a hand holding my shoulder, keeping me back.

I could hear their moans now, that I knew them. Every roundness of them, every ripple. I scraped the walkway with my shoes as I turned back to the car. I sat, shaking, and then drove toward the office again. Without my presentation. Without—I don't know, maybe myself?

That night, I came home. Alan's car was gone. He showed up a half-hour later. I opened the door, uncharacteristically to meet him.

"How did it go?" he asked. And then, after a long, silent pause, "Is something wrong? You—you look so old."

I looked at his face. I didn't have the heart to tell him, he did, too.

Kendra Tanacea

Diagnosis

The sky is a gray X-ray. Here's the round moon
with cancer shadows. What looks like a church spire

is the spine with bone spurs and bulging discs.
It seems like an ordinary night,

I look like a woman with healthy hair, in a brown coat
that looks warm. Even as branches grab at the sky,

plum blossoms snow down like asbestos.
Sometimes the moon is a bullet hole,

sometimes the ultra-bright light from an otoscope.
The more the bones fail, the more I become this cool

exhale of menthol that hangs in the air. Everything sinks
so fast, like this moon over Telegraph Hill. I remember

a love so distracting that I slammed the car door on my own leg.
But that was only skin. My right hip keeps catching,

then giving out. Tension, inflammation? Or maybe
I'm carrying things too heavy for my frame.

Lesions and uncertainty. Radiation may help,
the way the Condor's Club red neon penetrates this fog.

Erin Jones

Remembering Winter

It's November in Florida. We blanket
the tangelos, praying for frost to kill
something, especially the mosquitos

that nurse at our ankles when we walk.
We're craving the anxiety of Maryland
black ice, and our childhood game

of wading into the front pond
until our feet turn to ghosts in our boots.
Even the animals are suicidal

in northern winter. They watch you take out
the .30-.30 your father gave you,
blankly staring

as they did when they stood in your headlights, defiant.
We remember the morning papers, always the same story
year after year: In Newark, a woman

stepped in front of a train during the morning commute,
her black down-jacket turning her
to shadow before the train swallowed her.

Evelyn Somers

The Mistake

Four a.m. It was cold, and she'd slept in her clothes so she'd be ready in case her father changed his mind. She lay for a second when her phone alarm rang, trying to think why it was going off so early and why she was still in her jeans. Then she remembered. Second day of the season. Her father and Caleb had to drive into the next county to her uncle's land, Bruce's, and that meant leaving at five. No later than.

She got up and pulled back the curtain and looked out. It wasn't really a curtain; it was a faded sheet, blue-and-white striped like ticking. Finally, after a year of the sheet being there, her father said last summer that he'd get her some curtains, but it was November now. She was fifteen, and everyone in Covington could not be spying through her window in the front of the house, so she had hung the sheet; she'd hung it when she was fourteen and the young father in the vinyl-sided Habitat house across the street had started coming out early to sit on his porch and smoke and watch her. She'd washed the sheet every few months since then, always thinking that soon she could throw it away. But the last time she'd hung it back up after washing, she knew she was done waiting for a lot of things. She didn't care anymore whether she ever had curtains. She could buy cheap ones somewhere, but there was no point; it didn't matter.

The street out front had a different, more emphatic quality of desertion at this hour and season. *Desolate.* She liked that word; she liked words people didn't use a lot. Though it was partly the darkness that made it look neglected, disused. There was a cell phone tower over in the distance, winking. Chelsea had never noticed it until this second, but it must have been there all along, invisible in the daylight.

How far? Three distinct points of red flicked on and off, but the off was not a total *extinguishment*; there was a faint, constant glow of red even when the points blinked out. Night was not over yet, not even close; it was still clamped down hard like a jaw. The window, if you looked through just the top pane, was an all-black canvas except for the red specks pulsing in the lower right quadrant and the ghost of herself, Chelsea, in a camouflage sweatshirt, her faint reflection—*miasmic*. It gave her a shiver.

She could hear her brother, Caleb, bumping around in his room. She went to wake her father.

The hinges yowled when she opened his door. There was a can of WD-40 right there on the floor beside the doorjamb, but he hadn't got to it, just like he hadn't got to the curtains. He stored up everything that needed his attention for later. Everything. People. Things that wanted repair. And just things—worldly goods. That sounded legal and significant. But to her father, Tony Arcand, all things were nothing unless he decided to bestow his interest on them. Mostly, he didn't.

Her father's window, which faced the back yard, was a canvas unlike hers. There was no cell tower. The dusk-to-dawn lamp next door shone over the yard like a dispirited moon. Things were piled on and around the patio. A dryer drum, a stack of sodden baskets. A green-and-black foam block target for bow practice. The sliding patio door that opened out to the back was off its runner, and they'd wedged a strip of Styrofoam in the crack and would hang a blanket over it, like they did last year, when cold winds blew. Frigid winds. *Glacial.* It could probably be fixed easily, but she didn't know how, and he wouldn't do it.

He sat right up and cleared his throat with a growl when she opened his door.

"Can I go?" she said. She'd walked into the room so he could see that she was dressed. Even had boots on.

"No," he said. "I need you to get on the Infobomb and buy a tag if I shoot another buck today." Before last year, he would have just brought it home without checking it and butchered it on the kitchen table; rules meant little to him. But last year he'd been caught baiting, and he'd paid three hundred dollars in fines; he was being careful.

"You could take me this time, instead of Caleb."

"No."

He was up, pulling on wool socks and Walmart thermal underwear and camouflage pants. There was a faint, faint iron smell from yesterday's blood on his clothes.

She went back to her room. Outside, the night would unlock eventually. The dark would let go, and the sky would whiten rapidly. The vault, the heavenly *firmament*. The ink of night draining away. Her father and brother rushing around now to beat it, even though it wouldn't happen for two hours.

Chelsea took off her boots and got back in bed, under the covers. *Black as the blood of night*, she thought. If you bled the night out, it became day. If you bled the light out of day, it was night. There was a whole lot of heavenly throat-slashing going on to make the days and the years and the seasons. Because life was blood, and the world was life. Her father had turned his back on it. She liked Covington High because the things they learned were not about this place here, Covington; they were about everywhere else—places she would never go. Right now, she liked school, anyway. She'd gotten As on most of her papers this term. Last year, Mr. Barron hated her because she was an Arcand, and she got a C-minus in math. And a D in Civics after she stopped handing things in; no one looked at them anyway. But Mrs. Hart, her history teacher this year, read their papers and stopped Chelsea after class to compliment her vocabulary and ask about her family. What she meant was, He doesn't mistreat you, does he? He doesn't neglect you? He didn't. Not entirely. But she knew Mrs. Hart wasn't the only one thinking it.

Their father taught art at the elementary school; he'd been there twenty-four years, and people knew he was going through the motions and didn't care anymore, if he ever had, though once upon a time, they said, he'd had talent. Covington was so small—he wouldn't have had the job anywhere else, not with his second-rate education degree and the bitter chip on his shoulder, but he'd gotten it because he was a local boy, one of Covington's own, and now was protected by tenure and because people felt sorry for him: Everyone knew their mother had run off with one of her Turner third cousins when Chelsea and Caleb were nine. People took care of you in Covington. *We have your back. We will never, ever turn on you.* Not as long as you didn't push things, and were grateful.

Caleb came in and got in bed with her in his hunting clothes. She was older by eight minutes; she was not a baby, and there was no reason her father couldn't take them both, or one on Saturday, one on Sunday. She knew how to shoot. Bow and rifle both. She loved Caleb. But she sometimes wished she was a lesbian, so her boy self would be herself, not him. She loved him, though. She wanted him to get a buck with antlers wide as a truck bed.

He moved over and spooned her, but it was more light embrace than pressure: chaste. "One boy, one buck. Tough shot, great luck. Memories are made of this," he crooned. Then he laughed and rolled away.

"You don't sound very much like Elvis." But she laughed, too. She was mad at Tony, not at her twin. He was just being silly to make her feel better.

Caleb left, and she thought about going back to sleep. Her bladder wouldn't cooperate, though. So she got up again.

Down the hall, the bathroom door was closed, water roaring. She knocked.

"Go outside!" shouted her father.

The stool in the other bathroom had backed up months ago. So he'd turned off the shutoff valve and they kept that room closed off. The stupid thing was that he'd come up on a farm; he'd cut his teeth on chores from sunup to bedtime. He knew how to do everything, inside a house and out. He could plumb, wire, tune a car, fix a tractor, drive a combine, hang drywall, mow and bale a field of hay. He used to do what needed done, even though he had always been focused on something else, somewhere off in his head. He didn't drink. People thought that, too.

She wasn't going outside in the cold and dark.

She went to the kitchen. Caleb wasn't there. In the back, probably, getting the guns out. She really had to pee. She was going to wet herself in a minute.

Below the sink, the pans were all tossed in piles. It leaked sometimes where the PVC joints were glued, so there was a Cool Whip tub under the elbow. The graywater ran down the kitchen plumbing into the basement and out a basement window into the yard. It was another thing Tony had done to avoid messing with the sewer. It wasn't too bad for the grass in summer, but if you walked out to that side of the house, you saw stuff that had gone out unintentionally with the dishwater. Noodles and bloated Cheerios in the grass.

She pulled out a two-quart pan. Down came her jeans, to her ankles. The cat, which had anticipated food, not this, watched like she'd gone crazy. She bent her knees and held the pan right under her pubes by the handle and felt it getting heavier as her stream poured in. She wiped her cleft with a dishtowel and threw the towel in the dirty pile. Not a drop spilled on the floor. *My aim's all right*, she thought.

Her bright *effluence* in the pan looked like lemon Jell-O before it set. She poured it down the drain, let it run out into the yard with this morning's coffee grounds.

She washed the pan and was setting it in the drainer when they came in, using the funeral-home murmuring they always did, since before Melissa, their mother, left. She was a night owl and slept until long after the rest of them. Now there was no one to wake, but they still did it—except the clomping of their men feet in muck boots belied the effort at stealth. Her father had not "seen" anyone since Melissa ran off. People asked this, too: "Is he seeing anyone?" They meant, *Is anyone taking care of you?*

He didn't talk much. Back when she and Caleb had had him for art, in grade school, he was the most silent teacher, and the only man besides the custodian. No one acted up in art because Tony scared them. He gave one- and two-word directives. He passed out paper and glue, walked around, saying nothing, tapping on your part of the table if what you were doing caught his interest. A tap more coveted than all the gold stars in all the teachers' desks in Covington Elementary. His attention was transitory, but if it settled for a second on someone's drawing he would have them in thrall forever. A few children with actual talent poured themselves out in his class in the hope of receiving words of approval that Caleb and Chelsea knew he would never give. Even the tap by your paper meant nothing. It was what he did in the evening when he was reading or watching TV and something struck him. Tap, tap. His mind had alighted on that thing, in the world, and for just a second, he'd stepped outside himself and considered it. For a while a few years ago, he'd had a real-life project. He'd bought a 1980s single-wide for a thousand dollars and put it out on their small acreage south of Covington. The water and electricity were hooked up, and he'd taken some of his stuff out there; he spent many of his evenings and weekends at the trailer, leaving them alone.

Chelsea stole a look at him going through his things, making sure it was all there. Latex gloves and knife for gutting the deer. The

56

two *insubstantial* polyester blaze-orange vests. Flagging tape, if they needed it to mark a trail. He looked nothing like Caleb, who was big boned and had a reddish tinge to his light-brown hair and peach fuzz. Tony was handsome. The smallest of men, but riveting to look at. Dark hair and unsettling light eyes. Thin as a whip. There was nothing to him but bone and cables of muscle. Hands and feet too large for the rest of him. Perfectly shaped facial structure under his November beard. A smile that came almost never, that stripped and ambushed you, and you could see that he was and always had been on the edge of feral indifference to anyone. That he somehow calculated, consciously or unwittingly, exactly where the line was between civilized and not, and was walking it with impeccable balance.

Caleb poured brandy in the flask—the only time Tony drank was when he hunted. Just sips, to warm him. There were the half-gallon-milk-jug urinals on the table. *A pan works.* Not in a tree it doesn't, though.

Now Caleb was making sandwiches, not looking at her because he knew she was angry.

"Get me some of those peanuts, Chelsea. In a bag," said her father.

"Why can't I go?"

"There's no place for you to sit. I've got two one-man stands up there. No place to put you."

"There's the ladder stand out at the trailer."

"Well, there you go. It's out south. That doesn't do us any good."

"You could have moved it up to Bruce's."

"I might need you to go on the Infobomb and buy a tag," he repeated.

"It's my tag you want, isn't it? That's why you won't take me."

He didn't reply, and she filled a sandwich bag with peanuts and zipped it and threw it on the table.

"Answer your phone," he said.

"You might just as well buy a tag now."

"Waste of seventeen dollars if I don't get another buck."

"What did you do with all those antlers?" she asked. Years and years—decades—of racks with the skull tops still attached, some of them Caleb's, a few that their mother had shot. They'd all been arrayed at one end of the laundry room in the basement, but they'd disappeared.

"Hung them out at the trailer," he said.

Caleb was putting the drinks in the Igloo, but he looked up at her and nodded, giving her a sign she couldn't interpret.

It was five-fifteen. The house was mute as a stone. She loved Caleb, but having a twin didn't save you from what Tony Arcand had showed her, what the children in all the classes he'd ever taught could have learned from his remoteness if they'd been paying close attention: that to be alive … human … was to be indissolubly wedded to your aloneness. By yourself, or in a classroom with twenty children, or in the "bosom of your family." Single, isolate, without a chance, ever, of freeing you from your *self*.

But that was only a half truth. It was how she felt sometimes. Feelings were *capricious*, inconstant. Her anger this morning. Her love for her brother.

Her desire to go with the men.

The cat wound through her ankles, serpentine mink with a hungry mew. She fed it and then went to the back room and tried the gun safe. He had enough rifles, she could find one to use.

The door wasn't pushed in far enough to lock. The safe was invariably locked. She'd seen Caleb hand the key to Tony when he came out with the guns. That was what Caleb had meant when he nodded at her; he'd left it open. Inside was where her father kept the other key, the one to the trailer. She took it and took out the Winchester 94 that her mother had used. It was a lever-action gun, unscoped, which was why they didn't use it. There were round-nose bullets for it. Chelsea didn't love guns like Caleb did, but she knew this gun was a classic.

The door to the safe clicked shut, and now there was no putting the rifle back. She didn't think she had pushed it—but it was so early, and nothing was quite clear.

She would have to hurry, and she didn't know how she would get out to their land. She threw some food in a drawstring sports bag and shoved a liter bottle of Coke in it and found another camouflage jacket and an orange hat. She didn't have enough layers on, but it would warm up; she had to hurry. Then she thought about a tag. But she didn't have Tony's credit card, and it didn't matter because she wasn't sure she could even find a way to get out there before the sun rose. She had a momentary pang about disobeying; but what was there to disobey? He hardly noticed her most of the time, didn't know what she did, where she was.

She stepped outside, and the cold slapped her face. *You fool.* For a second she paused and wondered what she was doing. In her gloved hand, though, she clutched the gun case. And it was a dry cold, not the kind that seeped into you, and there was almost no wind, and when the sun emerged, it would be a perfect morning. The clear black sky was salted with stars, and she noticed again the throb of red lights from the cell tower. Was that what it was? A cell tower? On and off. *Incessant.*

Across, there was a light on in the vinyl Habitat house. The Potters'. The man who smoked on the porch was Kyle. They had two five-year-old boys who were also twins, Bradley and Brick. When she was thirteen, Chelsea had watched the boys once for a few hours for their mother, without getting paid; she'd been worried but not surprised that their fridge held only half a package of hot dogs and two six-packs of beer.

She set the rifle case at the end of the porch and went across the street and knocked.

No one came, so she knocked again, and then she heard the thud of steps, and the door creaked open. She'd expected the mother—her name was Katie. But it was Kyle. He had a moon face with a sharp widow's peak, and a thin-lined mouth and slanted eyes that looked shifty—a *perpetual* smirk. Chelsea had been taught a degree of formality, and she was used to people calling Tony "Mr. Arcand" because he was a teacher. "Mr. Potter?" she said.

He stood squinting at her in torn, black sweats.

"My dad and brother went hunting, and my brother just texted me. They're having some trouble."

"Trouble?" He seemed not to know who she was, or that he used to watch her through her bedroom window.

"My dad is Tony Arcand. Across the street?"

"Someone get shot?" he asked nervously.

"No, no. No one's hurt. My dad needs me to bring him his other gun. But I can't drive."

"It's *five-thirty.*"

"I know. I'm sorry. Could you take me out there?"

"Where you going?" he said, sounding more confused than annoyed. She must have awakened him.

"It's out past the county shed."

"This an emergency?" he said. "My van's barely running, and I ain't got no gas."

"I'll give you thirty dollars." She pulled off her glove and dug in her pocket; she held out a ten and four fives that she'd taken from the oversized coffee mug where her father always kept some cash.

Kyle looked at the money. She saw it in his eyes: fifteen minutes out and fifteen back; one of the fives alone would cover the gas.

"You'll be back way before church," said Chelsea. Knowing they didn't go.

"OK," he said. "I'll get my shoes and jacket."

The Potters' van was an old Grand Caravan. Tony said he'd rather drink a bucket of worm spit than drive a Dodge. There were two booster seats for Bradley and Brick in the backseat, which was filled with plastic bottles and crumpled fast-food bags. She climbed in the front and settled the gun case with the stock end on the floorboard in front of her and the barrel angling back. The bullets were in her bag. Some belt or rod was torn or bent or giving out, and the van made a metallic grating as they drove. The gauge showed three-fourths full, and Kyle Potter didn't offer any explanation for having said he was out of gas.

They drove out on the gravel, Pink Elephant Road, that met the state highway. Kyle stank. It wasn't him; it was his jacket, she decided, something that had spilled on it and grown putrid. It was a stomach-churning smell, worse than the staleness of the van, which erupted whenever he moved his arm. And he kept moving: grabbing his iPhone and looking at it every time it burped at him. Chelsea wanted to take the phone and throw it out the window, but she couldn't, so she turned her face away, trying to breathe past the stench.

They rattled by a cluster of houses: a flash of light from a lamppost in one of the yards and a group of boxy shapes in the dark. Then the headlights washed over a dead possum in the other lane—swollen-belly white with a bony tail. She knew it was dead because it was in the road, but they could "play possum," too, lying stiff as corpses on their sides with their rat mouths open and a dead stink emanating from the anus. She and Caleb had once seen a possum big as a terrier—they didn't usually get that large; they didn't live long enough. Born the size of an insect, they groped their way blindly to their mother's pouch and suckled and grew and were weaned and bred and ate people's garbage, and carrion, and got preyed on by coyotes or hit on the road and died. Their only protection against death was mimicking death. It was like she felt about being an Arcand: The sole defense against what people thought of her father was that she, too, was an Arcand, so screw them all; who cared?

Tony said the male possums had forked penises and the females had double-hole cooches to match. When she was twelve or thirteen, a few years after their mother left, Chelsea had found some pornographic pencil drawings in the top drawer of the chest in his room. They weren't there anymore—he had taken them to the trailer, or he'd destroyed them. They were of muscular, naked men and women like a fantasy illustrator would draw, sometimes one woman with two men and sometimes several women with one man, and some of the men had forked penises and were doing two women or doing one woman who had two openings, and in other drawings there were more bodies than faces, and the mouths were open in ecstasy. If you followed lines of the bodies, you could not always trace them to a head, as if the wanton indulgence of the sex and the bifurcated genitalia had somehow spawned other bodies, bodies that didn't even need heads because their only purpose was pure physical gratification. She didn't tell Caleb about the drawings; she wasn't sure how they made her feel. She was proud that they were good. Some of the women looked like their mother. And she was upset, sometimes, that her father wouldn't do what normal people would do in his situation. Quit drawing porn. Get a girlfriend.

"I better not hit a deer," said Kyle.

They hadn't seen any deer, just the dead possum.

They were still in the city limits. There was the water tower, to the east. A little further on, a bucket truck loomed in the headlights with a sign that said MEN WORKING IN TREES, but they'd both been there for months, the sign and the truck. And then the gravel hit the highway. She touched the Winchester in its case and thought about her mother for a second. Before Melissa had left Tony for her cousin, she'd had an affair with the school band director. Chelsea and

Caleb and Tony were not the first to hear this, but eventually they did because in Covington, what was known to even a few people was rapidly known to all.

Kyle turned the van into the blacktop, and something in the steering or the axle squealed in protest.

"What's wrong with your van?" said Chelsea.

He mumbled something and looked at his phone again, and the stench flooded out from his sleeve. It wasn't cat piss or vomit but just as revolting. It was a smell she couldn't identify, but it evoked a memory that hovered just out of reach.

"What's your brother's name?" Kyle asked.

"Caleb. We're twins," said Chelsea.

Kyle looked over at her. "Twins," he said, "will screw you up. If I'd known it was going to end up twins, I wouldn't have gotten with Katie."

"My brother and I were easier than most single babies."

"Who says?"

"My mother."

"Y'all aren't normal."

At sixty-five, the van vibrated and roared like a belt sander. Kyle's voice came to her above the noise.

"You don't hunt?" he was trying to ask her.

"I do," she said.

"How come you didn't go, then?"

"I don't know. I just didn't. I've got a project for school."

"What year are you?"

"Sophomore."

She could see him trying to figure out her age. Sixteen? Fifteen? He was gross.

"You know that teacher at the high school? He shot his hand off hunting when he was fifteen. He was going to be a professional piano player. He was a prodigy. *Was*," said Kyle.

"Pianist," said Chelsea.

They came around a curve where gravel met highway. People spun out here and ended up in a ditch if they weren't careful. A hundred yards up the road was the county shed.

"It's the next on the left after the road shed," she said.

"Better be careful with that gun," he said, looking at her as though he guessed what she was up to.

Then, "I don't get how your dad's an art teacher. He looks like a mountain man. Can he ...? What kind of art can he do?"

She lied. "Sculpture. Wood carving. He made all our furniture. He makes sculptures out of deer antlers and sells them on the Internet. For thousands."

"Huh." He didn't believe her.

Now they were at the turnoff. The van squealed again as they skidded onto the farm road a little too quickly. It was bumpy and washed out, almost bald of gravel.

"This road sucks," said Kyle and slowed the vehicle. He moved his arm, and the odor seemed at once to engulf the whole van. She was drowning in it. She thought she was going to retch up whatever was in her stomach—nothing; she hadn't eaten a thing. She reached around into the backseat for a Walmart bag to throw up in.

"Hey!" His right hand came around and grabbed her arm, as the van swayed and jolted. She understood—he had something in the back seat. Money. A handgun. Drugs? Something he thought she was going for. He jerked her arm toward him, gripping it so hard she could feel bruises blossoming. "What do you think you're doing?" he hissed. He squeezed tighter.

"I was just—," she tried to explain when he finally loosened his grip, but she didn't finish because the van's front wheel on the driver side plunged into *the* pothole, the deep one, the "pothole from hell" that Tony always veered to the right to avoid.

They careened left, headed off road, toward a barbed wire fence. "Shit, I can't steer!" shouted Kyle.

He braked hard, and the van rocked to a stop in the grass, throwing them both forward. But at least the seat belts worked, and they were both buckled in.

If the van had airbags, they didn't deploy.

"Fucking must've broke the tie rod, fucking pothole. What did you have to mess around in the back seat for?"

"I thought I was going to vomit. I was looking for a bag."

"Puke in your goddamn lap," he moaned. "Look at this. I'll have to get it towed, and we don't even have the money to tow it. It'll be four, five hundred to fix it."

Everyone called Lucas T., of Lucas T. Towing, whose dog rode in the seat next to him on his calls, a cross-eyed border collie named

Atwater because Lucas T. had rescued him from the river. Someone had thrown that cross-eyed puppy off the bridge, and by a miracle, it struggled or floated to the bank, where Lucas T., out fishing, found him dead and gave him CPR, and Atwater came back to life and was the most loyal dog anyone in Covington had heard of. And smart.

"I got Lucas T. in my phone," she said. From when Tony had made her call once.

"I'm not calling him."

"Then get your friend to come and get you," said Chelsea evenly.

"What?"

"Whoever's been texting you this whole time. Your girlfriend? Or your drug buddy?"

He glared at her as he pulled the steering wheel back and forth angrily. "You're as messed up as the rest of your family," he said. Then he started going on again about the repair and the tow cost and the twins ruining his life. Now he was just ranting.

She couldn't stand it. It was already almost six, and it would be light in no time. She wanted to be in the stand before the sun came up. She wanted to see what her father and Caleb would be seeing, the woods and the deer at sunrise. She just wanted to see. It didn't matter if she killed a deer. She had nothing to field-dress it with, and she wouldn't be able to drag it out herself unless it was small, and no way to get it back home. She hadn't even thought about how she'd get back. Walk until someone picked her up. You couldn't hitch a ride with a dead deer.

She hesitated ... made a sudden decision. She unbuckled her seatbelt and opened the passenger door; she pushed the barrel end of the case toward Kyle. "Keep it," she said, feeling frightened at the thought of what she was saying but also exhilarated at her own boldness. "Sell it to pay for the tie rod or whatever's wrong with it. The van was basically broke down anyway. You know it was. So now you've still got a broken-down van, but you've got a gun too, and thirty dollars."

She got out and pulled her hood up, and her zipper up to the top of the jacket. She grabbed the sports bag. *Leave him without the bullets.*

"What the hell," he said. Then, "How do I know this gun's worth anything? What about your father?" But she ignored him and slammed the door and started walking.

The cold recognized her warm blood instantly and wrapped around her like a winding sheet.

The trailer was on a ridge surrounded by cedars and scrub trees and a lone black walnut that was bare now, but its fall crop—what the squirrels hadn't carried away—rolled at her feet. The green hulls had blackened, and if she'd had a sack with her, and time before the *imminent* sunrise, she would have picked them up because she and Caleb loved them. Melissa did, too.

She got the key out of her pocket, but the door wasn't locked. She wanted to see if he'd left another rifle out here. She wished for a second that she had her mother's gun, but she stomped the wish down. If he only had another gun here, and ammunition ... his bow, she wouldn't be able to pull it.

Inside, she smelled the odor before she turned on the light. Her eyes tried to make sense of the confusion. There was the forest of racks with skull tops spread over the living room floor. They took up most of the room. He'd mounted and hung one rack of antlers. There were kits for mounting some others but no sign that he'd been working on it. The possum—was that what she smelled? The odor was more like the stink from Kyle's jacket, a smell that kept tickling her memory—had emerged from the sea of antlers when she'd turned the light on. It must have been gnawing on the shreds of hair and hide still attached to the skull tops. She'd seen one do that in their basement. She didn't know how it could have gotten in. It couldn't have been here that long, or it would have died of dehydration.

She expected the animal to dart back into the forest of antler points or to fall over prone and play dead. But she pulled the screen door wide anyway and pushed the stop out to hold it and edged in to the other side of the living room. She wasn't afraid of it—just worried she wouldn't be able to chase it out. "Hey! Get out!" she yelled, waving her arms and lunging forward threateningly. To her surprise, it scurried into the dark.

She didn't find a gun—there wasn't much in the trailer: a chair, a tall stack of plastic cups. A tool belt. Cans of Kilz. A bag of trash that the possum had dragged out all across the kitchen. There was no time to look around if she was going to be in the stand before the sun was up. She locked the door behind her and followed the trail she knew from the times Tony had brought her out here. Down from the ridge, along a shallow creek. Her phone barely emitted enough light to see. She'd left her gloves in Kyle's van and had to keep switching hands. Her right in her pocket. Now pull it out, take the phone in it, and warm the left. Tony had the silent step of a natural hunter, but she was awkward and only half knew the way and was probably frightening off any deer in the area. She cast her phone light on the ground in front of her and saw the double-crescent prints of a deer's cloven hoofs—so delicate for an animal that could outweigh her by fifty pounds.

Was she lost? She recalled an old, stricken oak with gnarled branches knotted with black galls. It should be somewhere, but she hadn't seen ... and then there it was, spreading *grotesque* like a ghost tree on her left. Either it was so black that it stood out against the darkness or the night was starting to break up. She could actually distinguish it without a light.

Just beyond was a clearing Tony had made with a chainsaw, and the ladder stand on the north side. The metal rungs froze her fingers as she climbed. She had no seat cushion, so she crouched on the latticed platform; it, too, was freezing, and she didn't want to sit unless she couldn't squat anymore, but finally she had to. Her top half was OK, but her legs were cold, and her fingers and toes were frozen.

She was just in time because the blood was let, the day was here. A spectacular, frostless morning. The dryness was like a blessing; she couldn't have taken it any colder. The sun was a sliver of fire through the trees: bright heat, growing, emerging, staining what she could see of the sky. Everything was devoid of human sounds except her jacket rubbing when she moved to try to stay warm. But a few brave birds called out, and there were small movements nearby, and the chittering of squirrels, awake and hunting for food. Everything on the ground beneath and in the branches around her wanted food. That was why men used to go out in the woods with guns like the one she had handed over to Kyle, but now it was just a ritual where you shed blood easily, taking without offering the required price. Tony must know this. It could be why he'd stopped after mounting one pair of antlers.

She wondered what he would say about the Winchester. She remembered something now: it wasn't just any .30-30. It was an antique gun that had been her grandfather's before it was her mother's.

It was probably—certainly—worth more than the Potters' van, though Kyle Potter would never figure that out. He was poor and stupid. Every mistake he made got etched in his brain like a blueprint for his next move. The course of his life was to run again, and again, disastrously, in those grooves he'd etched. He'd sell the gun for a few hundred dollars and waste it all on the beat-up van or cigarettes or cheap shit, whatever. But, possibly, Tony wouldn't notice for a long time that the rifle was gone. And it had belonged to her mother, who had deserted them, so rightfully it was Chelsea's. Hers to shoot, hers to lose.

A shot blasted—not too close. A mile off, maybe. Caleb and Tony were a county away.

For some reason she was thinking again about Atwater, the miracle dog, when she looked down, and there was the buck. He stood facing her tree, nervously, stamping. Strong chest, with the white at his throat, the wet dark eyes and the symmetrical, curving antlers like an elaborate pronged headdress balanced between his erect ears. He was not a large animal. He was perfect. His sides rose and fell, breathing. She counted his antler points. Eight, one broken at the tip. He shook his head slightly and stamped again. He was afraid, why didn't he run?

Would she have shot him if she'd had the gun? It didn't matter because the thing was, she had given the gun away.

And then, all at once, she felt hollow and terrified. Fear colder than ice and burning, in turn. Her heart pounded, and her breath stopped like her body had forgotten how to breathe. Then, finally, at the edge of passing out, she breathed again, but she was shaking, awash in heat and sweat. She'd made a mistake. Worse than anything Kyle Potter would dream of doing.

Something was happening. But she wasn't sure what it was. Some force outside her own deciding was at work, bending things in a bad direction. It had been happening since she awoke, starting with red lights outside, with Caleb leaving the gun safe unlocked. It had continued with Kyle Potter and the smell, the *fetor*, that caused her to react and run him off the road and made her relinquish her gun. It had slowed her down because of the possum in the trailer. *Something* wanted that gun. And she'd been supposed to hang on to it. She didn't know how or why she knew this. The buck. It had come because she didn't have the gun. A messenger. To make her understand what she'd done, and what she must try to do to repair it.

She scrambled down the tree, skipping rungs, dropping to the ground. The deer leaped and was gone the second she moved. She ran back along the trail and up to the ridge, past the trailer. Her phone flew out of her pocket; she heard it hit the dirt, but she kept running at full stride. *Make him still be there, make the van be there, make no one have come yet, not Lucas T., not anyone, make the gun be there with him.*

Make him give it back.

Steven Chung

Lake-Effect Snow

We found flakes on fire hydrants
that will never save a life.

Sunday, talk of cigarettes
to heat our systems.

The lake no longer frozen midwave,
we dipped the dust of our fathers

past our ankles, below sight.
We jumped in like driftwood,

hoped to deposit ourselves on
a different bank. Morning:

this city still too cold for whispering
away into vapor. Even the homes burn

only freeze-frame by freeze-
frame. So we warm our lungs

with the endings of fire, remember
our fathers not as their bodies,

but as songs scattered from town to town.
They are loved by the schoolchildren

making snowmen
out of ash.

Kerri French

32 Weeks

Still dark, I listen for the flap
of wings as I walk beside the river.

Before I was sick, before the doctors
said my body would not sustain hers,

I sat each afternoon on the hill
behind the cathedral, a foal napping

in the field as anchored narrowboats
quietly shifted close to shore.

It went on like this until one day
the foal was gone, its mother

standing alone beneath the trees
as I walked to the hospital in the rain.

Now I walk until the birds
land beside me, their blue wings wet

where the river skims the path.

Dwight Hilson

Royal Ruby Reds

1986

 —Thank y'all for calling Billy Stans' Alamo Fruit, located deep in the heart of Texas, home of the world-famous Royal Ruby Reds. My name is Darlene; how may I help you today?

 Hello, Darlene, this is James … no, Jim, please call me Jim K—. I want to order some of those Royal Ruby grapefruits.

 —Well, sir, you've called the right place. I'd—.

 I grew up on Royal Rubys. My dad was a customer, still is, I think … if my stepmom hasn't canceled—.

 —Why Mr. K—, I'd just be thrilled to death to help you enjoy our delicious—.

 They're the best, without a doubt. You know, I ate my first Royal Ruby Red in the sixties.

 —Oh, sir, (laughs) you can't possibly be that old.

 No, really, you can look it up, I mean him, John K—, my dad, he's in your system, probably one of your best customers, certainly in New York City.

 —Is that where you're calling from, Mr. K—, all the way from New York City?

 Please, Darlene, call me Jim.

 —Are all you New York City folks so nice?

 No … well, I can't really say.

 —Mr. K— (whispers conspiratorially), we're not supposed to address customers by their given name. Now don't get me wrong, I would, but Mr. Stans would never let me hear the end of it.

 No, that's OK wouldn't want to get you in any trouble. I'm just glad you're still in business. I'd been away for a while and, and I remembered those big red boxes, one used to come to our apartment every month, like clockwork ... I grew up on those grapefruits. You see—.

—*Well, then, why don't we get started with your name and address?*

Yes, of course, like I said, it's Jim, James K—, ### Fifth Avenue, New York—.

—*Now, I see a J. K— in New York—oh, wait, that's a John K—.*

Yup, that's him—my father, I mean. He started ordering your grapefruits in sixty-six, I think, right after he was diagnosed. He was diabetic, you see—needed the sugar when his insulin went out of whack. You had to know the signs, though; he'd act silly, and then like he was drunk, and if you didn't give him some fruit—something sweet—fast, well, he could collapse like he'd been shot.

—*Now that sounds just awful.*

Yeah, but those Ruby Reds did the trick. I mean, you couldn't use them in an emergency, took too long to cut one up, but the juice worked fine; we always kept a small pitcher filled with fresh-squeezed Ruby Red. I wasn't allowed to touch it, the juice, but once I tried one of your grapefruits. I remember, well, the color, for instance, that pale red, almost magenta, none of the others had that color—not California, Florida—and so juicy; you could squeeze out half a glass after eating all the meat, I mean, damn, they're something special. Of course, my dad ordered other food by mail, like artichokes—"Mr. Choke," it said on the box—from California, and huge, never seen an artichoke that big in a store, big enough to fill a mixing bowl, but then—.

—*Mr. K—?*

Huh? Oh, I'm sorry, Darlene. I got carried away a little bit. I was going to say I never saw those again after I went away to school ... but the Royal Ruby Reds, those were in the fridge whenever I came home, even after my parents split.

—*And they're still just like you remember, the best grapefruits in the world. Now—.*

God, I can't wait to try them again; I didn't see any when I was last at my dad's apartment, but like I said, the stepmom runs the show, and, well ....

—*Would you like me to use that address? ### Fifth Avenue, in New York City, Mr. K—?*

Yes, that'd be great, Darlene … and, say, do you still ship them automatically during the season?

—*Why, nothing would make me happier (laughs), and Mr. Stans, too! We attach an invoice and return envelope to each box, easy as pie.*

Right…a grapefruit pie.

—*Oh, Mr. K—, you are funny. It's really been such a pleasure chatting with you today, and we can't thank you enough for placing your order with Billy Stans' Alamo Fruit.*

1992

—*Thank you for calling Billy Stans' National Fruit, how might I direct your call?*

Oh, hi, um … I'm a Royal Ruby Red customer, and—.

—*Let me connect you to that department—.*

Thank y—.

—*(Music)*

—*Hello, my name is Shari-Lynn. Do you have an account number?*

Yes, I think so … but I don't know what—.

—*You can find it easily enough on the invoice attached to the box for your most recent order.*

I'm sorry, but I didn't save my last box.

—*That's perfectly OK, sir; I can look that up for you … last name?*

Then why …. Right, thank you, it's K—, Jim … James K—, New York City, but that's not what I'm calling about. Hey, would you know if Darlene still works there?

—*Darlene, sir? I can't say I know a Darlene, not here at least (laughs). But we've been growing like weeds in a wheat field.*

OK, I was just wondering … I remembered her name, that's all, last time I called, she took my order a few years back and we had such a pleasant conversation.

—*Now, I see a Mr. John K—.*

No, that's my dad … I mean *was*—.

James K—, I found you, ### Fifth Avenue, New—.

Yes, that's me, but I need to change the address; you know, got married, moved to the suburbs ….

—*Well, congratulations, Mr. K—I can certainly help you with that. May I have your new address?*

Thank you, it's #-A Sound View Road, Stamford, Connecticut, but ….

—Let me just read that back to you … (repeats address). We'll start using this address with the new season delivery in November. Is there anything else I can help you with?

No … well, yes. I'm not sure how to say this, but … my dad, John K—, he died last spring.

—Oh, Mr. K—, I'm so sorry to hear that, please accept our condolences.

Thank you … Shari-Lynn, was it? He loved Royal Ruby Reds, started getting them when I was a kid—I told Darlene that story, how I remember the red box arriving each month through the winter. I tried buying a red grapefruit at a supermarket once, but they weren't the same, tart and tough and dried out. Guess only Billy Stans customers get the best fruit, right?

—Yes, sir, we mail out to every state in the union, even Alaska and Hawaii.

I ….

—Sir? Mr. K—?

Oh, I'm sorry, I was just thinking about something … the box, actually, that Royal Ruby Red box. It's strange, but after my dad died … he died last spring? Sorry, I said that already, well, after he died my stepmother was moving out of the house and she found one of your boxes—one of the Royal Ruby Red ones, tucked way in the back of a closet cupboard. I kind of expected she would've kept it for herself, but she gave it to me. Anyway, inside were letters, hundreds of letters from World War II. Can you believe he saved every letter written to him during the war? He was sent to the Pacific, Burma; almost got killed. That box also had every letter he wrote to his parents and sister, hundreds of them, letters from his friends sent overseas, teachers sending updates, and girlfriends, lots of girlfriends—seems he had one in every port. He ended up wounded, in a hospital, in Calcutta, no less, for six months. All these years, and that box remained hidden; he never mentioned it, not once, and he sure never talked about his injuries or anything else from the war years. I've got the letters now, still stored in that Royal Ruby Red box, been waiting to find time to read them all. Expect they might answer some questions.

—Well, I've never heard anything like that before.

Yeah, it is pretty crazy, but there's another selling point for your grapefruits—the box makes a perfect letter-storage box.

—I never thought of that (Laughs). But, sir, I'm not sure I can remove your father from our customer list. That's managed by another company,

and I think you'd have to contact them directly ... or maybe your stepmother should—.

No, that's not going to happen. And now that I think about it, it doesn't really matter anyway.

2000

—*(Recording)* THANK YOU FOR CALLING RED TERRY'S DIRECT FRUIT. ... FOR RED'S FRESH GLOW ORANGE CUSTOMERS, PLEASE PRESS 1. ... FOR GEORGIA SWEET ONION CUSTOMERS, PLEASE PRESS 2. ... FOR ROYAL RUBY RED CUSTOMERS, PLEASE—.

—*(Recording)* IF YOU'D LIKE TO PLACE AN ORDER, PLEASE PRESS 1 ... FOR ALL CUSTOMER SERVICE—.

—*Thank you for calling Red Terry, how may I help you today?*

Oh, yes, I have a question about my standing order; this is Jim K—, account number #####.

—*Thank you, Mr. K—, I'd be happy to assist you. Let's see—are you sure about that account number? I'm not showing it in our system.*

Yes, that's the number I wrote down last—.

—*I see the problem. That's your old number Mr. K—; we assigned you a new Red Terry account number after Billy Stans' National joined the Red Terry family of companies.*

I guess I knew something had changed when I didn't hear a Texas accent, and—.

—*(Chuckles.) We're in Iowa now, order processing and corporate, but your grapefruits are still shipped out, as always, ripe off the tree from South Texas.*

The box is different, too—still red, though.

—*Yes, it is. So how may I help you today, Mr. K—?*

Right, here's the problem—my standing order is for nine grapefruits, and this time you sent me eighteen ... along with a whole set of spoons.

—*(Proudly) Why, yes, that's our way of saying thank you for being such a loyal Royal Ruby Red customer.*

OK, sure, that's wonderful, but you see—I'm sorry, what's your name?

—*Marilynne, it's Marilynne, Mr. K—.*

Thank you, Marilynne, I should've asked earlier, but you see, Marilynne, there's no way I can eat that many grapefruits in a month, not even Royal Rubys, so I hope you can—.

—Don't you worry, Mr. K—, like I said, that was just a gift. Next month you'll receive your regular order. But we do hope you'll enjoy those Red Terry grapefruit spoons with our compliments.

Yeah, spoons … you know, we had those when I was growing up —I mean spoons with a serrated front edge, just like what you sent. Never used them, though, didn't have to. We had a housekeeper, Mary, used to fix my dad's breakfast; she'd use a paring knife to cut each section, sawing around the segment walls to loosen perfect little chunks of grapefruit flesh, amazing. Why use one of those spoons to grind and twist, mangle the fruit, when you can just lift out nothing but the meat?

—(Laughs) That's a good—.

Mary would cut up multiple halves; guess she thought she'd make sure there was always a grapefruit ready when my dad wanted one. But I wasn't stupid, if I saw one ready to go and she wasn't looking, then away it went. Of course, it became a habit—not stealing Mary's handiwork—no, I mean, cutting all the sections. When I was a teenager they, my parents, sent me off to boarding school out in the boondocks of Massachusetts, and believe it or not they had grapefruits there, not Royal Ruby Reds, more like those crappy Florida ones, the ones with yellowish, mostly mealy fruit. I'd eat them, though, like I said, out of habit, or maybe they reminded me of …. Anyway, I'd use their lousy cafeteria knives and carve out the sections just like Mary used to do. I must've looked like a moron; the dean of students actually made fun of me when he saw me in action one morning. He liked grapefruits too, but would use his pocketknife and slice around the outside between the rind and fruit, then dig in. But you did that and you had to eat pieces of the section-dividing rind, which is just nasty and bitter, even in Ruby Reds. One of these toothy spoons would've come in handy; students weren't allowed to own a pocketknife, that's for sure. That dean … what was his name? Crocker, that was it; everyone used to say he was a *crock of—*. Well, he could've kicked my ass out of school when I got caught with Daphne in my room, girls were strictly verboten in the dorms, but when he called me in to his office, all he wanted to talk about was my silly grapefruit-prep technique. It was like he thought my handiwork represented some weird example of discipline, future potential. Crazy, right?

—(Silence.)

Marilynne—you still with me?

—*Umm ... (hesitates). Yes, Mr. K—.*

So the dean, Dean Crocker, he let me off the hook with just a suspension. If you think about it, my life could've been a total mess if not for Royal Ruby Reds. Maybe I need to teach my kids how to properly cut a grapefruit—.

—*(Relieved) Oh, do you have children, Mr. K—?*

What? No, no, not yet, we're trying, but ....

—*Well like I said, Mr. K—, your next shipment will return to the normal amount, and by the way, I notice that your credit card will expire in a couple months . Would you like me to update that information?*

2007

—*(Recording) THANK YOU FOR CALLING TERRY DIRECT. PLEASE LISTEN CAREFULLY, AS OUR PHONE OPTIONS HAVE CHANGED: FOR HOUSEWARES, PLEASE PRESS 1 .... FOR KITCHEN APPLIANCES, PLEASE PRESS 2 ... FOR FRESH GROWN FOR YOU, PLEASE—.*

—*(Recording) THANK YOU FOR CALLING FRESH GROWN FOR YOU. FOR RED'S FRESH GLOW ORANGE CUSTOMERS ....*

Dammit.

... PLEASE PRESS 1 ... FOR GEORGIA SWEET ONION CUSTOMERS, PLEASE PRESS 2 ... FOR ROYAL RUBY RED CUSTOMERS, PLEASE—.

You've got to be kidding me.

—*(Recording) IF YOU'D LIKE TO PLACE AN ORDER, PLEASE PRESS 1 ... FOR ALL CUSTOMER SERVICE—.*

—*(Foreign accent.) Thank you for calling Fresh Grown For You. My name is Aryan, how is it my pleasure to assist you today?*

Oh, great—.

—*Thank you, sir, who is it with I am talking to?*

Something tells me you're not in Kansas.

—*(Laughs) No sir, but Fresh Grown For You delivers many customers in—.*

Right, I get it ... say, you wouldn't be anywhere near Calcutta, would you?

—*Oh, no, sir, Fresh Grown For You is located—.*

Excuse me, Aryan, but I have a complaint.

—*Yes, sir, I am most pleased to*—.

I'm sure, I'm sure. Look, my name is Jim K—, account number ##########, and I want you to credit me for this last batch of grapefruits.

—*Whatever was being the problem, Mr. K*—?

Simple. These were not Royal Ruby Reds, you're sending me crappy Florida grapefruits or from some other godforsaken place, and worse, you're still charging me the full price.

—*I am sad for your displeasure with these Fresh Grown For You grapefruits, Mr. K*—.

Look, Aryan, I've been a customer for over twenty years, and I know what's what. You guys … I mean, not you, but Terry Direct, they're just trying to extend the season, probably costs them nothing to buy these things, bet they pick 'em up for pennies at the local Shop Rite. But I don't like to waste my money. I ….

—*Terry Direct wishes a guarantee for your happiness, Mr. K*—.

A guarantee? Yeah, that would be nice … a guarantee. Not sure how that could work. Funny, though, Royal Ruby Reds always used to make me happy. Not these crappy imposters, mind you, but the real ones, big and heavy and filled with that thick, sweet fruit. Christ, did you know you can squeeze out half a glass of juice after you've scarfed down all the fruit? Probably not, no way Mr. Terry's gonna send any to old Aryan when they have the balls to deliver batches of shit to loyal customers. Am I right? I was actually excited when the box arrived, I couldn't remember getting any grapefruits after early April; but then I sliced into one and it was like trying to cut a coconut. I'm sure I sound like a lunatic, but they shouldn't try to screw their customers, there's plenty of companies that that's all they do, like the goddamn drug companies, for instance. And they don't give you a choice…at least I can cancel my grapefruits if I want. Not my wife's medication, though, not a chance, they just keep raising the price every year and my company keeps raising my deductible. I bet you don't even know what that is, a deductible. Doesn't matter, what choice do I have? I don't want to think what would happen if she …. Well, anyway, I don't let her see the grapefruits when they arrive, keep them down in the garage fridge. She sure enjoyed them, too; that was one of the reasons I first ordered, so she could taste what I'd been making such a fuss about—all my Royal Ruby Red stories. Sometimes when an order arrived we'd make a race of sectioning out all the fruit, see which of us could hollow out the most grapefruits. Then we'd squeeze them all into a Tupperware and spoon the chunks as desired, sprinkle a little sugar. Had to stop when she was first diagnosed, her medication … what was it? Doesn't matter. Can you believe that you can't eat grapefruits on the stuff? That's when I started hiding them in the garage. Probably should've canceled my order right then, but … . That was all a few years back; she can eat grapefruits on the new medications, but I think the acid would throw her off, she really needs protein, stuff that'll ….

—*Please to excuse me, Mr. K—, but I am not understanding what you wish of me, sir.*

Yeah, I'm sorry, Aryan; I didn't mean to get carried away there. Listen, I know it's not your fault. Just credit me for this last shipment and put it in the system that I don't want to receive any grapefruits but genuine Royal Ruby Reds …. No, wait, just set it up so you don't send me anything after April, and we'll call it a day. That should be easy, right?

—*(Silence)*

Recently

—*(Recording) THANK YOU FOR CALLNG BAKER & HOOD NATURALS, PROVIDERS OF ONLY THE FINEST FRESH-DELIVERED PRODUCE. TO ENSURE CUSTOMER SERVICE, THIS CALL MAY BE RECORDED. TO PLACE AN ORDER, PLEASE PRESS "1"; FOR ALL BILLING ISSUES, PLEASE PRESS "2"; TO REPORT A DELIVERY PROBLEM, PLEASE PRESS—.*

—*Good afternoon, my name is Crystal, how may I assist you?*

Umm ….

—*Sir? Can I help you?*

I'm sorry, guess I didn't expect to talk with a human being so quickly; last time I was connected to someone … someone in India, I think.

—*That was a different company, sir.*

Do you still sell Royal Ruby Reds? I found an old invoice with this eight-hundred number and it connected me—.

—*Yes sir, and our Golden Sunshine and Coastal Orange grapefruits, too. Baker & Hood is America's finest purveyor of farm-fresh produce; we started selling Royal Ruby Reds just over a year ago. Are you a current customer?*

Yes, I think so. I'd receive the grapefruits every month, but—.

—*Name, sir?*

79

It's K—, James K—.

—I see a Mrs. J. K—, in New York—.

Yeah, well, I'll be damned … no, I mean, that's my father—no, stepmother.

—I don't see you in our system, but as a prior customer, you should've received our product catalog.

But I never needed a catalog before; I was a regular customer … for over twenty-five years.

—Yes, Mr. K—, this has been a problem since we acquired the Ruby Red brand.

What? I don't understand.

—Customer files were sent to our list-management division, but we can't access an old, I mean, previous customer file here at order processing in Memphis, at least not until an order is placed.

Wait … are you saying I don't exist until I buy something?

—Oh, of course not, sir, but have you moved recently?

No, not recently, I moved last year, after my wife …. It was such a crazy year, too much to do, I moved to a condo closer to the city, but, well, I can't remember when I ate my last Royal Ruby Red.

—Why, nothing would make me happier than to take care of that right this instant, and, as a loyal customer, if you order a full season of delicious Royal Ruby Reds or any other full season of Baker & Hood Naturals products, we'll throw in free of charge a complete set of ….

Laura Lee Washburn

Faces

"[The face] is pierced with greedy holes"
−Jean-Paul Sartre

Sometimes looking at the magnification
of an insect or seeing up close
from an aquarium's tunnel
the mouth and other orifices of a pale
bottom-dwelling creature, one can't help
but feel repulsion. We imagine that mouth
sucking or crunching some other vertebrate's
death, knowing, though not acknowledging
the brutality of our own maws,
from the baby's teething screams
to the mutton ground in molars.

The eye above all rejects nothing.
Though it may close, we know
not to trust its avarice, and so
draw the hands up at horror. Only pinched
fingers keep the nose in check. Grab
and snatch, our mouths send
the emissaries of the lips and tongue out,
such is the importance of their needs.
I am thinking of my face as the flat pale face
of the skate or the ray, pressed
against the world, capable of almost anything.

Ösel Jessica Plante

When I Come Back From the Dead

There are no doorbells. The tulips greet me
with the same empty cups I've never been

able to drink from. The porch lights,

left on all night, have battened their faces
against the confusion of moths.

There was a time when any hand—your hand—

was the entire world at work on its old
dissertation about love. That word locked

in page after page of thinking. The ambulance

inside me has only just turned
off its siren. I've learned to hover, to fly

backwards into the ravaged heads

of cardinals. The way love works is
darkness, darkness, darkness, let there be

one atomic and particular sun. My body
spoke fire into itself, an opal ring

was lit. The world then reversed its grip.

Staci R. Schoenfeld

The Alligator Girl Becomes

Nights the girl slips into the alligator skin
she relishes the weight of husk—how her arms
and legs fit, how the surface welcomes her,
wraps her frame in its reptilian hug.

She remembers countless field trips
to the Everglades, her classmates shrieking
as the gator's mouth was held shut by
the guide's hand, proof of man's superiority.

She felt bad for the creature, on display
against its will for kids who would kill
it rather than listen to the soul song
of its bellows. The gator's cold eyes

always drew her in. Her mother says
the girl's skin is too thin. A gator's hide
is thick. Impervious. She still hasn't figured out
how to work the eyelids. She'll need them

to swim with her eyes open for predators.
For prey. Nights she dreams of flight
she understands she is becoming.
She's tapped into the genetic memory

of that common ancestor that kept her kind
close to the earth but saw her kin take to the skies.
They learned a different kind of freedom.
She grows adept at flicking her tail,

clacking her jaws, the high walk
and low crawl. Practices her log
imitation in the bathtub, snout
above water, breathing in. Out.

The night she leaves for good,
she tries on the prom dress her mother
bought after making her lose
fifteen pounds in time to get a date.

She smooths the dress down, enjoys
the slide of satin over scale, each bump
still visible through fabric. Her mother
would tell her to hide the lumps with Spanx.

The girl twirls for the bathroom mirror
one last time, then shreds the dress
with her claws. She won't need it where
she's going—back to the swamps.

She lowers first her head, then her front
and back legs into the toilet bowl, her diving
form a perfect ten, and with a snap of her tail,
she flushes herself away, leaves not a trace.

Jason Namey

Barked Hoarse at a Bottom-Lit Pool

A man tried to stab me yesterday and now I have no shadow.

I had walked into a deli to decrease the pastrami in central Florida and some lazy-eyed, street-torn rot I'd never met followed me in to try and poke my kidney with a switchblade. I shimmied aside and he hit my shadow in the leg and it ran off screaming then he ran off screaming.

Today's a hot, family-free Florida Easter Sunday. I'm standing at the living room window, watching waves in the pool loop like measuring worms. The neighbor's daughter, Anna Saturday, is practicing her jackknifes in *my* pool while *her* parents have a cookout with no invite sent my way. We let her swim whenever she wants as long as she cleans the leaves out. Secretly, Elle, my wife, thinks Anna will date her son—I'm supposed to say *our* son, but she had him when we met—but her son's fifteen years old, homeschooled and mucusy, while Anna's near matriculated at UCF, so good luck, hotshot. I've never once seen her clean the leaves out.

If I had to describe Anna in one word, I would say she's symmetrical.

She is full of skittish sideways glances and responds to everything with "You, too." Her wet yellow hair ropes over her shoulder like the tail of a dog.

I could use a swim, but don't want her to see me without my shadow. I keep thinking I just need to find the right shade of light that will bring it back. I've tried every light bulb in the house. Last night, I looked up how expensive it would be to put in black carpet. Elle and her son might fight that. They love to gang up on me.

Over meals, they sit close and creak secrets like lovers. They eat breakfast in their underwear; I won't even leave the bedroom without socks on. He watches a fitness video called *The Vietnam War Body: 5th Edition* and crawls through swamps with a large whittled stick, shouting tangos and foxtrots. He chases me around the house with it, the stick. Poking and jabbing. He tells me he's going to stab a gator. I tell him I don't think *either* of his sticks are big enough for that.

They left last Thursday to visit Elle's twin sister. Her husband had died and they went to fill the empty space and spent odors.

I drove them to the airport and stopped on the way home to buy a handle of tequila and liter of lime juice, a five-pound, bone-in ham, and a loaf of rye. When I get hungry, I sandwich the ham with bread and spicy mustard. When I get thirsty, I sip a margarita. I'm currently sipping a margarita.

If I had to describe Elle in one word, I would say she's buttony.

I sit on the couch to catch the replay of a weekend golf tournament, some affair with sun-dried skin and sundry hats.

One night, years ago, I woke up to a dog barking at turned water. The lights lit the pool a fluorescent blue. The Saturdays' dog, then a puppy, stood on the deck, shouting, staring at the slithering dark shade of an alligator toeing the floor. The surface rippled. The floating leaves rose and fell like lily pads. The gator walked along the bottom and the dog followed, barking himself hoarse, barking bruises in his lungs. He thought the gator was his shadow ran off. Maybe it was.

A knock on the sliding glass door.

I stand and look. Anna, bent-kneed and shivering, rubs hands against goose-pimpled arms. She quickly waves and mouths, "Towel."

I show her the one-second finger and walk to the laundry room, hesitate, walk to the bathroom and grab my shower towel—throw it in the dryer for thirty seconds and fold it twice to feel freshly unhampered.

She basks in its greedy fur, rubbing her neck and hair.

She smells like chlorine and tanning oil, coconut, some shampoo's stubborn tangerine scent. Coal smoke and beef char waft the fence from her folks grilling and cocktailing, rubbing it in my face. When Anna dries her calves, I see concrete chalk pool-decked to the palms of her feet.

"Do you have the eardrops?" she asks.

I hand her the brown dropper bottle we keep by the door, filled with rubbing alcohol and vinegar. Her water-wrinkled fingertips overlap mine and feel treaded like tires. She tilts sideways and carefully puts the drops in one ear, lets them stand a few seconds, then turns her head and does the other.

"Thanks Mr. Corduroy," she says, handing me the bottle back; some dripped solution cools my hand and smells like peroxide. She gowns the towel and goes to lie in the sun, inserts earbuds that sprangle from an iPhone.

"Pool's looking pretty leafy," I shout.

"You, too," she replies with a hollow smile I take to say she knows I said something but not what. Or means to give that impression.

Elle told me not to come because I would make things worse. She said, You'll just make things worse. She said this to me, my wife.

I wouldn't have made things worse, but this way she gets two weeks off and a chance to visit her sister, and I get some quiet and a chance to play the victim. If you know how to look at things right, you always get what you want.

If you don't know how to look at things right, you try to shiv guys like me for no reason.

If you really don't know how to look at things right, you don't invite me to your Easter cookout.

If you're Anna, you look like you could use a cold margarita.

Maybe she would be impressed that I didn't have a shadow? It would be something that distinguished me from her handsomer, well-shadowed peers.

One time while I swam laps underwater, Rocko escaped and got into the pool and started to tread water directly over me. When I tried to swim around him to come up for air, he followed me from above. He thought I was his shadow. That he had to follow it or lose it again. He tracked me like a quail. My lungs felt like they were sucking the oxygen from all my cells, but each time I prepared to make a run for it, I looked up and saw these four feet jutting with unkempt claws, scissoring the water. Eventually, I couldn't hold my breath any longer and launched myself off the bottom, and that night Elle cotton-balled alcohol over the lines on my back.

☾

I mix two drinks and finger through my Steely Dan CDs, pull out *Aja*, and find a T-shirt that snugs my arms. No time to trim that hairy inner bicep, but those shivers of grey sideburns bring out my driving-range tan. Balancing the drinks, I slide the door and spill some sticky green down my thumb.

The towel lies folded neatly over the chair back. Pink, plastic sunglasses shadow the table, hers, forgotten.

I sit and recline, the rubber still damp and pimpled with drops of either sweat or pool water. I can smell the sweet-lingered scent of salt and tanned skin, lotion and sunburn. I gulp a margarita and close my eyes.

I wake to wet pricks against my cheek.

The Saturdays' golden retriever is licking my face like a scab.

Anna comes around the fence in a pastel blue sundress, skin slightly pinked. "Rocko!" she calls and runs over, tugging him once by the collar.

"Hey, Anna, tell me everything you know," I say drowsily.

She forgets the response and laughs, skips back across the yard. Rocko checks his reflection in the pool, then chases after Anna, nipping her heels.

"I did when I said hello," I say to myself and close my eyes while I finish the second drink, arms heavy with liquor and sweat. When I set the cup down, it trips over her sunglasses and rolls across and off the table, unscarred shatter-proof plastic. It rolls into and ripples the pool.

Her sunglasses. She might need them. I should bring them over.

Hey, notice anything different about me? Anything rendering me unique among the men you know and, therefore, most attractive?

I stand, take a minute to steady myself, then walk to the bottom edge of the yard and around the fence, careful not to lose my footing and foot into the canal.

Empty chairs jut from the grass. Tall trees shade their yard. Empty beer bottles and loose napkins spread blades of grass. The after-image of an aged Easter.

I take broad steps up the inclined yard. When I get to their patio, I gently knuckle the back window. I try to shade my eyes with my palm and look in, but, shadowless, the sun goes brightly through my fingers.

Jack: improver of Easter cookouts, comforter of sisters-in-law, with no Easter cookout or sister-in-law in sight.

I knock again but can't squint inside. In the window, my reflection looks back at me.

I amble slowly down the grass like a morose schoolboy.

I stand at the living-room window and stare out at the pool. As night moves in, I turn on the underwater lights. The pool, blue bulbous and bulb lit. If you stand directly over the source, no one can see your shadow, it melts infinitely upward.

I keep the living room dark. It brings a certain quiet. The whole house smells like old newspaper. Alone, me and the dust beneath my fingernails.

Sarah Freligh

The Pedophile's Wife

He picked daisies
from a vacant lot
the day he proposed.
He wanted children
and when I couldn't give him any
we took in foster kids: boys
with bitten fingernails,
the glazed eyes of beaten dogs.

He liked to wrestle them, tickle
their ribs until they begged
for mercy. Summers
he showed them
how to wrap their hands
around a football and throw. Nights
he went to their rooms
when they cried.

I remember the daisies
looked like faces
bent and trembling
in his hand.

Sarah Freligh

Why I Despise the Martini

Because I carried trays dangerously
weighted with them, stemmed glasses
like big-bodied thoroughbreds
tapering to slender legs. Because
when you looked down instead
of straight ahead, booze sloshed
over the lip. Because I believe
a martini should be sipped
by women wearing veiled hats
and white gloves, hair arranged
in low chignons or French knots, not
drained in three glugs by men fresh
from playing eighteen holes under
a July sun, insatiably thirsty
for attention from their college-
girl waitress: *Hey baby, hey*
honey I need another even as gin
levels continue to rise in the brain,
wiping out neighborhoods
of glial cells, flooding cities
of gray matter while down below,
no evacuation plans are in play:
The heart is staying put, but
beating slower now while
the liver sighs and braces
herself to deal with the waste.

Kim Magowan

Pop Goes the Weasel

One by one, Nina's friends from her moms' group have gone back to work. It's a march Nina watches with chagrin, since the most interesting mothers bail first. Raunchy Iris started working part-time, but switched to full-time after telling Nina that her days at the bank felt like her days off.

"I just don't have a twenty-four-seven/stay-at-home mom in me!" is the consensus.

At the reunion party in May, when the ten babies (all spring birthdays) are a year old, Nina and Becky are the only holdouts still not working. Nina would gladly trade Becky for any of the other moms. Officious Becky makes her own baby food, jamming roasted yams through a potato ricer and freezing the puree in ice cube trays. Becky corrals Nina into exchanges ("I'll make yams tomorrow, and you do mashed asparagus").

At the reunion picnic, holding Jonah between her knees, Nina describes the aftermath of one of these baby food exchanges to Iris. Nina's husband Nathan, making cocktails, assumed the Ziploc of green ice cubes was some gourmet experiment of Nina's—cilantro or mint-infused ice—and squalled when informed that he had just put frozen mashed peas into his gin and tonic.

"Like with all my free time, I'd make specialty ice cubes," Nina tells Iris. "Who am I, Martha Stewart?"

Iris laughs, though her eyebrows raise. Their angle conveys that, unlike the working moms sprawling around them on Guatemalan blankets, Nina does indeed have free time.

There's a big dollop of boring involved in being a stay-at-home mom. There are long hours of kneeling in playgrounds, on that rubbery surface that seems to have replaced, within the parameters of Portland, Oregon, all the playground concrete, that makes Nina feel like she is perching on a deflated ball. No matter how many showers she takes, Nina's hair is always full of sand. There are moments when Nina longs to work, when she calls Manuel, her business partner (they are event planners, a team for the five years prior to Jonah's birth). She says, "I miss you. Talk grown-up to me."

But in general, Nina enjoys pushing Jonah's stroller for miles in quest of *pain au chocolat*. She likes having nothing more pressing to do when Jonah naps than to glue-stick photos into his scrapbook. The repetitive tasks sedate her: folding laundry, stenciling stars and crescent moons along the baseboard of the nursery. Nina has felt no sustained urge to follow the lemmings back to work.

Until her stepdaughter Laurel comes to stay for the month of June, and lands, like a cat with claws, in Nina's lap.

Laurel has, of course, always been a factor, but primarily she's an abstraction.

When Nina met Nathan, he was married. As a favor for her college suitemate, Cathy O'Neill, Nina planned the party for Cathy's thirtieth birthday. So, four years ago, she flew to the Bay Area for the weekend: Berkeley, where Nathan lived, the party in the Brazilian Room that he attended (he and Cathy worked in the same architecture firm). Nathan immediately caught Nina's eye. In his orange linen shirt he reminded Nina of Buenos Aires, of the way her father and her uncles dress.

"They look like hibiscus flowers," she explained to Nathan, over champagne.

Nathan seemed both flattered and concerned that he was being mocked. "Don't know if I was aiming for hibiscus."

Later, Nina learned his wife, Alice, had dressed him—"Wear that shirt I got you in New York"—before deciding, typical Alice, that she was seeing silver sparks, a migraine must be coming on, so she couldn't attend Cathy's party.

In those heady days of falling in love with Nathan, his daughter Laurel gave Nina pause, more than his wife.

Alice was easy for Nina to rationalize: self-absorbed Alice, too preoccupied with her artwork to pay attention to her husband; in the aftermath of their divorce, too crazy and weird to waste guilt upon. Nina liberated Nathan from an untenable situation.

Laurel is trickier, then and now. It's one thing to fall in love with an unhappily married man, itching for rescue; it's another to fall for the father of a ten-year-old. It seemed officially *wrong*; it seemed, moreover, like a pain in the ass.

As her partner, Manuel, put it, "There are plenty of unencumbered men out there." Why saddle herself, at thirty, to inconvenience?

It's hard for Nina to explain what makes Nathan worth the hassle. He is smart but not brilliant. He is good in bed but not extraordinary; she's had better lovers. She wonders how much of the draw stemmed from her initial impression: across the redwood-paneled room, his orange shirt.

Despite the fact that Nathan grew up in Denver and is solidly American, he reminds Nina of her father, of her uncles, of a particular way all three of those men, four if she folds in Nathan, chase pleasure. There is something irresistible about Nathan's enjoyment of things: a *tarte tatin* Nina dressed with fresh whipped cream; Nina's naked body. Even silly things, like the way he raves about Nina's lemongrass shower gel: "This is the best thing I've ever smelled!" His capacity for pleasure disarms.

The downside of this, Nina is discovering, is that Nathan has limited tolerance for distress.

She thinks of him as a "tickle daddy." He's the kind of father who attacks his child right before bed, tickling the kid into hysterics, and then hands him to the mom. He isn't the twenty-first-century, sling-wearing father most of the moms in her group married. When Iris' son Ricky defecates, Iris hands him to her husband. Nina can tell that Iris thinks it's strange (those raised eyebrows, again) that Nina is always the one who changes diapers.

Nina can only return to the orange shirt: We marry what is familiar.

To Nina, fathers were not present and responsible, but they were fun. They swooped in when one's mother was broke and pissed off, and they carted one to Patagonia for Christmas. They had a string of blade-thin girlfriends, they gave one opal earrings for Christmas, and they were, like the red and gold sparks in those opals, bright and flashy.

No doubt it's the half-Argentinian in Nina who makes her proud she "gave" Nathan a son, like some old-time British queen, though of course logically she knows it's the X- or Y-sperm that determines the infant's gender. Still, when Jonah was born, Nina felt that she scored. Take that, Alice the narcissist!

Now, Nina wants a daughter. Girls' clothes are prettier, and there are so many more appealing options for names. She broached the subject of a second baby with Nathan: "I don't want Jonah to be an only child."

Which, for once, made his eyebrows lift. "What about Laurel?"

More proof that Laurel, until this summer, has always been an abstraction.

When Nina first met her, Laurel was nearly eleven, almost as easy to win over as Nathan. Nina took her to a store in Russian Hill where they sampled candy displayed in glass jars. Afterwards, she sent a care package of Laurel's favorites to her summer camp (Swedish fish, chocolate-covered strawberries). She bought Laurel a cardigan with porcelain buttons, a green vellum book, a fountain pen, *The Golden Compass*, ribbed stockings. Nina is good at presents; she made a career out of having perfect taste. She thinks of Laurel's responsiveness as akin to physical chemistry. Why exactly Nathan's hands make electricity travel along Nina's skin is unfathomable, too, can only be inadequately explained by pointing to stimuli like shirts.

Eleven-year-old Laurel struck Nina as a cat, winding herself around her legs. She reminded Nina of what her mother, always cynical but more so after her divorce, says about cats: "They have a knack for seeking out the one person who doesn't like them." Laurel has her dad's pretty hazel eyes; she asks, deferentially, what book she should read next. Within the parameters of Thanksgiving breaks or weekend trips to the Bay Area, Nina has always enjoyed petting Laurel.

Fourteen-year-old Laurel is another sort of cat altogether. She's practically feral.

"Alice can't cope," Nathan told Nina when he came back from visiting Berkeley in April, freaked out about his skeletal, miserable daughter. "We need to take Laurel for part of the summer, to see if we can help. See if we can get her back on track."

They were sitting on the couch, drinking wine, watching Jonah roll around his exercise mat. Lying on his back, Jonah reached up to grab one of the toys suspended on the plastic arch above him, a cloth turtle. Nina watched his fingers clutch and miss.

Laurel in her house for a month?

Fairytales are notoriously hard on stepmothers, so Nina had recast herself as a fairy godmother. On Laurel's short visits, she waved her wand to magic up, instead of ballgowns or pumpkin chariots, a set of German markers with ten different shades of green; she taught Laurel how to bake scones. But a whole month of a depressed teenager with an eating disorder? The thought made Nina's mind go blank, an exposed photograph.

"Alice can't cope," Nathan repeated.

It was a familiar comment, but it wasn't delivered in his familiar tone: derisive, inviting Nina to mock messy, inept Alice. Even before Nathan continued, "We need to give Alice a break," Nina processed that he was speaking not out of scorn, but out of sympathy.

"You can't just leave her with me," Nina says as Nathan puts on his jacket.

"Nina, I have to work."

"But I am not responsible—"

He's out the door before she can finish the sentence.

In the kitchen after Nathan flees, Nina mashes bananas for Jonah. (He has four teeth now, but still only wants pureed food. He inspects Cheerios and the other finger food Nina scatters on his high chair tray as if they were diamonds or bird bones. They are interesting to examine from various angles, but he refuses to put them in his mouth.)

Nina considers her sentence, trying to come up with the words that might complete it. "I am not responsible," fill in the blank. For your daughter? Nina catches herself introducing Laurel to people as "Nathan's daughter," rather than "my stepdaughter."

The truth is, Nina could have just ended the sentence, "I am not responsible," period. She is, after all, Nina Durante (now Durante-Haven): Nina who crashed her college suitemate's Mazda (this is partly why ten years later, Nina organized Cathy's party, practically for free; she owes that woman a car); who before their college commencement ceremony, as they were lining up in their caps and gowns, did lines of coke with Manuel, her good friend and classmate long before he became her business partner, never mind that it was ten a.m.; who ended up in Portland, Oregon, back in 2008 because she followed a musician boyfriend there. Nina is organized (her scrapbook catalogs every food Jonah has ever sampled, in chronological order), but she has never been responsible.

There's a reason Nathan, four years ago, was so alluring to her, beyond the beacon-like shirt, which has probably gotten, via nostalgia, too much credit. He was willing to give up everything, wife, kid, firm, for her; to move six hundred miles, for her. For once, Nina was the magnet, rather than the metal filament being drawn; that power exerts its own kind of compulsion (being compelled by one's capacity to compel).

Now Nina, who has never, for fuck's sake, been anyone's notion of responsible, has to look after not just her own thirteen-month-old, but a fourteen-year-old girl who is as skinny as a carrot peeler, whose mother is a nut, whose father has no idea how to talk to her. Laurel may not, in any fair sense, be her responsibility, but she is without doubt Nina's problem.

"God, the tension in this house: it's like buttah," says Manuel when he comes over, doing the Jewish-mom-from-the-Bronx accent that he and Nina have used with each other, for obscure reasons, since they first met as freshmen at Princeton.

Nina sighs. "Can I come back to work? Pretty please?"

"Seriously? Because you know I could use the help. I am very willing to exploit your desire to escape that kid and Mr. America, if you're serious."

Nina contemplates Manuel. He's still beautiful—he is one of those men who will always be beautiful, even when he's old, and has a mane of snowy hair—but at thirty-four, his age is starting to show. Under his eyes are blue shadows. One of the twin daughters of his ridiculous wife doesn't sleep. Nina can't remember if it's Ulrike or Heidi, but one of the two ends up in his bed almost every night, jabbing him with her propeller limbs. This kid is six now, but the wife (Nina doesn't like to think of Elizabeth by name) lets her sleep between them almost every night, and wimpy Manuel won't put his foot down.

Manuel first entered the grown-up land of marriage and step-parenting. Nina was perfectly happy being single before Manuel fell in love with absurd, married Elizabeth. At first Nina hadn't taken the affair seriously. Since their days at Princeton, she'd seen Manuel with any number of WASPy girls. Half of them had boyfriends. She was fully prepared, once again, to offer a shoulder, to pour Manuel wine and laugh about some narrow, *commedia dell'arte* escape through an upstairs window, scaling down lattice work, at the sound of the husband's car in the driveway.

But this time he surprised her: Elizabeth left her husband, and suddenly Manuel was a stepfather of sticky, insomniac twins.

In the sixteen years she's known him, Nina has never so much as kissed Manuel. There was a tacit sense in college that the two Latin kids, so visibly brown at Princeton, should be friends rather than lovers. "Spread the sparkle," said Manuel their freshman year.

But when people said to them, "You two will end up together someday," and she had laughed and rolled her eyes, Nina nonetheless believed they very well might. She could even picture their *New York Times* vows profile in the Sunday *Style* section: friends and business partners for years who suddenly looked at each other and realized, You're the one. Until the advent of the wife, she had thought Manuel believed this, too.

Two months after Manuel's desertion through marriage, Nina met Nathan.

"I don't know what to do," says Nina, stretching out her hand, and Manuel, after a pause, pats it.

"Poor girl," he says.

Nina says, "Who are you calling girl, boy?"

Then she sees Manuel is looking out the glass doors, watching Laurel on all fours, crawling with Jonah on the grass.

Laurel is sweet with Jonah, whom she hasn't seen since Thanksgiving, when he was six months old. She gets him to eat non-mashed food, an irony which Nina contemplates: This emaciated girl, who cuts her own food into pieces and then smaller pieces, finally entices Jonah to put a feared Cheerio in his mouth.

"How'd you do it?" asks Nina, amazed.

A trip to the community center and pool is a proposition for which separate imperatives need balancing. On the one hand, it is horrifying to see Laurel in a bathing suit, her ribs on countable display. But once Nina settles on a lawn chair and watches Laurel hold Jonah by the armpits and bob him up and down in the water, she feels less conscious of judgmental eyes. Laurel sweeps Jonah's hair out of his eyes. It's getting too long, but Nina can't bear to cut it. ("Get that kid a haircut," Nathan said one night at dinner, and Nina and Laurel both said "No!" at the same time, then glanced at each other, surprised.)

Laurel is having so much fun that Nina wants to take her place. Even though Nina feels self-conscious in a bathing suit these days—more than a year after pregnancy her stomach is still soft and flabby, webbed with silver stretch marks—Nina gets in the pool. After twenty minutes Jonah is hungry, so they get out. She opens the Tupperware of Cheerios, but Jonah pushes them away. The last Nina looked, Laurel was reading, but now she's gone. Her beach towel is draped on a slatted lawn chair.

Nina lifts Jonah onto her hip. The door to the community center is cracked open, and when Nina looks in, she sees a group of people sitting in folding chairs, watching a speaker at the podium. Or rather, "speaker": It takes Nina a second to realize that the people are deaf, the woman in the front is signing. Bouncing Jonah on her hip to keep him quiet, Nina watches, first the woman and then Laurel, sitting in the back row. After a minute the woman stops signing. The people in the audience raise their hands and flutter their fingers.

Now Laurel catches Nina's eye. "Did you see?" Laurel whispers, when they leave the room. "Did you see how they applaud?"

From another doorway, Nina spies on Laurel and Jonah, playing with his terrible toy. Laurel turns the crank, churning out music. Nina braces herself for the harlequin clown to burst from its metal box. Pop goes the weasel. Even as a child, Nina hated that toy: the way it would bob on its spring, arms outstretched, cheeks rouged, its expression deranged.

One of the goals of this summer is to get Laurel interested in food again, to alchemize food (more wand work) into pleasure instead of a minefield. So Nina asks Laurel to help her bake a *tarte tatin*. She tells Laurel to squeeze lemon on the vellum-thin slices of green apple.

"Why?"

Nina has to look at the girl closely to realize that this is not sulky backtalk. It strikes her that she hasn't heard Laurel ask a real question all June.

But she used to: The pretty girl Nina first met four years ago was full of questions. Mostly about quality: What made that piece of cured meat more expensive than this one? Why were those boots $300? "Feel how soft this leather is," Nina said. "Can you taste how much sweeter and more buttery this prosciutto is than the Spanish one?" Laurel was so invested in learning, and the experience of being an information-delivery system was so gratifying, that it was hard for Nina to spot the landmine questions, the ones she needed to deflect, or to answer only cautiously: "Why did you fall in love with my father?"

Now, Nina explains that the lemon preserves the apples in an acid shield. Otherwise, the apple will turn brown and bruise.

Laurel looks struck. Her eyes widen as if Nina has told her something very private.

Nina shows Laurel how to layer the apple slices, each C curling into another C, working from the outer circumference to the center. Laurel overlaps them by just two millimeters, the way Nina demonstrated. It takes her a long time to get to the center. When she does, Laurel hesitates, her fingers suspended.

"Is it okay if the last apple slice is horizontal instead of vertical?"

Nina nods. When Laurel places it on, Nina says, "It's a moustache!"

Laurel looks up, and Nina recognizes the look: This time it's Laurel checking her expression for mockery or disdain.

At dinner that night, Nathan compliments the tarte, and Laurel beams. Nina watches her lips close around the tines of her fork.

When Nina first found out she was pregnant with Jonah, after three months of trying, she couldn't reach Nathan all morning. On a construction site, he had turned off his cell. She had other people to call—her mother, her father, Manuel—but none of them could be told until she alerted Nathan that they were having a baby.

This time, Nina feels no need to follow such protocols. As soon as she pees on the white stick and sees the double lines, she calls Nathan. Again, he doesn't pick up.

She finds Laurel in the second bedroom, which Nina now thinks of as Laurel's room. Laurel has her back to her. She is brushing her hair, looking at herself in the mirror.

"Hey, Laurel, I have some news."

While she tells her, Laurel watches Nina's eyes in the mirror. "Wow," says Laurel, and then, "Congratulations."

"Thank you! I thought I might be, because everything was starting to smell terrible. Like people had poured buckets of urine on the street."

Laurel hiccup-laughs. "Have you told Dad?"

"Nope, I couldn't reach him. You're the first." Nina takes the brush from Laurel's loose fingers. "Do you mind?" She starts to brush Laurel's hair. "I hope she's a girl. I could name her after you."

"You want to name her Laurel?"

Nina feels a pang. It might be her fault, after all, that Laurel regards herself as so very disposable, that it's within the realm of possibility that her half-sister would have not just her last name but also her first.

"No, I was thinking about Daphne."

Braiding Laurel's thin, fine hair, Nina tells her the story of Daphne. A nymph, she attracted the attention of the god Apollo. "People think these nymphs and mortals are so honored to have a god infatuated with them, so happy to fall into the god's arms. But half the time, that's not the case. The girls say no, but the gods don't give a crap. They want what they want."

"So what happens?"

"Well, the gods rape them." Nina feels Laurel stiffen. She pauses to get a better grip on Laurel's hair, then continues the story. "So this nymph, Daphne, ran away from pursuing Apollo and called on her father to help her. Her father was a river god; I forget his name. To stop Daphne from being captured, he changed her into a laurel tree."

Laurel turns her head so suddenly that her hair pulls loose from Nina's fingers. "Seriously? That's the best her father could do? Turn his daughter into a tree? Does she have to stay a tree forever?" When Nina nods, Laurel says, "You're kidding!"

For some reason, Laurel's outrage hits Nina as hysterical. She laughs; she can't stop laughing. After a minute, Laurel laughs, too. It has been years, Nina thinks—since before her marriage, since before Manuel met his beautiful, stupid wife, when they used to go out clubbing together and found themselves in some corner at three in the morning, Nina laughing so hard Manuel had to hold her upright, laughing so hard she felt boneless—it has been years since she has laughed like this. Laurel says, "Why not conjure up a motorcycle? Or a get-away chariot?" and Nina loses control all over again.

The two of them wipe tears from their eyes. "Fathers," Laurel says, shaking her head.

"But listen, there's more," Nina says, and tells her about the laurel tree. Its leaves were used to crown victors. Roman emperors wore wreaths of laurels; so did Olympic athletes. She says, "So your name is a symbol of victory, of achievement."

Laurel looks at Nina. It's the most searching look she's given her all month. Nina holds her gaze, and Laurel must find something in her eyes, some answer to a silent question, because after a minute, Laurel nods.

Nina puts down the brush. Laurel's half-braided hair is unravelling. With both her hands, Nina places an invisible wreath on top of Laurel's head. Nina envisions Laurel surrounded by the roomful of deaf people from the community center. They stand around Laurel in a circle, their arms raised, fluttering their fingers in silent applause.

Pat Daneman

Overdue

Today I'm wondering if babies born late stay late
for the rest of their lives. I've grown to hate Brenda,
my sweet neighbor who delivered her girl last week—
two weeks before the date circled in pink crayon
on her calendar. The weight I carry sinks lower
every hour, as if my boy is already filling his pockets
with stones. He spins and paddles, but does not
seem ready to begin the final dive. I imagine him
missing the school bus, missing every bus
and train and plane—running, always running—
looking at his phone, knapsack bobbing
on his back, briefcase in his hand. I see him
sitting in the principal's office for coming into class
after the bell. Apologizing to a stern boss lady.
As a heel traces the curve of my belly, I see
a woman in a white dress waiting at an altar.
I change her look of fury into a knowing smile.

Katherine Gordon

Truth Tables in the Seventh Grade

No one ever bothered to explain
why we had to fill them in. We did
what we were told. Our notebooks
sagged under the weight of grids
freighted with true and false.
We considered every possibility.

Except, of course, the possibility
we suspected but couldn't explain
that while proving a problem false
took just a theorem, QED, this did
not mean our lives would fit in grids.
Love was complex, we knew from books.

I loved the boy who sprawled a book's
length from me in math, that possibility:
his mouth, punk boots, those messy grids
of girls' names he drew on his jeans. Explain
if you could why anything he said or did
wasn't proof he'd love me in time. False

hope is still hope, that logic said. Its false
voice spoke from chalkboards, the books
in my bag. I watched him talk. Did
he look at me? I held out the possibility
he'd turn to me, professing love. *Let's explain
the transitive property*, teacher said, drawing more grids.

After class, girls made fortune-teller's grids
of boys' names and the places we'd live. *False
or true, false or true*: the game would explain
our future. We slipped the good ones in books.
Bad ones we threw away. Possibility
was what we counted on in everything we did.

Back to the boy who never kissed me. He did
so many drugs his eyes glazed to grids,
but I waited anyway for the possibility
he'd come to at last, realize how false
those girls were, and turn to me, book-smart
and unloved, say *Is love transitive? Explain.*

It didn't happen: our blank room, a false entry
in the grids. I lost faith in possibility when
logic books wouldn't explain what to do next.

Tara Kipnees

Never Say Never

This is what it would be like to meet Justin Bieber: He would walk up to me, hazel eyes locked into mine, and hug me like they do in airports, and our hearts would swell with the lashing of waves from a thousand seas. And then I could say, "Death: Take me away! I have lived!" And when death takes me, it wouldn't even be an all-the-way death, just one of this world, where things can be touched. But there are other worlds, too. Other planets. Like Jupiter—that's just air. You can't even walk on it. So I think that's where we would be, somewhere like Jupiter, somewhere we could float, and if you went there, you could feel us, *know* our love existed and still exists, know it's enveloping you, now (not *know* know, but the you that could be there—hypothetically), know it's inside you, too, just like it was inside us. Know that people are good, and all they need is to love and be loved in return, and if you can find that, there is nothing you couldn't do: You could move mountains. You could rearrange the stars in the sky to spell out your name. You could whisper things to the future that would reach people like a breeze, and whisper things in their ears through that breeze, things they will understand, like a fragment of a dream that bobs up to remind them of this moment, and then they will wonder if they are in it, now (the dream), and they will feel happy, believe life could be like a dream. Or maybe they will believe it is a dream. Either way, it wouldn't matter.

Lying in bed when everyone else is asleep—is Robbie awake, too? If he is, what's he thinking? Is he laughing at that *SpongeBob* episode where Patrick asks Squidward if mayonnaise is an instrument? He made me watch it yesterday so he could prove *SpongeBob* is the best show ever, and I tried not to laugh because I told him before I think *SpongeBob* is dumb, and when he's older, he'll see it's just a dumb kid-thing. Maybe he's thinking about his best friend Benny, and how he wants to punch Benny in the face every time he comes over and starts shoving Yodels in his mouth whole and does this armpit-fart thing while he's still chewing? Is he thinking about Mom and what he'd say if he saw her?

You can never tell with people what they're thinking, night or day. Personally, I like night better. I like the silence of it, if you could even call it that. It's like if you're quiet enough, the air hums (or is just the heat evaporating through the pipes of the radiator?), and the walls creak like they're old and having trouble breathing, and the neighbor's cat's meow sounds like someone far away bleeding out, and the random purr of tire against asphalt makes me wonder who's driving and where they're going, if they might stop in my driveway and beep and wait for me to climb out in my Jeff Lakes Summer 2009 T-shirt and the wool socks my grandma knit and take me to Reno. Or maybe somewhere still, with a lake and no wind and a sky swelling with stars.

Roberta's advice about taking a good selfie (the pics that get her the most likes on Instagram): First, make it seem natural. If that means taking multiples, fine—as long as it doesn't seem that way in the picture you decide to post. Even though everyone knows that it probably took you multiple times to make sure the picture came out perfect, you still can't make it look too perfect or staged. People have a sixth sense when it comes to sincerity.

Then we took a few sample selfies together, though I was bummed she didn't post any because we weren't anywhere cool (another prerequisite for posting). Which then led her to lighting. We were in my basement, so she noted the lighting there (fluorescent) was less than ideal. All this selfie talk stressed me out and felt like a lot to take in, so after Roberta left, I smoked a Camel out my window until Meredith yelled, "Something smells up there," which made me flinch and drop the majority of the cigarette straight down into the polyester begonias Meredith sticks in the mulch instead of planting something real. Luckily, nothing set on fire. If only we had actual flowers that used photosynthesis and didn't miraculously survive Nor'easters and I wouldn't have had to worry about this stuff.

P.S. I only took two puffs of the cigarette. I don't want this to turn into a habit.

Dad's holed up in his bedroom like every other night. He got a letter. Probably from Mom, who writes every few years or months, though he never tells me about the letters. Hopefully tomorrow I'll be alone at some point so I can read it and look at that picture of Mom that he keeps in the drawer with all her letters, tucked away under folders with titles like "ID Documents" or "2013 Tax Return" or "Second Mortgage." In the picture, taken from afar, she's standing in an umbrellaed seascape holding an ice cream cone, rivulets of blonde hair reaching across her face as if the wind had just picked up (nowadays, people's hair only reaches that way in pictures if they're posing in front of a strategically placed fan, which Roberta has actually done). Anyway, my mom is wearing white shorts and a blue halter top that matches the ocean, and you can't tell if she's smiling. My mother: Mona Lisa. Really, I've spent hours trying to figure it out, if she's smiling or not, and it's impossible.

I could never produce a look that mysterious, not even in my dreams. Plus, I look nothing like my mom, except for the eyes. Both of us have green eyes. Sometimes, when I straighten my hair and it falls like brown curtains along my hollow cheeks, my dad's eyes linger on me, and I know he is seeing her. But I look rougher than she does, darker skinned with my dad's square chin and slightly crooked nose, and my body isn't all contours. I like to imagine what it would be like to have a body like hers: soft hips, breasts like clouds. When I'm naked, I hold my breasts as if I were Justin and he were standing next to me, and I try to imagine what I would feel like through his fingers. I wonder if he would like the slope of skin above the tight brown knot of my nipple, or the way my breast is the exact shape of a cupped palm if you hold it from below where it rises from narrow ribs.

Things that bother me about Roberta: Roberta and her toothpaste. How she drains it till its body is flat and rolled up, all its guts expressed by steamroller fingers. I know I'm being dramatic, and I'll admit it's hysterical to watch her at first. But then she'll stand there every night ,breaking a sweat over it. It's weird that sluts usually have a reputation of carelessness, because Roberta is the opposite of careless. For one, she's a miser. For another, she refuses to swim in the ocean because of a Belmar shark attack she heard about on the news when she was six. Most of her nightmares since then have been shark related, except after Les Turchin (who is *very* allergic to cashews) accidentally ate a cashew that got baked into the bottom of his friend's "nut-free" homemade chocolate-chip cookie and spent junior prom struggling to regain the capacity to breathe. For three weeks after that, Roberta's nightmares were largely cashew related. But that was it. I have no idea why the shark attack stuck over the cashews. An allergy seems a lot more commonplace, especially if you spend the majority of your time on land. *Plus*, the shark attack victim didn't even die. She just lost a hand and maybe part of her arm. Not to say that losing a hand isn't a big deal, but the girl got to be really popular after that, and probably had all these articles written about how she's a hero or something when really all she did was get eaten. And not even all the way. I know that sounds insensitive. But this is my diary and I think everyone deserves at least one place to sound insensitive and not be judged. If I ever get famous, I think they should turn that into a quote. Like on my IMDB page it would say Kimberly Harris, and then you could click on a link to my Top Ten Quotes that would read: "1. Everyone deserves at least one place to sound insensitive and not be judged. 2. [... so on and so forth ...]."

Last night I lay in the bathtub and slipped low under the water, eyes closed, but there was still light coming through, and I thought if I was very still, someone could walk in and not even know I was there. I thought how easy it would be for a person to disappear. Sometimes I think I'm already gone. I think Justin knows that: We are all gone, already. I think that's what makes us so right for each other. I think when we meet, that's what we'll both feel, like fossils holding each other's bone hands.

Update: Mom needs money. Mom's ex-boyfriend cleaned out her debit account and rode off with her car. Mom's ex-boyfriend is a douche. Mom loves us all but doesn't want to visit and confuse us. She's still not ready to be in our lives regularly. Mom is working as a hostess at a fancy restaurant. She is meeting lots of interesting people and trying to make connections for her art. It's tough these days. People are only spending money on things they need, and no one needs art. Mom is one month sober and listens to Billie Holiday or eighties Madonna (depending on her mood) when the urge hits.

Not that this matters, but Mom is probably prettier than any of the girls Justin has dated. I wish she were here. I think I could be happy anywhere with her: a couch, Dunkin' Donuts, the park, Sears picking out a dishwasher since ours basically combusted, just us talking about stuff like if I'll ever get asked to prom, and if I do, what I would wear, or if prom is just a stupid tradition, anyway, and if I'd be better off getting drunk in Roberta's basement with a bunch of guys from the skate park. I'd also want to know if you're supposed to believe a guy who says he loves you right before he asks you to have sex (not that that's ever happened to me, but in case it does). And, obviously, why she left us. Once in a letter, she wrote: "Painting fills the holes inside me like a light, or a really smooth pavement that's warm and viscous. No, not like pavement, actually, now that I got into the description. It's more like a soft liquid that travels with patience but agility, across the surface of me and, without even thinking, sinks into the cracks it reaches, covering them so completely, with no seams, and if you were to run your fingers across them, you wouldn't even know they were ever there." It's an old letter, though, and I wonder if she still feels that way. If she were here, I would ask. That's just one of the millions of questions I'd want to ask. And I do in my dreams when she picks me up from school and the guys on the basketball team walk past us on the front steps and yell, "MILF" and, "I'd tap that like ...." but I don't mind. All I want her to do is take me home and show me the picture she painted of us at the Brooklyn Botanical Garden when I was five, the one where we were holding hands in front of a lily pond, and the air was warm and the wind so faint it could have come from the batting of an eyelash. I remember feeling happy then. I wonder if she was happy, too, even if the feeling went away right after. I like to think she was happy then, in the tiny parenthesis of that moment.

I knew it the second Rochelle showed up in a little gold dress, blinking through ten pounds of Kmart lashes, that she wasn't over Trey. Whatever—Trey cheated on her with that refrigerator in a weave, but to be fair, Trey was plastered, plus his parakeet, which his mom bought him when he first moved to L.A. so he wouldn't feel alone, just died. Later, in his apartment, he brought that up to Rochelle when she asked him how he could cheat on her after all they'd been through, and then pointed out that Trey never even named the parakeet, and once fed it Twizzlers for a whole week just to see what would happen. Trey explained that he didn't expect it, but once the parakeet passed, it was really hard falling asleep without the rattling of it clambering along the side of the cage at night, and every time he came home, and there was nothing perched on the plastic twig he chose at Petsmart for its realistic coloring, he felt like his heart was freefalling through a night sky. He explains that all this, the rattling, and the twig, and the freefalling, are just signs that what he really misses is the companionship he could never until now admit he wanted from Rochelle, and on a side note, he actually feels really bad about the Twizzler situation, which wasn't his most shining moment, or week, or whatever. Then Rochelle kissed him pushed up against the kitchen table, the expired bird's body behind them in a white toilet-paper cocoon, and it cut to a preview of next week's episode (the refrigerator is back with a bad attitude and a worse weave and has a run-in with Rochelle; Trey gets a tattoo of his late parakeet; Trey's best friend, Troy, splatters a protein shake on his bare abs; Rochelle gives a homeless woman a makeover). The show is horrible. I know. I would never admit to watching it, except that sometimes I can't stop. I'm trying to think what I even like about it. The drama, the suspense (mainly with the romantic relationships, which are always a hair away from either full-on orgy or homicide), the way the girls cry and next week bathe in champagne wearing feather boas. It's hard to tell.

I can't just stop believing because Michael Kreppler shat on my dream. You can't stop believing in your dream just because Michael Kreppler shits on it. His name sounds like a shit. *Fuck Michael Kreppler.* What does he know about Justin? What does he know about me? What does he know about love, and fossils, and fate? I guess if I tried to give myself head and could never quite maneuver that way but got close enough that I'd still think it was maybe in reach if I tried a little harder, I would be pissed off at the world, too. He unclipped the Justin keychain from my backpack zipper while I was in the bathroom, and when I came back and realized it was gone and started looking through my stuff for it, he and the entire chemistry class started cracking up. Fucking morons. Of course Mr. Peltzer, who's ancient and hard of hearing plus oblivious, had no idea what was going on, and I had to wait till the end of class to fish the keychain out of the garbage where Roberta told me Michael threw it. I realize going through garbage makes me look desperate, but what else was I supposed to do? Pretend I didn't care? I bought that keychain in fifth grade with my first allowance money. It was the first Justin-item I ever owned, and I've kept it on my backpack every day since. Roberta says I should take it off, that I don't need to announce anything to the world with that keychain. She has a point. Most of the girls who like Justin are younger, or considered losers if they're our age, but I doubt love cares what other people think.

I didn't cry in front of Michael or Roberta or anyone else in school, but when I got home, it was like a monsoon exploded out of me. Maybe it's true, what Michael Kreppler said, that I'm not Justin's type, that it's never going to happen and I'm just a pathetic groupie, and he's shocked someone so smart could be such an idiot. But I know I can't give up on us. That's what people want you to do. They want you to give up the good things in your life. They want you to believe love is something that can be broken, like a plate or a carburetor.

When Robbie knocked on my door for dinner, I made sure to wipe my nose and eyes and to push the sticky hair off my face and take a few deep breaths. Robbie still gave me this look like "Are you OK?" and I just smiled and walked with him to the kitchen while he stared at me suspiciously. I think I got away with it, though. At dinner, I made a point to be extra perky, and even told some jokes, and smiled a few times at Meredith (which was probably the hardest part, because then she would smile back at me with her horse teeth, and I'd imagine having her as a stewardess and how terrifying that experience would be for people who are used to seeing other people with human-size teeth).

In general, I don't like Robbie to see me upset. That's the only way he knows our dad to be, and I don't want him thinking that's the only way a person can turn out. Most of the time, I have faith Robbie will be OK. He's a different breed, though. He's the only person who gives me faith that deep down, somewhere, even if it's, like, scarred over, people want to be good. He's always doing things like tattletaling on himself over something completely normal for a nine-year-old, like when he planted a stink bomb with his friends under the neighbor's porch and Meredith needed to lecture him about how it's normal not to tell your parents everything and that he should really spend more time outside shooting at birds with a BB gun. Robbie likes Meredith more than I do. It makes sense, since he wasn't even two when she married my dad, and she's a good cook and kisses Robbie on the head almost constantly. Truth be told, I'm surprised she married my dad, though how could she have predicted how he would end up? Just because I hate her doesn't mean I can't feel bad for her (IMDB quote #2).

I was seven when my dad came in my room early one morning and sat on the bed. All I could see was his profile, which reminded me of an aging parrot—aquiline nose, silvery black hair greased back like a crest over his head—and he said: "I'm getting remarried." "To who?" I asked. "She can't have kids, but she'll love you like her own," he said, stroking my hair with his wide, callused palm (back then he was doing roofs to pay the bills and writing a novel he said would make us rich). Then he disappeared through the door åßframe, the fabric of his pants rustling in a familiar murmur that comforted me and made me believe everything would be better. I look at my dad now and wonder if he's the same man underneath. He gazes into empty spaces, still as a mannequin holding a Camel Light between his lips, and doesn't hug Meredith anymore when she leans over a boiling pot, cleaning a wooden spoon with her apron. He used to read me Greek mythology before I went to sleep and tell me of the many books he has read that he will one day give me when I am older and wise enough to appreciate them. We sold all the books at a garage sale five years ago.

I don't think Robbie remembers her at all. I showed him the picture of her, but it felt like he was looking at one of those pictures that comes inside a new frame that's meant to hold someone else's picture. Nothing moved in his eyes. Sometimes I get angry because he can actually forget her. But then I'm not even sure that I'd want to if I could. It's worth noting that every time I try, that's when it gets really impossible and she's all I can think about. It's kind of like how people on diets are always thinking about cake, and I'll start remembering even more than I did before. The time I didn't want to go to nursery for some crappy reason involving a monster who lives in the arts-

and-crafts closet and she didn't even argue and took me ice skating. The indentation under the bulb of her nose that I'd skim with one tiny finger while lying with my head on her lap. The lavender way she smelled, even after working all day in that deli that smelled like an armpit stuffed with bad cheese. How she could flirt her way out of any ticket. Once, she rear-ended a cop, and right before rolling down the window she winked at me and said, "Take notes" (IMDB quote #3).

Whenever I bring her up to my dad, he just says, "Spilt milk." As if my brain were a house that needs cleaning. Sometimes, I get this dream where my mom and I are walking in a field and ahead of us is a thick fog, and as we get closer to it, she starts walking faster, getting yards and yards ahead of me each second, and when I try to catch up, my legs start feeling heavy, like two anchors stuck in the mud, and she won't turn around so I yell, "Take me with you!" but she can't hear me, or if she can, she just doesn't want to turn and I can't tell which way it's supposed to be, if she wants to go alone, or if she just didn't think to look back because how is she supposed to know my legs turned into anchors? After I yell for a while, I realize she's not coming back, so I stand there watching this blurry silhouette turn into a faded inkblot of head and shoulders till that's it, she's gone. I hate that dream. No matter how many times I've dreamt it, it always feels like I'm alone there for the first time, trying to pull my legs out of the mud to follow a ghost.

Mallory Chesser

Sin, Guilt, and Casserole

We circle the buffet table ladling food onto Styrofoam plates. In East Texas, weight is directly proportional to devotion to God. It is Sunday, and my church is having yet another covered-dish supper, because canned goods—cream of chicken, cream of mushroom, cream of celery—form the basis of Christian fellowship. When Jesus instructed his flock to be the salt of the earth, our congregation took him at his word. We scoop up some of everything, "Just for a taste," and the beige and brown juices run together. If grape juice and crackers are the blood and body of Christ, perhaps these gray vegetables are his organs. If this melted cheese gives Brother Wade a heart attack, he'll be one step closer to an eternity with God.

This could be any given Sunday of my childhood. We used casserole to welcome visiting preachers, to comfort the grieving, to celebrate the secular holiday of Christmas, which has nothing to do with Jesus, whose birthday is unknown. My theory: because we denied ourselves most pleasures of the flesh—fornicating, drinking, dancing, wearing shorts in ninety-degree weather—we used food as a substitute for all the fun we weren't having. For some reason, the sin of gluttony carried no shame, perhaps because the seven deadly sins are a Catholic construction, and we were not Catholic. And we were no mere Protestants. We were the Church of Christ—not to be confused with the Church of Jesus Christ of Latter-day Saints, whose members are better known as Mormons, or the Church of God, whose members are Pentecostals, more commonly known as the people who speak in tongues and get bitten by snakes. Churches of Christ consider themselves to be direct descendants of the original churches established in the New Testament. The term "non-denominational" is insufficient.

First Major Transgression: Age 16

My first big sin was fooling around with J.C.—not Jesus Christ—in our dormitory at the Academy for Socially Stunted Geniuses—not actual name. The door was open, per the open-door policy for male and female students during visiting hours, and I had to roll onto the floor whenever we heard footsteps coming down the hall. Closing the door would have been the better solution, but J.C.'s roommate would have notified an RA if he'd walked in on us with the door closed. "Conduct unbecoming" was rampant, as you might expect when you remove sixteen- and seventeen-year-olds from their homes, ship them upstate, and put them in a dormitory at a public university. The handbook officially stated that when students of opposite genders mingle they must be "upright at all times, with both feet on the floor."

I would be reminded of this policy later, in my sophomore year of college, when a favorite professor distinguished between vertical and horizontal sins in roughly this way: "Growing up Baptist, I divided sin into two categories. There were the vertical sins—brawling, drinking, and dancing—which I wouldn't get into too much trouble for, but the horizontal sins—I won't elaborate—were a no-go." I remember feeling smug at the time. Though already a backslider myself, I felt vaguely proud that I'd been raised in a religion that was so hardcore. As I'd always suspected, other denominations were less committed to their beliefs than *my* church, which preached that there was no sliding scale for sins—you could go to hell as easily for a little white lie as for killing a man. I may have been a hypocrite, but I felt a sort of halo was conferred on me for being the worst of the best, the softest of the hard.

Variations of my first transgression were repeated throughout my junior year of high school: in the music practice rooms on piano benches, underneath a stairwell of the social sciences building late at night, just before curfew, and, more brazenly, behind a thick column outside the basketball stadium. Although we never went "all the way," in the teenage sense of the term—*No, J.C., a sock cannot be used as a condom*—this first major sin was shortly followed by not answering my phone when members of the local congregation called to see if I needed a ride to church. I still attended intermittently my first semester away from home, but only on Sunday mornings, and everyone knows that missing Sunday night services is the first symptom of backsliding. Sitting on the hard, cushionless pew, hymn book in my lap, I could feel their eyes on me, noting my makeup, checking my hemline—*If you have to cover your knees with a Bible when you sit down, that skirt is too short.* After services, I cringed from their attempts to welcome me, sure they had an ulterior motive for inviting me out to lunch. It seemed better not to go to church at all. Once you've given an inch, you've given a mile. It's an all or nothing religion.

But I was still a Christian during summers, and one weekend a month, when I went home. I dreaded being unmasked as a phony at church, or being scolded for non-attendance by my parents. They knew, of course, that I wasn't going to church often, but chalked it up to me being shy. We were never a family of communicators, as if by not talking things over we kept them from being real. Big conversations with my mother were brief and took place when we couldn't see each other's faces: 1) The driveway one night, three days after I got my first period: "I need you to buy me some pads"; 2) The movie theater, right before the previews started: "Wouldn't you have better luck finding a boyfriend if you went to church?"; 3) A car ride after a personal crisis: "If you get like this after every breakup, you need to tell me the next time you're dating someone." My father let my mother do the talking, and my mother timed conversations so that we could escape difficult subjects quickly. Rather than circumventing the awkwardness, this avoidance of conversation put me on high alert. I agonized over the moment when my parents would call me out as a backslider, but more than ten years later, I'm still waiting for that other shoe to drop.

Teen Evangelist

Perhaps I've projected high expectations of me onto my parents, then imposed them on myself. While the rest of the church adhered to the letter of the law, my parents abided more by the spirit. To fit into the frame the church provided, I created my own brand of churchiness, beginning a dogmatic period that lasted through my early teens. I spent long nights on AOL Instant Messenger, talking to online friends in glamorous places like Canada, Cypress (the island), and Oklahoma, explaining that the Church of Christ was the one true church and most people were going to hell, even if they thought they were Christians. One contact, Cody, had a conversion but didn't know what to do—his mother wouldn't let him have a Bible. Google was pretty new then, circa 1998, so it was not easy locating a church for him. I probably asked Jeeves, then my search engine of choice. When Canadian Cody suddenly vanished, never again to appear on my list of available contacts, I believed that his mother was punishing him for the hours spent online talking about the Gospel. In retrospect, he probably found a cybersex chat room.

I don't blame Canadian Cody. My zeal at the time was no doubt offensive. I had nightmares for days when my soccer coach, popular at the local Baptist church for fun young people, suddenly died in a fire while sleeping, but my grief did not take the form of sensitivity. I went to the funeral, and a few friends and I later discussed the tragedy at a sleepover. Samantha, a girl who was part of my coach's youth group at church, expressed her sadness that he was dead, but joy that he was in heaven now. Strong in my conviction, I couldn't let this stand.

"I'm sorry, Sam, but Coach M. was a Baptist. I know you are, too, and that's why I have to tell you this. As bad as the fire was, the place he is now is a lot hotter."

Poor Samantha. The other two girls at the party, Church of Christ kids like myself, may not have been impressed by my lack of tact, but they couldn't disagree. I don't remember their reactions—I have the vague impression they said nothing—but Samantha kept to herself most of the night and walked home early the next morning. At the time I thought I was performing my duty, but now I see that I was, probably still am, a know-it-all. I was a thirteen-year-old crusader, brandishing my religion as a weapon. My virtue was a license for cruelty.

Second Major Departure, or College, the Early Years

The realization that I might not agree with the faith I was born into was slow in coming. Throughout high school, my devotion ebbed and flowed with the seasons—a semester away, a summer at "home," "home" now implying not only family but my entire belief system. As a freshman in college, when the falling away began in earnest, I started questioning decisions made by the elders at my family's church. I took issue with the rhetoric of my preacher, the constant condemnation of outsiders. Unsure about my own status within the church, I listened with greater objectivity. I detected little concern for the wayward friends and neighbors we invited to Gospel meetings. Instead, I sensed a joy behind the fiery language, the pleasure church members took in pointing out sinners. They told their stories of encounters with the "unwashed," or "unwarshed," in East Texas: company time-wasters at the water cooler, neighbors who ignored invitations to worship, stubborn in-laws in other denominations. But in Bible class, we'd always been told to "Hate the sin, not the sinner."

At first I was perplexed, but the feeling didn't last. I stopped trying to find a place to worship away from home. Like many college freshmen, I read Ayn Rand with fervor, gave myself terrible dye jobs, only wore a bra on special occasions, and went as bad as I thought I could—spending every Saturday night at live reenactments of *The Rocky Horror Picture Show* with sweet transvestites and beautiful creatures. I had smoked at least two unfiltered Pall Malls and been mistaken for a prostitute. (I had been walking to the 7-11 at ten p.m. in Houston's Third Ward wearing a plaid shirt and denim skort. I wanted a Slurpee.) I owned five different colors of fishnet stockings and had two gay friends—I felt transformed.

I kept a running tally of the church's hypocrisy when I visited home. In addition to sermons that made me squirm, announcements from the pulpit indicted cheating spouses and members with poor attendance records. I'm reminded of a memorable announcement years earlier. I paraphrase: "Brother Rick was pulled over for speeding and caught with several ounces of marijuana in the back of his Jeep. Although the elders made attempts to meet with him, he did not wish to discuss the matter. We are withdrawing from this member. If you see him at the grocery store, offer to pray for him, but don't be too friendly." Brother Rick and his neon blue Jeep eventually repented and went to a more liberal congregation a few minutes away.

Where was the love? "Above all, keep fervent in your love for one another, because love covers a multitude of sins" (I Peter 4:8, *American Standard Bible*). Was I the only one who took the love scriptures seriously? I was no Pollyanna asking for the glad verses, but it seemed logical to give equal weight to the positive passages, hypocritical to follow the negative more faithfully. To make matters worse, I was enrolled in a freshman great books course called The Human Situation, and I had fallen deeply in love with Thomas Hobbes. I began quoting from *Leviathan* as obnoxiously as I had previously quoted from scripture, and Hobbes' definition of "vainglory ... commonly called pride and conceit," resonated. Wasn't I vainglorious? Wasn't that how I was raised? Finding satisfaction in my own goodness—now a thing of the past—seemed just as bad as being a liar, a murderer, or a Baptist. Taking self-righteous pleasure in the sins of others, in their eventual eternity in hell for not heeding your warning, seemed worse. I had learned a new word from Friedrich Nietzsche in my great books class—*schadenfreude*—and I was sure it was at the root of most sermons.

Sunday School as a Source of Shame

My origins as a smug intellectual began at the age of four; I was the only kid in Sunday school who could recite all the books of the Old and New Testaments, and quickly rose through the ranks—by age ten I was dominating scripture memorization contests, getting the most gold stars for completed Bible lessons, and winning engraved Bibles. I now find it strange that the sin of pride wasn't discouraged. Perhaps because I was shy and quiet, they didn't see the signs; maybe there was no maniacal gleam in my eye.

What my teachers mistook for piety was bookishness and curiosity, easily transferable to excelling in school, leaving home (and church) for a math and science academy, and experiencing a crisis of faith as soon as I was exposed to new ideas. The debate over whether one can be educated in science and philosophy and still maintain faith in God is not important here. The problem, for me, was that it was so easy to shift priorities—biology for Bible verses, education for righteousness. If I could get equal satisfaction acing a test, if I applied the same skills I had used in Sunday school, didn't that cheapen my earlier accomplishments and call into question my motives? I wasn't a Christian—I was a baby Bible scholar. My doubting, college self was wracked with guilt. Even in my best years, I had been nothing more than a show pony; in my most sinless state, I had been smug.

Of course, guilt is a staple of Christianity, both of the Southern Protestant variety with which I am familiar and, according to friends of "the other persuasion," of Catholicism and most forms of American Christianity. Another professor tells a story passed on to him by an old friend of his, a reformed Church of Christ-er like myself. The friend was returning home after a Christmas visit with his family, several years and many reflective poems past his break with the church, when he passed a lone Church of Christ in a one-Dairy-Queen town. Like most buildings owned by conservative Churches of Christ, it was plain and lacked a steeple, but the members had modernized by getting one of those marquees where preachers post pithy sayings. This one was dressed for the holiday season: "Don't be sad you didn't get what you wanted for Christmas. Be glad you didn't get what you deserved."

Third Major Transgression: Sherry, Rum, and Outsider Status

Age nineteen. Experimental drinking of cooking sherry at my grandmother's house while she was out having her hair set. I intended just to taste it, but I finished most of the bottle within half an hour, dancing around the living room and watching for my grandmother's sedan to turn up the driveway. Afterward I shuffled the bottle to the back of the cupboard and hoped she wouldn't remember it was there.

I had been looking through her kitchen cabinets for something to eat when I happened upon the sherry. Most of her groceries came in a can, unless she was expecting company, when she pulled out all the stops. That day, as I foraged for food, curiosity pushed me further. What had my grandmother been eating since my grandfather had died and she no longer had to prepare meals tailored to his health restrictions? Something drove me on, cabinet after cabinet, drawer upon drawer. In the back of a cabinet at floor level, next to the oils and vinegars, I located the cooking sherry. Shock, experimentation, inebriation—and curiosity. Why would my grandmother have sherry? At Thanksgiving a few years later, my uncle told a story that shed some light. My grandmother had recently baked a rum cake for a housewarming party, putting in so much rum that my uncle claims the alcohol didn't cook out. My uncle also claims that my grandmother ate most of the cake herself, until she was red in the face and had to be taken home.

At the time this image of my grandmother surprised me. But over the years her memory has slipped, and so has her filter. Her wisdom has become not only sage, but graphic: "There's more room out than in," she advised my brothers after the man next to us had an accident on an airplane. In the same vein, her anecdotes have become more earthy: "Mama would let us say damn, and hell, and chicken shit, if you stepped in it. That's a bowel movement, not a cuss word." My grandmother reminisces fondly on her time as a Baptist, telling the story of how in the early years of their marriage, my grandfather, a staunch member of the Church of Christ, made her walk to church until she converted to his religion. (The Chesser surname is prevalent among Churches of Christ in the Golden Triangle of Texas, which includes Beaumont, Port Arthur, Orange, and the cities in between. Specifically, the Chessers are from in between, a little town infamous for its ties to the KKK.)

My grandmother may be as much an outsider to the Church of Christ as I am, though she wouldn't say so. She has been chastised by elders for listening to church hymns set to instrumental music—at home in her own living room—and frequently misses Sunday night services, due to the aches and pains of old age. She once confessed to me that she used to shop in the next town over so that church members wouldn't see her buying alcohol for her rum cakes. I can imagine the announcement: "Sister Chesser's Mercury Grand Marquis was seen parked in front of J.B.'s Liquor Store. Attempts were made by the elders to get Sister Chesser to repent, but she did not wish to discuss the matter. We are withdrawing from this member. If you see her at the grocery store, offer to pray for her, but don't be too friendly."

All or Nothing

Sophomore year became a time of parties, of semi-naked lawn cartwheels, of school-sponsored movie nights with wine and cheese. By senior year I settled into a classier version of the party girl; I was the model student who mingled at alumni and donor functions, drinking wine instead of Everclear punch. By most standards I was good; by my own I wasn't. The greatest betrayal of my faith was my love of books by authors who didn't need God, my preference for knowledge over obedience, for the company of interesting, educated people over "good" ones. Even the cheese I ate was a betrayal—it wasn't melted into a casserole and served with a spoon, but cut into wedges and arranged next to fruit, to be picked up with tiny tongs and placed, no more than three cubes at a time, on a tiny, clear plate. I was a traitor to my culture, my congregation. I stopped trying to reconcile with my faith. I was fallen.

Black-and-white thinking may be the most lasting legacy of my upbringing. Then there were wolves and sheep, sinners and saints. Now there is married or single; behind or on schedule; publish or perish; succeed or fail. However, this totalizing thinking—mine and the church's—may be a failure of language. Biblical rhetoric, especially quoted in sermons like sound bytes, can be alienating, absolute, and final. Just as I struggle to put my experience into words, sermonizing language fails to capture reality. Commandments to live by leave little room for people to breathe.

I've seen other members flounder and fail. Just last year, my mother reported that the church withdrew from a woman in her sixties who chose to stay with her husband after discovering he'd been married before. During my childhood, a man who had been attending for only a few months suddenly killed himself; the rumor spread that he had been a closet homosexual, struggling with guilt. It isn't uncommon for girls to have babies out of wedlock. Because premarital sex is absolutely forbidden, using birth control is a premeditated and less forgivable sin. A seventeen-year-old girl a few grades ahead of me got pregnant by her first boyfriend, and was soundly condemned in Bible class by her sister. Within two years, the younger sister was pregnant, too. My saddest memory is Timothy, the brother of a friend at church. Like sex, alcohol is absolutely forbidden, and parents don't teach responsible drinking. In his first year of college, Timothy drank so much at a party that he died of alcohol poisoning; his friends were too scared to call an ambulance.

By the time Timothy died, about a year after I finished college, sin and I had an uneasy truce. I stayed away from home to avoid feelings of guilt. If I didn't go home, I didn't have to lie. Still, I wondered whether the problem was with the all-or-nothing attitude of the church or the weakness of its members. Why is the Church of Christ apparently so interested in alienating young people? Many congregations are dying, along with their elderly and infirm members. Without compromising beliefs, couldn't preachers soften the rhetoric and sell the message to a new generation of sinners? I've answered my own question: "compromise," "soft," "sell"—no.

Usually my apostasy feels final and absolute, but I never really get away. One of my greatest challenges with this essay was handling tense—what should be past and what should be present? The church still exists, though I am no longer a part of it. I wonder whether to call myself a Christian, and if someone can be a Christian without a church. When I first moved for graduate school, five years after completing college, I went to the local Church of Christ one Sunday morning. I hadn't been to church on my own in years, and like the cooking sherry, the visit was experimental. I teared up during the service, perhaps due to nostalgia. I wept openly when I got home. Most likely I was crying about the pathos of my situation: displaced from the life I'd had for the past nine years, returning to church in search of a home. The experiment didn't take.

I think about a new religion, but I've been taught to view the other major denominations—Baptist, Methodist, Lutheran, and don't even mention Catholic or Episcopalian—as lesser, inaccurate, insufficient. Ironically, the black-and-white thinking my church taught me is what keeps me home on Sunday; I can't live with the contradiction of calling something a sin and doing it anyway. Instead of returning to church, I live with the twinge that there may be literal hell to pay. I can't rejoin the fold, but I can't embrace friends who've never given much thought to spiritual matters. By living too long in this liminal state, my not-knowing, I risk paralysis. In looking back, have I turned into a pillar of salt?

Holidays with the family still entail visits to their church. I look at the preacher without flinching; I monitor my blinks. To keep up appearances, I still take Communion—not wine, but Welch's grape juice—but I usually don't sing. The old members greet me as a friend and ask careful questions about my life and work, avoiding the subject of church. There is no need to tell them I prefer to sleep in on Sundays. Sometimes when they hug me, I want to tell them Jesus would have liked Sister Patty's chicken enchilada casserole.

John Paul Davis

Ode to My Potbelly

This deep-voiced citizen,
hallowed weight,
curled & sleeping above my legs
& cock, my belly
grows when I am happy,
pouches out over my belt,
fits snugly in the concavity
between my love's back & ass
when we lie together.
I will not have a boy's
body again, my ribs
will never crater
around my tummy
or make a bowl
when I lie down naked
again, all the power
in my abdominal muscles
waits, a secret
beneath the sacred bloat
of my gut. Sometimes I wake
in the night & my love
has burrowed a hand
under my shirt, & it flutters
like a rabbit on a hill
amongst the cornsilk-soft
hair that surrounds my navel
like a crop circle. It leads
me through all my days, my prow

were I a ship. The cyclops
blinkless eye of my belly button
susses out my destiny
as I veer whichever direction
my belly tilts. It tugs
me toward the world's menu
of celebration & pleasure
like a grown dog
who knows how long the leash
is, & how hard to lean
to urge his master
toward the good smells
& the singing.

Margot Wizansky

Repentant

Barefoot boy of fourteen
who sat in church on the sinners' bench,
guilty of slingshot-sin, ordinary sin,
popping toads with a stick,
fighting his brother till both of them are bloody,
pilfering peppermint from the country store,
the reverend preaching damnation,

and on the twenty-first day
of his repentance, when he runs out
through the fields, kneels
in his praying ground beside the old hickory,
watches dark branches splay
against a pink immaculate sky,
the meadowlark's song
lifts him off his knees,
something takes hold
of his skin and all his parts and fibers,
raises his arms to the rising sun,

the sky rippling exaltation, the song
swelling in his head: *I'm here! I'm here!*
I'm here and I'm staying! his heart
beating time and his mouth rounding
like a trumpet's bell as he leaps
and dances home
hollering through the corn.

J. David Stevens

The Babies

I never watched *Happy Morning Fun Time*. I grew up outside Albany, and we didn't get the downstate channels. Crystal looked hurt when I told her. "Buster Benheim?" she said. "Kiki Chou? Teddy Tompkins?"

We were waiting for a table outside P.F. Chang's—one of our first dates, though I already knew how I felt about her. At the request of the justice system, I'd quit dealing eight months earlier, and my bank book was tapped. No cash for ramen, let alone chain Chinese. My landlord, Mr. Horoschak, had started telling me he wasn't a Sister of the Poor. I'd promised to review my portfolio.

Crystal hummed a few bars then shuffled three steps. "I still know the songs." She described the show—singing and dancing and stories where Old Mr. Sunbeam talked about people being friends despite their differences. There were five kids total: Buster, Kiki, Teddy, then the black girl and the Mexican, Wanda Jones and Jesus Dolor. The restaurant neon made Crystal look younger than she was.

Don't get me wrong. She wasn't obsessed with the show. I'm just setting a baseline to explain the babies. Not that anyone could explain the babies—I'm more providing context. You marry a person, you marry their past. So, yeah, the show came up in the decade after we said *I do*, but not a lot. I wouldn't call it special.

The babies were lined up on the basement couch. I still don't know where she got them: a robot that looked like a juice can with arms, a Potato Head missing its feet, a Barbie naked except for pink elbow-length gloves, and a cross-eyed panda with a T-shirt that read I ♥ AKRON. Crystal had faced them toward the radiator beside the utility sink, where a grown man in a yarmulke and yellow romper sang a song about ice cream and being nice to immigrants. He did a little dance, too, stepping over the chain that ran from his ankle to the radiator, the romper barely holding in his junk. Buster Benheim. I just knew. Crystal laughed and clapped, my Ruger on the couch beside her.

Some things in this world there's no response for. I cleared the gun and dropped the magazine into my pocket. When the song ended, Crystal found a pill vial in her blouse and pushed two fingers between the dough of Buster's lips. She coaxed him down to a cushion on the floor. He was already lit. His eyes bulged. After a second, he swallowed.

"Crystal," I said.

She laid a finger over her mouth then headed toward me, the land of misfit toys still watching Buster.

"Where'd *he* come from?" I whispered.

"The Internet."

I frowned. "What did you give him?"

"Nothing he didn't want to take."

At least that part made sense. Somewhere behind me, a sound came from the wall, a soft tapping I'd never noticed before, maybe the pipes. "We should call the cops," I decided. "You can say he showed up this way. We'll claim self-defense."

"I don't know. The babies love him."

"What babies?"

"*Our* babies," she said, like I was joking.

For the record, Crystal couldn't have kids—the price of past indiscretions. I'd talked about adoption once, but she shut me down. Her own mother had kicked her out of the house when she was fifteen. Family was a vexed topic. "And we got our babies ... how?"

"I rescued them."

"Rescued?"

"From the car in the river." She waited for a sign of recognition. I glanced at the couch. "On TV they say the babies drowned, but they didn't. I was there."

Three weeks earlier, a mother from Scarsdale had broken into the Peekskill Yacht Club and driven her Range Rover into the Hudson with her four kids strapped inside. The cops said she'd meant to die, too, but panicked. The story got legs. Reporters pretended to do their job. There'd been an unfaithful husband, postpartum depression, Xanax and Prozac, a woman on the edge. People took sides. The oldest kid was five years old, the youngest twelve weeks.

Crystal patted my chest. "Do you want lunch? I'm making corn and chicken nuggets." She slipped past me and up the stairs.

We met at an outpatient facility in Hartsdale. Crystal was four years sober, a volunteer. My participation was less optional. There was no rule about dating, though most thought it a bad idea—two wrongs not making a right.

Sometimes we talked about things we'd done. Crystal had been a maid at some big Manhattan hotels, and the guests had quality meds. She would fill her pocket with pills then gulp a handful late in the day. Mostly, she wouldn't look at what she was taking. "I loved not knowing," she said. The pills could make her float on her train ride home to the Bronx or numb her feet and set her chest on fire. "One time I threw Viagra into the mix and swear I grew a dick." She shook her head. "Maybe I wanted to die. Who knows?"

I was less hardcore, drank too much, a little weed. But I wasn't an addict, at least not as I understood things then. I know it's the standard line, but what I needed was cash, and if I was lucky about anything, it's that I had just unloaded three bags of product when the cops grabbed me. Possession, not distribution. The judge gave me rehab.

Truth is, I would have gone back to my old life. I was almost thirty and clearing a tax-free grand per week. My client list included high-schoolers and college kids only. Everyone had money in Westchester, and nobody wanted trouble. I took the gun for show—in case a teenager acted teenaged—but I never used it. Things seemed good.

Back then, I had no sense of risk, and it's fair to say the planet would have shed few tears had I stopped answering roll call. But Crystal changed that. Even before we were exclusive, she wanted good things for me, which may not be a lightning bolt to most people but turned me around on the spot. Why else would I take a job at the Yonkers Costco where she worked? Why else did I imagine her face the night I dropped a shoebox of high-grade stash into a Dumpster behind the Central Plaza Best Buy? It didn't take long to understand I owed her—a debt she'd never try to collect. Some people might have another name for that. I called it love.

The chicken nuggets were shaped like dinosaurs. A pot of uncanned corn steamed on the stove. Crystal put two nuggets and a spoonful of kernels on three plates. She ducked into the refrigerator, surfaced with a bottle of milk, nuked the bottle, then shook it hard. "You have to get rid of hot spots," she told me. Delusion-wise, I figured the trick was to observe without going all in. Did I help carry plates to the basement? Sure. Did I talk to the panda or Barbie as I gave them their nuggets? No way. Buster had passed out. Crystal set a plate in front of the robot then cooed at Potato Head and uncapped the bottle, resting the nipple against his lips. I wondered why he was the baby.

Back in the kitchen, I flipped a tyrannosaurus on my plate so it faced another nugget—a stegosaurus. I pushed them together, but they appeared to make out more than battle. Crystal nibbled at some prehistoric breading. She went back downstairs and returned with the untouched remains of the babies' lunches, which she tossed in the trash. I suddenly noticed how clean the kitchen was. Spotless. She had this look on her face that made me wonder if she'd taken a couple of whatever she'd given Buster.

"You OK?" I began.

"OK" she said.

"That Buster." I whistled a little.

She didn't look at me. "The babies say *Happy Morning Fun Time* is their favorite show. They know all the songs."

"When did they—."

"You heard them singing."

"The babies?"

"Yes."

"I didn't. Sorry."

She nodded again. "They should know," she said.

"The songs?"

"They should know they're loved."

"Sure," I agreed. "Every kid should." I waited for more, but she stared straight ahead. I let things stew a second. Somewhere far off I heard the tapping again, reminded myself to check the bathroom for leaks when I had a chance. "Crys, you know he has to leave, right? He has to go home."

Her eyes narrowed. "I asked how long he could stay, and he said a million years."

"He was just talking."

"The babies heard him."

"He didn't mean it like that." I tried to move in front of her, but she angled sideways. "The babies will understand."

Her cheeks tightened, her body swaying. "I'm a little tired," she said. "I should rest."

"Sure," I said. Then an afterthought, "Can I do anything for the babies?"

She managed a smile. "They're napping, too."

The first thing I did was look up Buster Benheim. Turns out he'd made an industry of private appearances. Headshots on his website showed him in a yellow yarmulke, a blue borsalino, and a rainbow propeller beanie. Services included *Music Extravaganza, Story Time!,* and *Motivational Oratory*, with separate fees for each. There was also a category called *Misc.* with a question mark beside it.

His addiction history was almost surreal. If a thing could be swallowed, snorted, shot, or—in a couple of cases—absorbed through a sweat gland, Buster had tried it. He had survived two heroin overdoses and the drunken demolition of his Mazda Miata when it jumped a barricade on the FDR. In his twenties, he once stumbled into the Emergency Room at Roosevelt Hospital with the broken neck of a Cuervo bottle in his ass. The doctor who caught the case said Buster was lucky. Hemorrhage aside, his blood-alcohol level was tipping lethal.

He came from hedge-fund money on the Upper West Side. Buster's real name was Ezra Avigdor Wallach, but his mother rebranded him before his first audition at age two: Eddie Wolf. He landed some bit TV roles through his teenage years before the drugs kicked in, but Buster Benheim was the character people remembered.

His story got me thinking about the different levels of loaded. Some people couldn't keep a car between the lines after two drinks, but I'd seen guys knock back a dozen and drive home like champs. Same thing with crazy. As a matter of nutso, Crystal split the uprights. Certain circuits were shorting, but she'd known enough to invite Buster when I was at work. Where she got the shackles was anybody's guess. And I'd hidden the gun in a place I thought she'd never find—a gallon Ziploc under the insulation in a scuttle attic we never used. The rehab docs would have called her high-functioning.

Which raised questions. What could I explain? What did she understand? Would a few days make her better or worse? By the time I shut down the computer, the world was dimming outside. Crystal hadn't stirred, so I searched the fridge for bottled water and went to the basement.

Buster had slumped to one side, his head under the utility sink, the cushion stretching the romper tight against his ass. I nudged him with the bottle. "Hey." He stirred. I rocked him harder with my foot.

He groaned, pushed up, found the sink with his forehead, flopped down. Amazingly, the hairpins kept his yarmulke in place. I dragged him out and sat him with his back to the sink. "Hello," he said, as if starting a speech. His head swiveled. I lifted the bottle to his lips, and he licked it a few seconds before pulling, water dribbling down his front. After a while he got so he could hold the bottle himself. "I know you," he said.

"Don't think so."

"Sure." He squinted toward the couch. "Hi, kids," he said to the babies, then snorted.

"Drink," I said. He took another swig. "Eddie," I said.

He didn't respond.

"Ezra."

Nothing.

"Buster."

He inhaled deeply. "People love the B-man." He sang, "*Love is a big red balloon—*"

"Buster."

"*—tied with a string to your heart.*"

"Buster, look. I'm going to help. You hear? It may take a day or two, but I'll get you out."

His eyes locked on me, and he seemed to understand. Then his cheeks pulsed. I grabbed the romper, flipping him over the side of the utility sink before he hurled. "Aw, shit," he said, face down. "Aw, shit, man." He slid to the floor, managing to sit on his own.

I put the water back in his hand. "Slow," I said.

"We've been here before," Buster said. "You're in love."

"It's not what you think."

"No, I see it." His breath reeked. He reached toward my face, but I jerked away. His arm hit the floor. "Everybody loves me," he said.

"Buster—."

"You want extra? I can do things." He whispered, "Sex things." He thumped the back of his head against the sink. "I can sound like a girl." He sang again, "*Lyulinke mayn feygele. Lyulinke mayn kind.*"

I didn't know what the words meant, but I could hear what his voice had once been. I looked around the room—not much to see—radiator, sink, and couch, the furnace in a corner, one window barely big enough for sunlight on the far wall. The house was a rental after all. We didn't have money for furnishings. We were saving for our own place, though we were nowhere close, not even in Yonkers.

"I gave a guy a handjob," Buster said. "In Queens, off Union Turnpike." He lifted the water but didn't drink. "He had a room with my pictures. And he played my songs. Ten-thousand dollars. Good times." He ran his fingers through his hair, found the yarmulke, crumpled it in his fist. His bald spot was the size of an egg. "Aw, shit," he repeated.

Looking at Buster, I wondered about Crystal again. Maybe her brain was slipping back to some place before I knew her. Who could say? From the other side of the room I swore I could hear tapping inside the wall again—the whole house, I figured, going to hell at once. Buster ran a hand down his leg until he hit the shackle, a loop of stainless steel just above his foot, its other end secured to the chain. He prodded it with a finger. "If you love something, set it free." Then he laughed. "That's not a song."

"Buster, I'll get you out. I just need time."

"Whatever, man." He straightened and rolled his neck. "Hey, you think I could get something for the pain?" Maybe he meant his ankle. Upstairs, I found the handle of Jim Beam that my manager had given me the previous Christmas. Buster's face brightened at my return. "There's the stuff."

I broke the seal then watched him guzzle a few shots. "I'll leave the water. Try to make the sink if you puke."

Back in the kitchen, I checked off options. My only real solution was to keep Buster tanked while I decided how to help Crystal. Then I could sober him up, slip him some cash from the house fund, maybe suggest I'd done him a favor not calling the cops. Was it a good plan? No, it was not. I couldn't even leave the house. Just me and Crystal on our own. We had a few days to figure things out, maybe a week. A voice in my head said to be reasonable.

But what could I do? I loved Crystal. And I owed her. I couldn't explain the switch that had flipped in her head. But it would have been no different if she were paralyzed in a car crash or got bad news about a lump. Whatever she needed, I'd give. Just like she would for me. I'm not calling it an easy decision. The voice in my head did the math. Unreasonable equals crazy, it said. And I considered the possibility that I was—or almost—following Crystal down this path. But, in the end I knew I wasn't. I want to be clear. Everything happened in the light of day, mentally speaking. I might have been a lot of things, but bat-shit loony wasn't one. People who don't believe me are only trying to sleep at night. They want to pretend there're lines a right mind won't cross.

Crystal appeared sometime after dark to put the babies to bed. Buster's snoring filled the basement. He'd polished off half the bourbon and looked—hard to believe—content. Crystal gave me an approving smile, the kind one parent gives another. We carried the babies to the guest room bed, and she retrieved the afghan reserved for company, tucking each one in. In the hall she said, "They couldn't wait to come home."

I turned down the light. "So this is home?"

She looked at the guest room door. "When they were in the car underwater, I asked if they wanted to be somewhere else. You think I lied, but I never did. I said the whole world was underwater. I said even when they weren't underwater, they were."

"It must have scared them."

"They said they understood. Even the littlest one. They said if I took them home, they would never forget. They would always see the water." She touched my arm. "I couldn't leave them."

"No, I guess not." When she shifted toward our bedroom, I pulled farther down the hall. "I should stay downstairs," I said. "In case Buster needs anything."

I didn't plan on sleeping. The kitchen chair I set in front of the basement door was straight-backed and metal, no way to get comfortable. Even so, I couldn't tell how long I'd been out when the glass broke. For a second my mind tried to stop the dream world from peeling away. Then night whipped into me. I ran downstairs.

Buster had his head and arm out the window, the chain trailing behind him. One foot was still on the couch, which he'd dragged across the basement, but his other foot scrabbled against the wall for a hold. No way his gut would fit through the window, but that didn't stop Buster from trying. His body humped the wood paneling.

When I grabbed the leg still on the couch, he kicked hard and screamed, "Help." Then higher pitched, "Help!" What could I do? Somehow he'd gotten the chain off the radiator, but it was still tight around his leg. I grabbed and pulled—felt the adrenaline surge. Buster's legs shot away from the wall like he was flying. For a second he stayed that way, body parallel to the couch arm. Then gravity kicked in. He was still struggling, twisting his body, but the part outside the window didn't twist like the rest. There was a sound like a stick breaking, only muffled, before Buster's torso met the wall. Then everything relaxed and he slipped to the floor.

Behind me, Crystal screamed. She ran to Buster. He was alive but didn't look good, blood around his neck and face where he'd scraped over the window. His throat clutched like he couldn't decide whether to breathe or swallow. I expected Crystal to say something, but she got on all fours and started rocking. Buster's eyes moved around the room. He looked at me, and I didn't know if he was seeing, but I turned away regardless.

Don't ever let a person tell you what they'd do in a moment like this. You never know until you're there. Even before I thought about an ambulance, I did two things. First, I checked the radiator, which was still in one piece. Crystal's mistake had been using a barrel lock from our garage to attach the chain. Four numbers on the dial, and Buster must have worked the possibilities until it clicked.

The second thing I did was wonder how Buster held all that liquor. Some people couldn't have worked the lock sober. It was almost superhuman. Or maybe he poured the bourbon down the sink when we weren't looking. Maybe he was a better actor than anyone knew.

I went to the Peekskill Yacht Club to think about things one last time. There were maybe a hundred boats, some on shore, others tied to docks in the Hudson. Every summer, the newspaper ran stories about bluefish coming from the Atlantic, and I wondered how it might feel to reel in a thirty-pounder. I could imagine taking my kid out on my boat, landing a fish so big I'd need both arms to lift it. Not that I'd ever have a boat or a kid. But it felt good to pretend.

A cement ramp angled down the bank where the SUV must've gone in. I imagined the river at night, moonlight smoothing the water. In my head I saw the mother swim away, and suddenly I wished more than anything I could've been there—to save the babies or die trying. The babies had started it all, a beginning that couldn't be undone. A thousand paths moved away from them like a spiderweb of space and time, and one of those paths was mine. At home Crystal lay in the bed where I'd put her two days earlier. Now and then she'd lift a hand and sweep it across her face like she was parting a curtain. Or warning something away. Or trying to reach the surface.

Here's what I knew. The *Happy Morning Fun Time* gang had broken up. Teddy Tompkins worked for the Republicans in Kentucky, and Wanda Jones married a music exec in L.A. Jesus Dolor had gone off the grid. But Kiki Chou stuck around, changed back to her real name, Stephanie Lim, sold real estate in Ossining. She'd been married twice, divorced both times. No kids, I checked. I caught her on the street coming out of her office. I'd cleaned up as best I could, ironed a button-down and slacks. At the first mention of Buster, she drew back. "I haven't seen him in years."

Which I knew. Which is why I asked if she could give me just a minute to tell her about the birthday party. My wife had been a huge fan of the show—of Kiki, all of them—and the last thing she wanted was trouble for Buster. She'd been trying to help. But he'd shown up drunk. And when my wife mentioned an ambulance, he'd gotten aggressive. He refused to leave.

Stephanie Lim looked scared, but it was the right kind of fear. She didn't run. I pulled out my wallet and showed her a picture of my kids, some sample from a Utah photographer ripped from the web. I told her my family had left the house, but even so my wife didn't want trouble for Buster. She'd made me promise. I said, "He's in bad shape," and I told Stephanie if she could give me a few minutes, it might save his life. I told her that Buster had asked for Kiki specifically. I promised if nothing worked, we'd call the ambulance or cops, whoever.

She parked out front. Things were as clean as Crystal had left them. The tapping in the wall had slowed so much it barely registered. Stephanie Lim declined my offer to take her jacket. I could see the blue and gold pin on her blouse that said REALTOR.

Buster lay next to the wall by the utility sink, under a blanket, a bourbon fog filling the room. Plywood fit neatly where the window had been. Stephanie edged forward. "Eddie?" she said.

"We tried," I told her. "He won't answer to it."

She nodded. "Buster?" She moved forward more, held out a hand as if toward a flame. "It's Stephanie," she said. "I mean Kiki. Buster?" She knelt beside him.

Once an addict, always an addict. That's what the rehab programs say. There's never an end, just one trial after another. But what the programs don't tell you—what they might not know—is you can be addicted to anything. Every piece of the world is a barb waiting to snag in your blood. Pills. Money. Fame. Even love.

Kiki pulled the blanket away. "Oh, God," she said. But when she looked back, there was more than fear in her eyes. I wouldn't have believed it except I had come up behind her and saw her expression as the shackle bit into place. Even now, I think she understood.

The Missouri State University Student Literary Competitions

Moon City Review exists as a publication of Moon City Press, based independently in Missouri State University's Department of English. Remembering *MCR*'s origins as an in-house journal, we annually print one poem and one piece of fiction written by members of our student population, each selected by an open competition judged by a writer from outside our community.

Jeannine Hall Gailey, author of five collections of poetry, including the 2015 Moon City Poetry Award winner, *Field Guide to the End of the World*, served as judge for this year's poetry competition. Gailey selected senior undergraduate Soon Jones' poem "Generation of Vipers" as this year's first-prize winner. Of Jones' poem, Gailey remarks, "This poem illuminates the darkness that even children accumulate in the shadows, and the story of this young girl's revenge, unfolding in the context of a religious community, is very arresting. A disturbing but skillful poem."

We also congratulate thes four additional finalists were included in the poetry category:

Justine Dix
Shayne Jacopian
Jupiter Kieschnick
Willow Onken

For the fiction competition, *MCR* tapped short story writer and novelist Mary Troy to choose our winner. Troy is the author of several books, most recently the Moon City Press Missouri Author Series novel *Swimming on Hwy N*. Coincidentally, Troy chose Soon Jones as the winner of this contest as well, awarding her story "Mustard Seeds" the top honor. Troy notes,

> It is a short and powerful story. The writer manages to create an emotional response in the reader. Moreover, the story is not sentimental, as stories such as this can be, but is honest and true, and that means it is also funny. This is spot-on adolescent

humor, yet even those of us who are not adolescents laugh. Mostly, though, it is the last few lines, the lyrical and perfectly worded ending, that makes this one a winner.

In addition, seven other students were named as finalists for their work, and they include the following writers:

Brandon Ashlock
Anastasia Berkovich
Beth Fiset
Grant Haverly
Shane Page
Genevieve Richards
Breea Schutt

The following pages include both Jones' poem and her story. We are proud to present her work to you and for her to receive this exposure in this format. We know this is just the first you will hear from her.

Soon Jones

Generation of Vipers

Six of us folded templates of paper houses
while our parents held prayer meeting in the big church.
We were all without our allies, unbound to each other,
and one girl forgot to glue Tab A onto Tab B,
her roof collapsing.

I taunted till my belly was full with the sound of others
laughing at her. She hid by the curtains,
face against the wall,
cried alone the rest of the night.

Mrs. S pulled me aside, told me the girl's father had cancer
and shouldn't I, of all people, know better?
What would my mother think, undone by the tumors in her chest,
watching me make this poor girl miserable?

I did not apologize. Mom had been an artisan
of holding grudges, keeping accounts until the end.

Besides, for months that girl had pulled the bow
out of the back of my dress, tugged my zipper down
while we sang from hymnals at junior church,
whispered rumors during the sermons I was a slut,
smirked with her gang at my early breasts.

She did not know my spine was already
a knife sharpened, my tongue a patient snake.

Soon Jones

Mustard Seeds

For the third time in a day Abigail joins hands with her family and Brother Elliston, the traveling faith healer, to close the circle around Ruthie's bed. Ruthie wears a white dress and holds an illustrated child's Bible in one hand with a lamb embossed in gold on the cover, like Ma instructed, even though she prefers her black leather-bound New Testament Abigail gave her last Easter.

"If you have faith the size of a mustard seed, you can move mountains," Brother Elliston reminds them.

They bow their heads and the men take turns praying, promising God things they don't have and righteous acts they won't commit in exchange for Ruthie's life. Whenever Brother Elliston prays, Pa and Daniel throw their heads back and shout "Oh Lord!" at the ceiling while Ma amens under her breath.

Abigail meets Ruthie's eyes and smiles. She sticks her tongue out and makes funny faces at her little sister until Ruthie has to press her hand against her mouth to keep from laughing. Then Ruthie gurgles from somewhere deep in her lungs, and Abigail holds her breath. Brother Elliston breaks the circle and presses his round, bloated hands down on Ruthie's chest and she scrunches her face up and squirms. Abigail interrupts before he can start a new round of prayer.

"Don't push so hard. She can't breathe."

Ma crushes Abigail's hand until her bones hurt, but Brother Elliston moves one hand to Ruthie's forehead and raises the other to the ceiling and Abigail feels victory flutter in her stomach. Ruthie sucks in a deep breath and sighs.

"Lord Jesus! Help us our unbelief! Reach down and heal this little lamb so your name may be praised!" he shouts.

Afterwards, they let Ruthie rest alone and move to the living room. Pa and Daniel both sit on either side of Brother Elliston on the couch and Abigail sits on the ottoman. Ma comes around with a pitcher of sweet tea for refills; she ignores Abigail's outstretched glass before taking the pitcher back to the kitchen. Abigail pulls her empty glass close to her body and picks at her flowery skirt. It's the only one she has left, and Ma won't let her wear pants while Brother Elliston stays with them.

Pa leans his head closer to the pastor, as if inches mean holiness.

"Brother," he says, "will God heal our little girl?"

Brother Elliston takes a sip of the tea and wipes his brow with a yellow handkerchief.

"We must have faith. Even the tiniest doubts …."

Pa turns toward Abigail for a breath and then looks away. Daniel scowls at her. Ma's lips are a hard line.

Abigail opens her mouth to ask Brother Elliston if the tiniest doubt is stronger than the greatest faith, if it's harder for God to clear the lungs of a little girl than it is to move a mountain. Her heartbeat pounds hard and quick and she wants to fling mustard seeds in his round face and demand the miracle he promised her family. Instead, she closes her mouth and retreats to her sister's bedroom.

Ruthie hops up on her knees on the bed and asks, "Will you pat my back?"

Abigail smiles and as soon as she sits on the comforter, Ruthie lays across her lap. She cups her hands and pats firmly in a steady, alternating rhythm on Ruthie's small back to loosen the mucous in her lungs so she can breathe better.

When she was first diagnosed with cystic fibrosis, the doctors sold them fairy tales of people who'd almost lived to their forties with little trouble, and it seemed like so much time then. Now they said she'd drown before her tenth birthday, and the weeks ticked by in seconds.

Daniel opens the door and watches them for a moment before saying, "Abigail, I need to talk to you."

"So talk."

"In private," he says.

Abigail rubs Ruthie's back before tucking her into bed. She's already dozing off.

Daniel's bedroom walls are covered with verses on plain paper he printed at the library. His shelves are decorated with all kinds of theology books he'll never read, and nailed above his bed is a fiberboard cross he bought for a nickel at a yard sale. Ornamentally displayed on his desk are notes for the sermon he's been writing for months with one of his Bibles left open to a passage in Proverbs. Daniel will be sleeping on the couch tonight so the faith healer can have his bed, but for now the room is still his.

"Abigail, you need to get right," he says.

She stares at him, and then bursts out laughing when she realizes he isn't joking.

"Where can I get that?"

He clenches his jaw and says through his teeth, "We can't afford any unbelief in this house. Not when Ruthie is so close to dying. You need to get rid of that book. It's planting seeds in your head," he says.

The book is Meditation 101 that Abigail borrowed from her secular friend Katie down the street. When her mother found it, she slapped Abigail across the face and grounded her, but late at night Abigail snuck out of her room and rescued the book from the trash. Though her punishment is over, her parents still haven't forgiven her for bringing wickedness into the house. So she reads it late at night with a flashlight beneath her covers, sitting cross-legged and breathing deep from her belly, hoping enlightenment won't be as elusive as the Holy Spirit. Daniel knows she still has the book, but he doesn't know that Abigail also lets Ruthie read it and they do the breathing exercises together in secret.

"It's just a book; it isn't special," she says.

"Spiritual actions have consequences. Pa paid money we don't have to get Brother Elliston here to heal Ruthie, and if you don't throw away that book and turn back to God it's all going to be for nothing. Can you live with her death on your conscience just for a damned book?"

Abigail presses her lips together and walks around Daniel to open his closet door, and before he can stop her she pulls out a battered cardboard box tucked in a dark corner and upends its contents on the floor. Pornographic magazines spread like a liquid stain and color floods Daniel's face. Abigail slams the door behind her when she leaves, knocking scriptures to the floor.

☾

Dinner is meatloaf, mashed potatoes, and asparagus drenched in butter that doesn't make up for the fact it's asparagus. Ma and Pa thank Brother Elliston for the small victory when Ruthie joins them at the table, breathing without much trouble, but Abigail knows it's because of her own hands. Daniel refuses to look at either of his sisters.

"Tell us, Brother, when did you first learn you had the gift of healing?" Ma asks after the blessing.

Brother Elliston smiles and wipes his forehead with his handkerchief.

"When I was a young boy, my cousin Zeke was bit by a cottonmouth down at the lake. We lived way out in the country then, an hour away from any hospital. My brother went running to get our parents, and I knelt down beside Zeke and I placed my hands on him and I said, 'Jesus, don't let my cousin die. He's got so much left to give you.'"

Brother Elliston pauses. He chuckles to himself when Ma and Pa lean forward, like he already knew what they would do before they did it. Ruthie pushes food around her plate with her fork, never looking up.

"Then I felt this warmth in my arms, like the love of God was flowing through me. By the time Uncle Kent got out there, Zeke was dancing on his feet and praising Jesus. I've been doing the Lord's work ever since."

Ma quickly wipes tears away from the corner of her eyes, and Pa blinks rapidly and coughs into his napkin. Ruthie pushes her plate away. Her food is half uneaten, and she didn't touch the meatloaf.

"Dinner was good," she says.

"Thank you, dear," Ma says.

Ruthie climbs down from her chair and quietly walks away from the table while Daniel asks Brother Elliston to share more stories about his healing, and he complies, regaling them with tale after tale until nearly midnight.

Abigail wakes to the sound of whispers in the hallway and gets out of bed, afraid Ruthie is sleepwalking again. Many nights she has had to watch over Ruthie to make sure she doesn't wander outside or hurt herself, gently steering her away from anything sharp or dangerous.

She finds Brother Elliston standing outside Ruthie's doorway with Daniel's fiberboard cross clutched in his hand, pressed tight against his thigh. Abigail hangs back, hides in the shadows of the hallway, ready to attack if he goes inside her sister's room.

"Lord," he whispers, "I'll give it all back, every gift and every dime. Don't let this precious girl die. Just this once, let someone live. Help my unbelief. Give me faith."

Brother Elliston gets down on his hands and knees then, touches his forehead against the carpet. His whole body trembles. Abigail clenches her teeth so hard her whole jaw aches. In the darkness, they each pray for a miracle.

John McNally

Courting Disaster

Barbara was the first woman I had a crush on. She was in her thirties, divorced, drove a '66 Mustang, and lived in the mobile home across the street. Summers, she wore shorts and cheap flip-flops and loose cotton blouses unbuttoned low. "You like my car?" she asked me one hot, dusty day. "As soon as you can drive, I'll give it to you."

I was three years old. My own vehicle was a Batmobile pedal-car that I rode feverishly around the trailer court. I liked riding my Batmobile right up to Barbara's painted toenails. From my seated perspective, I would get dizzy looking up at Barbara, waiting for her to bend down and touch the top of my head. Even the sight of her Mustang parked next to her trailer made my heart pound harder because I knew that this meant she was home.

We lived in Guidish Park Mobile Homes, in a southwest suburb of Chicago, from 1966 until 1969. I was born in late 1965, so I remember nothing about my life before the trailer court. The trailer court is where my memory begins: my daily life finally, at long last, coming into focus. But my memories now of those years are like a reel of miscellaneous film footage spliced together—a few frames here, an actual full-blown scene there, very little of it cohesive.

Before Barbara, there were no women for whom I felt an irrational attraction. She and my mother would stand outside, near our trailer's propane tanks, and smoke Winstons. One of my earliest memories (one of the few extended ones) is of me sitting in my Batmobile while my mother and Barbara are talking. My mother looks down and says, "Johnny. Go inside and get me my cigarettes."

I don't want to leave Barbara, but I also don't want to disobey my mother, so I climb out of the Batmobile and run to the trailer, mounting the concrete block steps leading to the only entrance. My mother always kept her cigarettes in a special case that snapped on top and held a lighter in a pouch like a kangaroo carrying its baby. For years, my go-to Mother's Day present would be a new cigarette case.

Cigarettes in hand, I hurry back outside and give them to my mother. And then I start chattering on about my Hot Wheels, telling Barbara that I have a Hot Wheel that looks just like her car, and I wonder if maybe she'd like to see it. It's a purple Custom Mustang, and it's my favorite.

"Johnny," my mother says. "The adults are talking."

Barbara says, "Another time, sweetie," and winks at me. I love this woman. I truly do.

As early as I can remember, I had wanted to be a special little boy, a boy who did spectacular things, but for the life of me I couldn't think of any spectacular things to do, so I played with my Hot Wheels instead and let my imaginary characters who drove those little cars do all the brave and amazing things that I wished I could be doing— fighting bad guys, surviving cataclysmic events, and saving lives.

In the trailer next door lived a man I called Grandpa. Both of my real grandfathers and one grandmother had died before I was born, so the old guy living next door was the next best thing. He was a retired lineman for the electric company and was missing several fingers, which fascinated me. He'd let me look at the stumps and study them. We also had secrets, Grandpa and I. He would take me into his bedroom and show me a billy club hanging on a bedpost from a leather strap.

"This is my nigger beater," he said. "Some nigger comes in here to rob me, I'll take care of the son of a bitch. Believe you me."

He made me promise not to tell my mother what he had said or that he had shown me his weapon. I nodded. Of course I wouldn't. For one thing, I had no idea what he was talking about. I was three years old. He was speaking gibberish, using words I'd never heard. He showed me his collection of knives, too. He talked about his son being a worthless bastard. He told me I was a good kid because I didn't talk much.

"I don't like kids unless they're quiet," he said.

My mother wasn't fond of Grandpa. She hated how he would call me over to share his TV dinner and then complain about it later, accusing me of eating all of his food.

"I want to strangle that man," she would say, but she felt sorry for him because his own son wouldn't talk to him or bring his grandkids to visit him. She believed that he really did care for me, that I was the closest thing to family that he had. "Still," she would say, "I wouldn't mind choking him."

It was Grandpa who taught me how to court a girl.

"See her," he said as the two of us peeked out from a window inside his trailer. He gestured with his head toward a girl named Patty. Patty was a chunky girl, probably three years older than me. Grandpa said, "You want to get a girl's attention?"

I nodded, thinking of lovely Barbara and her Mustang.

Grandpa handed me a pair of scissors and said, "Call her 'Fatty Patty' and then chase her with the scissors. But don't tell your mother," he added.

"OK," I said.

This sounded like great fun. Normally I played by myself, but the thought of chasing someone with scissors thrilled me.

Grandpa slowly opened his front door for me to exit. Once outside, I held the scissors up over my head and yelled, "Fatty Patty!"

Startled, Patty looked up, saw me (a wide-eyed neighbor boy holding scissors over his head), and screamed.

"Fatty Patty!" I yelled louder and charged down the concrete block steps after her. Patty screamed again and ran away.

I chased her between trailers, across gravel driveways, and onto another street populated with people I didn't know. And then I lost sight of her. I was panting, the scissors still over my head. I heard Grandpa calling my name, so I returned, heart thumping, grinning.

"You did good," Grandpa said. "She'll never forget you."

"Fatty Patty," I said and laughed.

Grandpa laughed and said, "You hungry? Want to split a TV dinner with me?"

"Sure," I said.

Together, we ate Salisbury steak and mashed potatoes. He gave me sips of his coffee.

"You should have seen the look on her face," Grandpa said. He laughed louder. I'd never seen him so happy. "Serves her right," he said.

"Serves her right," I repeated.

Oh, how I wanted to give Barbara a ride in my Batmobile. Oh, how I wanted her to give *me* a ride in her Mustang. I wanted to hold her, sit in her lap, sleep against her. Forty years later, when I asked my father if there was, in fact, a woman named Barbara who lived near us and drove a Mustang, he said, "Barbara?" His eyes widened. "Oh, hell, yeah. She was a good looking woman, too." He paused, as though stunned by his own memory of her, a memory that I had resurrected by providing only the barest of facts. Staring beyond me, he shook his head and said, "*Damn* fine looking woman."

"I hated that trailer," my mother told me years later. "I used to wish it would burn down. Every day I wished that."

My Batmobile was my prized possession. Given my parents' income, which didn't amount to much, the Batmobile must have been an extravagant gift. I stowed the fake automobile each night in an aluminum shed that sat in the driveway. In the driveway also sat a white 1966 Rambler, a stick-shift with no air conditioner, and a VW van with no air conditioner or heater. A vehicle without a heater in Chicago was a monumental disaster, and to this day I have no idea what my father could possibly have been thinking when he bought it.

One Saturday morning, I walked out to the shed, opened it, and looked at the empty space where my Batmobile should have been. I stared at the space, trying to make logical sense out of a sight that was illogical. And then I screamed. My father rushed outside, probably expecting to see an abduction in progress.

When I told him what was wrong, my father said, "Son of a bitch." He looked around, as though the culprits were in sight, then said, "Come with me."

Dad and I walked up and down each row of the trailer court. Four rows away, I saw three boys standing over the Batmobile. "Look," I whispered. But even at three years old I knew it was possible for more than one boy in the trailer court to own a Batmobile.

There weren't many actual lawns where we lived, and the few lawns that did exist were mere postage stamp lots. This particular lawn had a fence surrounding it, but it couldn't have been very high.

My father yelled to the boys, "Hey! Where the hell did you get that?"

"It's mine," one of the boys said.

"The hell it is," my father said. Like a giant, my father stepped over the fence, walked over to the boys, and picked up the Batmobile with one hand. The entire time I thought, *But he said it was his*, and my fear was that we were now thieves. My father stepped back over the fence and set the Batmobile down.

"Go on," he said to me. "Ride it home."

I was too afraid to look back at the boys we may have just robbed. I sat down in the Batmobile and started pedaling, keeping pace with my father who said nothing as we made our way back to the trailer.

My days back then had a distinct rhythm. While my father was away cleaning strangers' rugs or washing their walls, I stayed with my mother and played with my Hot Wheels. At some point in the early afternoon, my mother and Barbara would have a smoke by the propane tanks, and I would stare longingly up at Barbara, who would look down at me and smile while my mother was talking. Grandpa would eventually call me over to share a meal with him and then complain about it to my mother. When my father came home, my mother would head to work at a factory that made corrugated boxes. With my mother gone, my father might listen to Herb Alpert's "Tijuana Taxi" on the record player or the theme to *Peter Gunn*. My brother, who was six years older, had his own life, and I don't remember seeing him around much in those days. At night, my mother and I slept at one end of the trailer while my father and my brother slept at the other end. I don't know why my parents had made this arrangement. Perhaps because I couldn't sleep in a room without my mother, to whom I was irrationally attached when I was three. Or maybe there were problems in the marriage. Just as I was unaware of Grandpa's racism, I was also unaware of my mother's deep unhappiness. I was unaware of most things, it turned out.

☾

If you read about trailer fires, you'll likely see the words "fire trap," and of the occupants' fates, you will often read, "They didn't have a chance."

A person has only two to three minutes to extinguish a house fire before it's out of control. A mobile home can burn entirely to the ground in five to ten minutes.

It wouldn't be until 1976 that the construction of mobile homes would be regulated by the government. According to the 2013 report on Manufactured Home Fires by the National Fire Protection Association, "The death rate was 57 percent lower for post-standard manufactured homes than for pre-standard manufactured homes."

A fire in Batavia, New York, that took place in November of 1969 illuminates the perils of pre-regulation mobile homes. According to the newspaper article, a neighbor heard screams for help coming from the trailer at four in the morning. When she ran outside, the trailer was already overcome with flames. She tried opening the door but couldn't. She awoke another neighbor, who called the fire department, but there was nothing left to do when they got there but put out the flames which had, according to a reporter, "melted much of the aluminum shell of the unit." The cause of the fire was not determined. It could have been an electric heater. It could have been a small gas stove. It could have been an oil-fired furnace. The newspaper reports, "Mr. Beakman, whose shouts had awakened Mrs. Piche, was found dead near the door at the front of the trailer. His wife's body was found in the hallway between the bedrooms at the rear of the trailer and Mrs. Ogden was found in bed in another bedroom near the center of the structure. All had died of smoke inhalation."

In late October of 1969, two weeks before I turned four, my mother got her wish. Our trailer burned down.

Here's what I remember: coughing and coughing, unable to get comfortable. It was night. My coughing, deep and croupy, woke my mother, and my mother, unable to see through the smoke, screamed for my father. My mother carried me to the other end of the trailer and then, gathering my brother, took us outside while my father, to my mother's irritation, mystifyingly changed out of his pajamas and into a pair of jeans and a shirt. My mother hurried us to Grandpa's trailer, pounding on his door and waking him up. Perhaps thinking they had finally come for him—they being all the black people who were going to descend on the trailer court to rob him—Grandpa answered the door holding his billy club.

While my mother used Grandpa's phone to call the fire department, my brother and I stood side by side and stared through a window at our trailer. At first, all I saw was smoke pouring from the seams and the occasional flickering of flames inside.

In the few seconds before the fire overwhelmed the trailer, my father threw three things outside: a bird cage, inside of which lived a finch named Dale; a Code-a-Phone answering machine; and a Von Schrader rug cleaner. And then, flames at his back, he leapt from the trailer, landing on his knees.

This is where my memory switches from grainy fragments to full-blown Technicolor. It's a clear dividing line in my life: before the trailer fire and after the trailer fire. It's like switching from a tiny black-and-white TV with rabbit ears to a high-definition color TV the size of a wall. The first four years of my life were like a short picaresque novel populated with odd neighbors and the occasional recurring relative. The fire, however, was like landing in Oz. It's when my subconscious and conscious minds finally clicked into place, one layered over the other, like the sun and moon during a lunar eclipse. As I watched the fire, I was keenly aware of what was happening around me. I felt, for the first time in my short life, like a sentient being and, thus, truly alive.

My father joined us at Grandpa's after saving the bird, the answering machine, and the rug cleaner. From Grandpa's window, I watched our trailer door, also on fire, fall off its hinges as though in slow motion. The flames lit up the trailer court. Once sparks began spitting on Grandpa's window, making a loud popping sound each time one struck glass, my mother took us across the street to Barbara's trailer.

The firemen, I learned many years later, were volunteer, and one of the reasons it took so long for the trucks to arrive was because the trailer was in an unincorporated area and there was confusion as to whose responsibility we were. The trailer was destroyed by the time they arrived and likely would have been destroyed no matter which fire station responded, although the fire itself continued to burn.

There came a point while trying to extinguish the flames when the firemen had to stop working because of a series of explosions coming from within the trailer.

"What do you have in there?" one of them asked my father. "Fireworks? Ammunition?"

"Why the hell would I have fireworks in there?" my father asked. Then: "Oh, wait. I know what it is."

My parents had stored jugs of wine under the kitchen sink, and, one by one, the bottles exploded from the heat.

My mother and father argued at sunrise when Red Cross arrived to help us. The Red Cross representatives had come with clothes and $165 in cash. My father refused their help. His own father had served in World War II and had claimed that Red Cross charged servicemen for coffee. This was, in my father's eyes, reason enough to turn them down. My mother, the more pragmatic of the two and often exasperated at my father, signed whatever papers Red Cross had asked her to sign. She welcomed their help.

By morning, all that remained of our home was a smoking heap of twisted metal and ashes, but before the sun came up and while the fire trucks remained outside, their lights swirling and swirling, I fell asleep in Barbara's lap while she sang to me. Although we had lost pretty much everything we owned, I was a happy little boy.

The temperature at which human tissue begins to combust: 572 degrees Fahrenheit.

The average temperature on Mercury, the planet closest to the Sun: 801 degrees Fahrenheit.

The average temperature at which a house fire burns: 1,100 degrees Fahrenheit.

The temperature required to cremate a body, after which only bone fragments remain: 1,400 to 1,800 degrees Fahrenheit.

Several days after the fire, I walked through the ruins and studied everything that had melted. I had the taste of rotten eggs at the back of my throat, likely from smoke inhalation, and I felt queasy each time I swallowed.

At the spot where I kept my Hot Wheels in a tiny plastic garbage can was a mound of melted metal. I could make out a few of the cars' shapes, but they were now merely part of some larger, misshapen object. It was the sight of my little cars, which I played with every day, that brought home the import of what had happened to us. Until then, it had all been a grand, surreal adventure.

Near the end of our trip, my father found the only possession that survived the fire intact: a wooden nineteenth-century crucifix that had once belonged to his mother. It lay in a bedroom closet, underneath a pile of ash. The crucifix, however, was unscathed except for the edges of the cross, which had blackened. My mother always interpreted the crucifix's survival as evidence of a Higher Being. I tend to think that the crucifix had been soaked in some kind of flame retardant, although I honestly have no idea how it survived while everything else perished. For years, whenever I wanted to return to the night of the fire, I would hold the crucifix up to my nose and breathe in the smell of smoke that it still retained, and the aftermath of that night would instantly come back.

"I wished it every day," my mother said when I was nine.

She confessed this right after she had told me that Grandpa had died. I felt nothing at the news of Grandpa. I had seen him only one more time when he came to visit us at my aunt's house a month after the fire. Mostly he complained that the fire had damaged his window and that my parents still owed him money for it. I have a Polaroid from his visit: I'm sitting on his lap and the two of us are smiling, my mouth rimmed purple from the grape punch I had been drinking. As for Barbara, I never saw her again, and she never gave me her Mustang. I couldn't say what became of her, but I eventually fell in love with other women, dozens of them, including my kindergarten teacher, Miss Mendoza, along with many of my classmates, until the pool of women I loved shrunk and shrunk as I got older and older.

I still remember trying to sleep as the trailer filled with smoke that night. I kept coughing, unable to catch my breath, and there was a horrible noise coming from my throat. I coughed and coughed until my mother shook me awake, and then I opened my eyes into thick smoke. My eyes burned, but I could see in the distance, through the smoke, flickering light from a half-open door in the hallway. It was like waking into a dream. Or death. My mother picked me up as though I weighed nothing. Within seconds, we were out of the trailer, along with my brother.

Had I not coughed, it was unlikely anyone would have woken up that night. Or so I told myself.

On the day that my mother confessed to me that she had wished the trailer would burn down, we were driving to a grocery store. It was summer, the car's windows were rolled up, and my mother was smoking. I stared at my mother. Had my mother set fire to the trailer? I knew she hadn't, but I couldn't not entertain the possibility.

The grocery store, Dominick's, was across the street from our old trailer court. I looked toward it every single time we drove by, wondering if anyone would remember the boy who had pedaled his Batmobile up and down the street or chased a little girl with scissors but who also, on what could have been his very last night of sleep, saved his family, becoming, for the only time in his life, the hero of his own story. My mother, on the other hand, never looked, even on the day she confessed her secret to me. It was as though the trailer court ceased to exist, as though we had not all almost died that late October night of 1969. But I knew better. I knew the opposite was true.

My mother crushed her cigarette in the ashtray. Country music was on the radio. A Charley Pride song might have been playing. Or something by Tammy Wynette, a twangy song about heartbreak and independence. Unlike my father, who talked and talked and talked, my mother was often silent. If I'd asked her what she had been thinking, she'd have shook her head and said, "Nothing," even as visions of flames filled her mind, the four of us trapped inside a burning trailer. My mother believed in karmic retribution.

"Be careful what you wish for," she told tell me as she pulled into the grocery store parking lot. In her version of the story, I wasn't a hero. She was the villain. "Be very careful," she added, as though my future truly depended upon such silent longings, those darkest of desires we keep to ourselves.

Angie Macri

As the city trees are dying, they build a jewel box

of glass and iron, copper verdigris,
each frame designed against hail
that happens in summers, frequently.

Weeks at a time, soot
hangs, soft coal from Illinois
so cheap. It can be midnight at noon.

Through what they could collect in glass,
the grown-up child in the garden
walks in the menagerie of plants,

what might survive.
The box has clerestories
as in the factories, as in a church,

for natural light in a city built
from fur for hats before silk, now
booming power plants for industry.

They wash the coal but still it's dirty.
It's pulled across the river by the ton
and burned in every furnace for heat.

As the city trees are dying, they build a jewel box

Inside the box, they set plants
like precious stones in soil
in vertical walls of glass, like elements

of a play full of mums
when a Tuesday is so dark no one
can see. From sulfur,

the child, grown up, enters
the garden through limestone.
Eight arches hold the weight.

Angie Macri

Eight arches hold the weight

of black, which is not quick,
not fast,
but smog—a slow swan
descending
in its own sweet time
to coat
each tree, street, name.
Of course
after all that time growing
underground,
coal would work that way,
unhurried.

Seam to ash, the back of coal
crosses the city
black as night at midday.
What will the sun break?
Nothing, speak
the city clocks
from the underside of day,
no lucky
stars to count, our pretty
pennies burning.
This is our history
that no one studies:

☾

soft swans that clutch
at noon, that draw
milk from water,
mesmerizing
the city grown from the prairie,
from this coal smoke.

Matt Dube

Paletas

Some ice cream flavors they can't explain. Corn. Cinnamon. Cumin. Cactus. Cicadas, every seven years. They squat their refrigerated truck on the edge where the neighborhood turns. You line up for fat and sugar and cold. To make the wait easy, they wire together a busted PA, play corridas and cumbia. You juke in line, and they try to identify whatever oppresses you, balance it with what you hope for. You are stagnant at your job, or else you're climbing again and your spouse wants to move. They measure that into molds, mix till it turns firm. Graduation, second marriage, taxes. Heavy cream and salt and the mounting energy of a wooden paddle. Somewhere in the line, one of you has a need: car note, student loan. Report from the physician's assistant, phone call in the night. Sheriff at your door. Something you can't take cold, sugarless. It's out there but they haven't found it yet.

Karen Donovan

A Gothic Tale

½

Aweto.

The knob at the back of his neck didn't hurt at all, so he didn't mention it to anyone at first. Excepting a slight wince when what was developing there broke the skin, he was pain free, but we were close to panic. We drew near, but his body was so hot we had to take turns holding him. It seemed that the growth exuded a natural opiate, because even when he lost all movement in his limbs, even when the prognosis was clear, he remained upbeat. Toward the end we had trouble understanding his speech, an unearthly mixture of humming and growling. *Shhhh, I'm growing my wings,* he might have been saying. But that is not what happened.

Karen Donovan

Levi Catches a Hedgehog

Artemis (or Diana) of Versailles.

Our path descends through sassafras and oak to a pedestrian way along the river. We descend with it. The Seekonk is wide here, separating all these East Side mansions and tulip trees from Rumford's industrial waterfront on the opposite bank. Your dog pulls us ahead, nosing leaf piles and gutters, recording whatever life form has deposited a remnant of text. Animal vegetable mineral: checkmarks in his index of scent. Never a lack of story. There's a kayak upriver, a little family fishing off the rocks. *I screamed. I was on my phone when he came over the hill with it in his mouth and I just screamed.* Later you will give me a cool sweet drink, and our conversation will be a sort of reckoning with motherhood. Levi stops and looks out over the water. It's not a true river, like the Connecticut, which goes in only one direction. The tide is pushing back in. It will run up as far as it can get before turning around again.

Noel Sloboda

Monuments

That last summer we spent with Nana
she promised our deeds were not crimes
since nobody owned the Earth—
though she made us swear

never to tell what happened
after our Saturday Swansons
when she rolled her rusty Caprice downhill
into strange neighborhoods. Unbuckled,

my brother and I crouched in back,
coiled like pogo sticks
ready to bounce if she pulled over
for a rock that took her fancy.

Our prizes snatched from roadsides
looked like cannon balls, helmets, or skulls.
It took us both to wrestle
the best ones back to the car

where Nana clucked impatiently
over the low grumble
of her engine. From our spoils
she erected cairns atop weeds

in the garden where, she insisted,
mother once grew poppies
as brilliant as the sunrise.
Decades later, my brother and I slipped

out of Nana's wake without a word
to gather every stone we could find.
Up and down alleys and avenues
we raided, collecting rubble—

until there was no more
my truck shocks could bear.
Nana's place years before had been
razed, and we had nowhere

to secret our haul. So we spent
the Devil's Hour casting
rocks into a canal bed
as if it was a wishing well.

Our fingers still smelt of loam
even after we scoured them
till they glowed in the dark,
brighter than any flowers.

Wendy Drexler

Untitled Photo #9
From a Crimean Diary, Circa 1920

Four Serbian woman stare straight out at me, right through
    the lens. Against the sun, against the wind.
Unsmiling, barefooted, wearing babushkas and dirndls
    over long, dirt-stained skirts. One of them

holds a bundle in the crook of her arm from which
    an infant's tiny leg, skinny as a dowel, dangles.
An infant accompanying her mother into the field,
    or from the field. Potatoes? I want something

to be growing in that field. Two shadows furrow
    the second woman's apron. Not shadows, I realize,
but the leg of a goat or sheep, and in the woman's right hand,
    a bucket. In her left hand, an axe.

The goat already dead, or soon to be. And what
    does it matter now, this long-ago pause
in the road, the four women, the infant, all long dead,
    and how little we know—a few stories, etched

in the breath—my assimilated Jewish grandmother, Millie,
    a French Levy, whose sapphire-and-diamond bracelet
I wore to my wedding. My grandfather Sam, a socialist,
    born in East Germany, who always said he was

from Russia to side with the peasants. Imported
    limes and lemons, cut a door in his warehouse for stray cats,

wore a suit and silk vest to feed the squirrels in city park.
      He named them after his three grandchildren, said

they always came when he called. When I was born,
      and the doctor told him he had a granddaughter,
he asked the doctor to please look again—.
      Let these Serbian women, my grandfather and grandmother,

these fragments and figments, stay. Let me forgive myself
      for not having asked, as day after day stiffened
into all these years, for all the stories, all the mechanisms
      of next and next and next—I'll never know.

Bronisław Wildstein

Susanna

She had never really got back to normal after her husband left her, twenty-three years earlier. Perhaps it was because of the tragic death of her brother Tadeusz four months later. "My little son", she had called him. He died in January. He had gone up to Gdansk, to deal with some Solidarity business. Irena called her a few days later, saying she'd not heard from him. Susanna tried to say soothing things, but she felt icy fingers clawing at her heart. It was so unlike Tadek. She tried to look at it objectively; she knew how psychologically frail she was after her husband's departure, knew that she should hold her emotions in check. She had to look after Adam, work, and go on with her underground activity. And now, on top of that, she had to look after her brother's fiancée as well, for Irena looked ready to fall apart at any moment. Susanna tried to be strong, tried not to give way to panic, but she could not control the trembling that shook her body. "Not him, not Tadek, please not him," she kept repeating silently to herself. She prayed, but while she prayed memories came to her those mysterious murders and "unknown assailants." She kept seeing the bloody face of Father Popieluszko, the priest they had killed.

The last time she'd seen Tadek had been on New Year's Eve, less than two weeks ago. She'd picked up Adam at about ten from a children's party at the house of one of his school friends. Benedict had asked to have him for a few days, and also before that, for Christmas, but in both cases Susanna had refused. Adam was sulking. For almost twenty minutes she plodded through the watery snow with him, trying in vain to cheer him up with jokes. The jokes sounded forced and he went on sulking. When they got home, she felt no trace of the few glasses of wine she had drunk earlier. Luckily Adam was tired and fell asleep almost at once. Susanna sat by him for a moment longer, gently stroking his hair. When she was sure he was asleep, she went into the other room and sat down in front of the dead eye of the television, vowing she would not switch it on. She ate some bread and cheese and washed it down with sour wine. As the alcohol slowly coursed through her, she examined the tapes in the cassette player, rejecting Kaczmarski, then, one by one, Wysocki, Kelus, and Cohen. She paused for a moment longer at Armstrong before rejecting him, too. She twiddled the radio knob but found nothing to hold her attention. The wine was finished. She made an effort to chase away memories of past New Year's Eves spent with Benedict, times they had spent together. Old times. She tried, as so often, to remember the bad things about him. His pettiness, his cowardice. And, as so often, she realised after a moment that she was only poisoning herself.

She sat down on the windowsill. Beyond the pane, Warsaw was dark and indistinct. Here and there feeble fireworks flashed. If it weren't for Adam, something inside her said. But the thought was unclear. Her life was over—she was just living its last sputterings now—and if it weren't for Adam .... With a determined hand she took a bottle of vodka out of the fridge and poured herself a glass. Then another, and another. The tightness inside her eased. But the ringing of the telephone brought it back.

"Happy New Year! We'll drop by in fifteen minutes," shouted Tadek. She didn't even have time to reply.

She turned on the television. In distant cities people were partying in the streets. But a minute later the screen was filled with the faces of the Polish communist leaders. She switched the thing off. As she did so, the door buzzer sounded from downstairs. Tadek and Irena and a group of their friends filled the room and the kitchen. She just had time to close the door to Adam's room.

"It was a good thing," Tadek was saying as he hugged her and clinked his glass against hers. "He didn't deserve you. He doesn't deserve you!" he sang. "You knew that perfectly well. Two different worlds in one apartment. In one bed. That's just about possible, I suppose, but living together? You constructed a sort of miniature Poland: the Solidarity activist and the disapproving man of the house who writes propaganda for the regime." Tadek's laughter was infectious and Susanna couldn't help joining in. Then her brother grew serious.

"But he hampered you, limited you, infected you with his ... his ..."—he groped for the right word—"... his scepticism, his lack of faith, that suspiciousness of his. He wanted to destroy everything you believed in. And his traumatic childhood experience was supposed to excuse it all. The wardrobe, when he was a few years old. But what about us? I don't remember our father. They more or less finished him off before I was born, after that he was just dying. I don't even know if I really remember anything about him or if I've just built up a picture of him from your stories about him. How do you preserve the memory of a two-year-old? I think I remember the funeral, and our mother crying. But that seems unlikely, too. And our mother? What was her life like? It was only thanks to you that I grew up to be someone halfway decent. You're the one who raised me when she no longer could. And him? After that trauma he had a good life. From when he was seven, all good things came his way. So they kicked him out of the university. Hideous repression! And what dreadful persecution to give him a job on the *Republic* so that he could sing the praises of the party—the incarnation of history's wise purpose. Protecting us from ourselves. And apart from that, what kind of person was he? He ran after every skirt that came his way. As you know. And finally got caught by a canny young wannabee journalist. How pathetic can you get! It's a good thing he's gone! You know," he said, lowering his voice and whispering into her ear, "it's important, this trip to Gdansk. Very important. But now"—he was shouting again—"let's party!"

Susanna shouted and sang with them. She felt almost good. They danced. Someone put on the soundtrack to *Cabaret*. "Life is a cabaret, old chum, come to the cabaret!" Susanna screamed.

"My wonderful sister," Tadeusz sang, hugging her. "Free at last. Young, beautiful, with your whole life in front of you. You can only be happy. You've got to be happy!" Susanna nodded.

When they left, she dragged herself to bed and sank into a leaden sleep.

Days passed and still there was no news from Tadek. Susanna lived in a dream state. She worked, did all she was supposed to do, and desperately looked for traces of her brother. Everything seemed to be happening somewhere beyond her. After consulting with some friends from the underground, she decided to call the police. They listened, took the photos she gave them, and promised to look for

Tadeusz. The photos duly appeared in the press, with a brief note about a search for a missing man.

Benedict was not so much on Susanna's mind during those days, though she called him as well, at his office in the newspaper.

"Yeeess?" His voice was hesitant.

"Tadek's missing. He's been missing for ten days. No one's heard from him. I'm afraid they might have arrested him. Your people." She didn't mention the thing she was most afraid of.

"My people?"

"All right, all right. Stop it. You know people, you have some influence. Try to find out something. That's all I'm asking."

"All right, I'll try. Though, despite what you seem to imagine, my possibilities ...."

"Just do what you can. I'll wait to hear from you." She put down the phone.

Weeks went by. Appeals for information about Tomasz Sokoł appeared also in the underground press. After a few days she got a call from Jerome, with whom she worked on the *Underground Weekly*. One of his colleagues from Gdansk had seen Tadeusz just as he, Tadeusz, was about to return to Warsaw. That had been almost three weeks earlier.

Tadeusz's corpse was dragged out of the Motława River at the beginning of March. She was summoned by her director, the editor-in-chief of *Portyk*. At the sight of the two uniformed policemen standing next to him, she thought they had come for her. I've got to get through this somehow, she thought; just as well that Benedict can look after Adam. But then they asked, "Are you the sister of Tadeusz Sokoł?" and she felt the breath leave her body. They showed her a horrific photo of Tadeusz's bloody face, beaten to a pulp.

Jerome drove her to Gdansk in his little Fiat. It could all be just a misunderstanding, she kept thinking. The thought thudded through her body as if through someone else's. Jerome pulled up on the other side of the street, opposite the red brick building of the Institute of Forensic Medicine. He would wait for her in the café at the corner, he said. She wasn't sure what she was saying. She gave the man in the lobby her name and her brother's. A man in a white gown and a policeman came and took her down some stairs. Murky-colored paint was peeling off the walls. At a signal from the man in the white gown, the man in charge downstairs pulled out one of the huge drawers that lined the wall.

Tadeusz's body, oddly short, was covered by a sheet up to the armpits. Someone had roughly, clumsily cut a piece of rubber into her brother's shape in order to brutalise it. The skin was greenish, the flesh seemed soft like custard. A broken bone jutted upwards, like a spike, through a deep gash in his arm. There were gashes all over his chest. Crushed and broken bones jutted out from what had been his face. Susanna took a step forwards, reeled, but managed to pull off the sheet. The legs were hacked off below the knees.

"What are you doing?!" shouted the man in the white gown, pulling the sheet back over the body.

"What ... what did you do to him?"

"It wasn't us. It must have been the boats, the propellers of the boats that sail along the Motława. Death was by drowning. We've been able to establish that." He must have said more, but his voice was receding. Susanna began making her way shakily towards the door.

"Where ... where's the ...." Following the direction in which the man in charge downstairs waved his arm, she bolted out of the morgue, pushed through the door of the filthy lavatory and began to vomit, kneeling in front of the toilet bowl. She vomited and wept, in deep heaving sobs, choking on the bile, her whole body wanting to dissolve in the dirt of that place, to be swallowed up in its spasms. It lasted a long time, but at last she got up, dragged herself over to the dirty washbasin, splashed cold water over her face, and rinsed out her mouth. When she returned to the morgue, she was almost calm. They took her back upstairs. She had to sign something, explain something.

Jerome was waiting. He asked no questions. "It was him," she said after a moment, stubbing out another cigarette. "They murdered him."

The official version was this: Tadeusz Sokoł fell into the Motława river in a state of inebriation on January 9, 1986. Death was by drowning. The body was noticed and fished out on March 6. The injuries to his body had been sustained through contact with the propellers of passing boats.

The drive back to Warsaw took almost eight hours. They hardly talked. The air in the car was gray from cigarette smoke, and from time to time Jerome had to open the window. They stopped a few times for petrol and watery coffee, exchanging meaningless remarks. It was only during their last stop, when they had passed Płonsk, in a dark hut called the Warsaw Inn, that Jerome, finishing off a glass of some undefined liquid, asked, "What do you intend to do?"

They sat looking at the night and at the lights of the cars swishing along the motorway.

"I'm going to find everything out. I know who did it, but I want the details. I'll do what I can."

"We'll help you," Jerome said.

Tadeusz was her little son. That was what she called him when he was just a few months old and she had to look after him. She was ten years old and felt the weight of her responsibility; she felt grown-up. Her father was getting worse and her mother had to spend more and more time caring for him, as well as running the house.

Susanna was pleased with her new responsibilities. Looking after her brother was absorbing—like play, but serious—and made her feel proud. She changed his nappies, bathed him, taught him to walk, tried to teach him his first words. She told him stories and he seemed to understand them, though he only babbled, or fell asleep listening to them. She was sure he took the stories with him, that they filled his dreams and—because in dreams you could do anything—constituted a dream world in which he was a participant. .

Even when she had to cry off play dates with her friends because of her brother—arranging her lips in a sort of pout, the way adults do, as she explained to them that she had to take care of the child—the feeling of superiority over her childish friends and their childish games made up for whatever natural regret she felt at missing out on these irrecoverable occasions for lighthearted play. They would be playing at grown-up life, while she would be living it in reality. She even suspected that they would make fun of her, not wanting to admit their envy of the serious burden responsibilities she already had to carry.

When she was taking care of her brother she felt, she was engaged in an important task: ensuring the survival of her family. At those times she would forget the sadness that had begun to fill the house, forcing out the joy of the previous year. Susanna remembered that joy. Especially the moment that heralded the happiest time of her life as a child: that moment a year and a half before, when her mother had told her, in a voice full of mystery but also brimming with hope, that Daddy might be coming home soon.

The winter was almost over, but wouldn't quite leave, though a warm breeze could be felt in the chill of the streets and the icy walls, waking the plants and trees from their winter sleep. The few times Susanna had seen her father, it had been through bars. A big man, a stranger, who awoke in her a strange muddle of emotions. He smiled, but his smile was so sad that she felt she would rather he didn't smile at all. Her mother explained to her that daddy was in prison because of a mistake, and that she would understand it all when she was older. For the moment she must be patient and not tell anyone about him. That was very important. If she didn't say anything, they might let him out. But if she did ....

Susanna knew that most children had two parents. And that it was better that way. It was sad at home. Not like other children's houses. Sometimes, at night, her mother would hide so that Susanna wouldn't see her crying. Susanna knew, but she didn't let on, not wanting to embarrass her mother. But the sadness infected her, too. It was even sadder after aunt Gienia got married and moved out—though of course it was more comfortable. While she was there, Susanna had to be very careful playing, and her mother kept having to move the sewing machine—a good, solid prewar one—on which she made things to earn a little extra to supplement her nurse's salary. The sewing machine took up a fair amount of space in their one room. Susanna dreamed of having a house like other children's houses. She wished her father would get out of prison and come to live with them and that her mother would stop crying. So she tried not to talk to anyone about it. But when the Miedziecki boy at the next desk over started making fun of her because her father was in prison, it was too much to bear. She went for him, crying as she pounded him with her fists. "My father will get out. It was a mistake. And then ... then you'll see!" The teacher pulled her off the boy, who was also crying, and yelled at her. Susanna wondered fearfully what the consequences would be. She had told about her father, after all. But a few days later her mother announced that they were letting him out. On Sunday she asked Susanna to pray for his return, and this time, in the church, Susanna tried to concentrate as hard as she could. She knew what her sins were, but she fervently promised God she would mend her ways. She believed she would. Next to her, her mother, on her knees, was hiding her face in her hands.

The following Sunday her mother took her to the prison. It was the first time she was meeting her father in a room without bars. He lifted her up and threw her so high in the air that for a moment she was frightened, but her mother's evident joy calmed her fears. She looked at this strange man, her father. An odd man, tall and thin. His face was prickly when he hugged her, but Susanna didn't mind. She had never seen her mother so happy—her parents so happy.

A month passed, and then another. The warm breezes had finally succeeded in chasing the winter away; trees in the parks and streets were bursting into leaf. Susanna was playing in the kitchen when she heard her mother cry out. For a moment she was frightened, but when she ran out into the hall, there were her parents, embracing. They stood there in the open doorway for a long time, clasped together, clinging to each other. The following day Aunt Gienia took her home with her. Her belly was already showing and Susanna knew she would have a baby. Uncle Stach went around the house whistling proudly.

Her parents came for her two days later; she was beginning to worry. Her mother had never looked so lovely. Susanna felt a stab of joy, but also a pang of regret that she would never look like her. Her father, too, was dressed in his Sunday best and gazed at them both with shining eyes. Her mother and Aunt Gienia fell into an embrace and then, for mysterious reasons, both began to cry. That evening they sat by the open window, with a view of some huge immobile cranes. Uncle Stach put a bottle of vodka on the table; Aunt Gienia brought bread, butter, and sausage, as well as pickles—cucumbers, mushrooms, and plums, each on its own little plate. Susanna liked the plums best, but she knew she mustn't eat too many. Aunt Gienia wasn't drinking; it would be bad for the baby, she explained to Susanna. Her mother drank a few glasses; the men finished the rest. They talked little, just slapping each other on the shoulder from time to time. Susanna went home with her parents in the warm spring evening. Laughing, they pushed their way onto a crowded tram. Dishevelled and crumpled, but still laughing, they extracted themselves from the crowds and made their way with a dancing step to the house. Susanna's bed was moved into the kitchen, which didn't please her enormously, but she knew it wasn't a thing she should make a fuss about.

She remembers those days as one long, unending holiday, although she was still going to school. It turned out that her father, too, wanted to go to school. To university, in his case. Before ending up in prison he had begun to study architecture. He wanted to build houses. "We have to rebuild this world," he would say to Susanna's mother, who gazed at him with a radiant expression. And he succeeded. When he came home with three tea roses Susanna knew something good had happened. "Come and congratulate the future architect!" he cried, presenting the flowers to her mother and hugging her. "I got in!" Then he seized Susanna and began dancing with her. "Daddy's going to build houses! And not horrible ones like those," he added, nodding in an unspecified direction. Susanna knew he meant the Palace of Culture. She didn't understand her parents' dislike of the building; it was huge and she liked it very much. It had been a gift from the Russians—our Russian comrades—and was named after the now late, though immortal, leader of the progressive world, Josef Stalin. A few weeks earlier Susanna had been on the top floor with her class, on a school trip. Warsaw was spread at her feet. She felt proud to be living in the capital and didn't have to wait years for a special trip to visit the highest building in Poland, like people from other, less important cities or—even worse—from villages. She looked down on the city which the Germans had wanted to wipe off the face of the Earth but which had rebuilt itself, cleaned up the wounds of its ruins and was soaring upwards, scaffolding everywhere, promising a radiant future.

"I'm going to build houses," her father kept repeating, "and people will be grateful to me. I'll show them that you can live in beautiful surroundings."

On Sunday Susanna proudly walked to church between her parents. Holding them by the hand. She thanked God and asked him to please make things stay that way always.

Not long afterwards something happened that worried her. In the evening uncle Stach dropped by. Her mother was doing her shift at the hospital. The men told her to play in the kitchen and closed the door to the room. She heard raised voices—most of the time just one voice, Uncle Stach's; her father's answers were rare and brief. They talked for a long time. She could make out individual words: "Poznan .... This time they can't just .... It's now or .... The blood ...." Her father was shushing her uncle and trying to calm him down. The hot June night filled the kitchen, bringing restless sleep and disturbing dreams.

In summer they would go to the country, to granny Ola's in the Niemiry region. The buses were hot and airless. They would pull up at the stop creaking and rumbling, raising clouds of hot dust, and the crowd would rush at them, shoving and shouting, children crying. They didn't always succeed in getting on. The driver shouted for people to stand away from the doors, which he couldn't shut because the people left outside would not give up but held grimly on, pushing, shoving, trying to force themselves into the solid mass of humanity inside. But in the end they had to give up, and stood there furious, panting and dishevelled, gazing at the departing bus, cursing and complaining. Her father was gasping for breath, her mother was trying to smile, and she herself wanted to cry. There were hours to go before the next bus. Once or twice her father had done a deal with some truck drivers. Her parents rode in front, squashed together next to the driver, with Susanna on their lap. But it was still more comfortable than the bus, where you had to stand jammed in a crowd in the suffocating, airless heat. In spite of this Susanna was sometimes able to ignore the conditions and enjoy the trip. When they had left behind Warsaw's ruins and the suburban chaos of houses and building sites, when the horizon was yellow and green with fields and forests, she forgot about everything else. Pines trees reached up to the sky and the sun glittered between the tree trunks, making the birches glow. But the best bit was when the bus stopped and you could jump straight out from its fug into the clean fresh air, like plunging into cool water and feeling the dirt of the city being washed off.

It was still quite a way through the forest to the village, but Susanna, even though she was tired, liked this part of the journey best. Especially when her father carried her on his shoulders. It was a moment she waited for. As she was lifted up, she would close her eyes and imagine herself floating in the air among the trees. She wished the moment would never end. But soon, all too soon, her father would put her down, panting heavily, mindful of her mother's wary and solicitous eye.

By the time they got to Granny's house it was usually dinnertime, and they were hungry. They each got a bowl of borscht with a big dollop of sour cream. In the centre of the table was a big dish of steaming potatoes with melted butter, which they would take and plop into their soup. Then each went about his own business. Her mother helped Granny and her aunts. Her father helped the men, but soon tired and went off to sit in the shade, where he would light a cigarette, coughing horribly. The others went on working. Susanna felt bad to be observing him at such a moment, which must be embarrassing to him; she knew he would not want her to see him like that. A father should be stronger. But she understood that it was just temporary; he would get better. He was strong; he just needed some time to recover.

He had to rest after prison, just as he would rest in the shade after the work in the fields, still too hard for him. The locals understood him. Sometimes they came up to chat, have a cigarette with him. In any case, Susanna had no time to think about it. Her cousins wanted her to come out and play. In the evening they would run home, exhausted, for a slice of bread spreadea with sour cream and sprinkled with sugar. The air turned blue and the sun hid behind the forest, leaving a red glow over the trees. The grown-ups would sit and talk long into the night. You could feel a tension that never went away, even though the heat of the day had gone and was resting in the darkness.

But it was beautiful—beautiful as never before, and as it never would be again. Her mother put on weight. One day, as she was walking arm in arm with Susanna's father across the fields, bare after the harvest, Susanna ran up to them and touched her mother's round belly. "You're going to have a baby," she announced with a sudden feeling of certainty.

"And you're going to have a little sister or a little brother," her mother answered, looking radiant, stooping down and putting her other arm around her. Susanna thought for a moment. "A brother would be nice," she said finally.

It was the beginning of September. The village was quiet. The fields and forests fell silent. Only the birds held their chattering conclaves, arguing in flocks before their flight south. Smoke crept low over the earth, smelling of juniper. But the adults' nighttime talk lost none of its intensity. That was their last visit to the village that year. It was time to go back to school.

Uncle Stach found some work down in the Zeran district. The tension Susanna could hear in the nighttime conversations spilled out into the streets. She could feel it even in school. The children would play at being their parents. They said that the Soviets would have to leave Poland. Someone remarked that the Jews would no longer rule over us. Karol said that Gomułka would save Poland; Zdzich argued with him, claiming that it would be the primate. The teachers seemed nervous and irritable. Even the christening party for Ala, Aunt Gienia's daughter, degenerated into a scene, a heated argument between the men. Susanna's father, who must have had a bit too much to drink, was shouting at everyone, saying they shouldn't be so sure. Uncle Stach tried to calm him down, and then Susanna and her mother took him home, still shouting. "They're just like children. They believe him. Have they forgotten that he's a Communist?" Susanna's mother tried to shush him.

It was autumn. One night her father didn't come home. Her mother was worried. When Susanna came back from school Aunt Gienia was there, holding little Ala. Uncle Stach also hadn't come home, but Aunt Gienia did her best to calm her mother's fears. Her mother didn't even look sad; her face looked rigid, twisted with pain. "One uprising's enough for me," she kept saying. Aunt Gienia also didn't seem very calm. But the men came back that evening, more confident-seeming than before. They looked at their women with tender superiority. For a long time, after her uncle and aunt had gone home with Ala, Susanna couldn't sleep, listening to the unusually loud, it seemed to her, rhythmical creaking of her parents' bed.

A few days later they took her to the huge parade ground in front of the Palace of Culture. It was a bit like the day the previous year, when Susanna had gone to the first of May demonstration with her whole school. Unlike her mother, she liked the first of May. She liked the fluttering flags and the great heavy red banners. She liked being part of the crowd; it made everyone in it feel even happier. Now, just as then, people were converging in the same place, flowing in from all the streets around, and though they were strangers, being in the crowd made them feel linked—perhaps because they were linked by a common goal. Seizing her parents by their hands, Susanna knew that they, and all the others who had come together to form the crowd, felt as she did: that they were participating in something that meant more than she could imagine. At the same time she realised that what was happening around her was different from the first of May parade, and much more important. People looked different, they moved and breathed and looked at each other differently. She knew she was participating in something extraordinary.

The streams of people became torrents, and then one huge sea, filling on the parade ground in front of the palace. They waited. And suddenly a ripple of enthusiasm went through the crowd and there was a burst of cheering. It was only a moment later that Susanna, up on her father's shoulders, realised that it had been prompted by the appearance, up on the tribune stand, of a funny-looking, bald little man. The little man started to speak, and his speech was just as funny as his appearance. But the crowd was enchanted. They cheered and clapped and chanted. Susanna gazed astonished at her parents, but they, too, seemed to be in a kind of trance. The crowd rippled around her.

There was something odd about it all. Here were all these people who felt they were living through an important experience, happy and clapping and cheering, but the funny-looking little man up there didn't seem interested in what was going on around him. At times she felt they had done a switch: that someone from behind the scenes had substituted a strange sort of puppet for the real hero of the hour, and that the tribune stand was the stage of a puppet show. But the crowd, this endless sea of the people, didn't realize this, and was cheering someone else, someone who wasn't there—someone who didn't exist. Susanna wanted to point this out to her parents, but they were waving their arms in the air, wild with enthusiasm like everyone around them. She wanted to explain it to them, but it was impossible; she couldn't break through their enthusiasm. So she decided she would just be happy for them, glad of their joy and that of everyone else there on the parade ground, everyone in Warsaw, everyone in Poland. The late-October air smelled of spring. Hope rose up from the whole country, like steam.

The crowd was reluctant to leave, even though the funny little man and his retinue had disappeared from the tribune stand. They wanted to stay together a little longer, to share their triumph, to feel the warmth of their togetherness. Finally they began to disperse slowly into the night, the air warmed by their enthusiasm.

That evening would remain vivid in Susanna's memory. But twelve years later, when she was running from the police truncheons in front of the university, trying to avoid the blows, and a few days afterwards, when she saw the same funny-looking little man on television, speaking in the Congress Hall of the palace of Culture, and he was shouting, yelling out names and making threats in a sort of feverish trance, images of that October happiness came back to mock her.

But that October day she was happy as she walked home with her parents. They were all happy. Her mother was fairly advanced in her pregnancy by then and was leaning on her father, who had his arm about her protectively, his other hand in Susanna's. She could see his smile by the light of the moon when it peeped out from behind the clouds.

But their October happiness was marred by disquiet. A few days later her father, together with a friend, lugged home a big wooden radio with a green eye. Her mother helped them set it up, and late at night they finally found the station they had been looking for. Her father was glancing around nervously. From beyond the hissing, whistling and buzzing, the green eye lighting up in rhythm to it, they could make out individual words: "About ... people have been killed, Soviet tanks have fired on ...." She understood what was happening. The army of our so-called allies was destroying the capital of Hungary, which wanted to be independent. Her parents' faces were immobile. "It's like the uprising," her mother said, and Susanna knew she meant the Warsaw Uprising, which her mother had survived by a miracle.

But everything was still so lovely. She awaited her little brother as excitedly as her parents awaited their second child. Her father was gone all day, combining work and study. He would return in the evening. He ate little. Then he would sit down with a cigarette and a cup of tea and gaze out at the darkness that enveloped the city. One day—her mother was not yet back from her shift at the hospital— Susanna realised that he was asleep with his head on the table, the smoke from a smouldering cigarette curling upwards from the ashtray in front of him. She put out what remained of the cigarette, burnt down almost completely to a pile of ash, and woke up her father. For some seconds he gazed wildly, uncomprehendingly, around the apartment. There was something strange in his face, but it was only much later, recalling the moment, that Susanna realized it had been fear. It lasted only the brief time it took for him to recognize her. Then it was gone. His face lit up in a smile and he hugged her to him, even as with his other hand he scrabbled for a cigarette in the pack on the table. .

"I'm so happy," he whispered in her ear. "So happy that I've got you, and your mother, and another child on the way. A little brother for you," he corrected himself, under her reproving gaze. "So many haven't had my luck, haven't known such happiness. I thought at once time that I, too—that I ...."—here he turned away from her to the window and took a drag on his cigarette—"... that I would never see you again." A violent fit of coughing seized him. He was coughing more and more. "But now I know that all the bad things that happened are over. I have you." He put the cigarette down in order to hug her again. "And your mother, Terenia ... you love her, but you have no idea what a wonderful person she is. You can only sort of feel that she might be. I met her during the war. What terrible times. But you knew what people were worth then, you could appreciate someone … like your mother …. We were separated, but we found each other again after the war. Your mother was unlucky; she was in the uprising. I was luckier. I had to escape from Warsaw a bit earlier. I'd never have survived the uprising. But she managed—although the uprising stayed with her. Still, that's all behind us now. In a couple of years I'll get my degree. Maybe your mother, too, will …. She used to dream of becoming a doctor. And I'll build. Before the war this was a beautiful city. Hard to imagine now. We have so much to look forward to, everything still ahead of us."

That was the best Christmas ever. Her father brought home a huge Christmas tree that touched the sky. The ceiling, that is. Susanna trimmed it with decorations she had made with her parents, chains and moons of colored paper, a few baubles and little candles, and a handful of sweets in bright wrappers. She knew she would be allowed to eat them on the last day of Christmas. At the top of the tree they stuck a star made out of cardboard and covered in shiny silver foil. Under the tree Susanna found a doll of the kind she had never had before. It had hair, and when she went to sleep she closed her soft silky eyes and said, "Mummy." Her father brought a pack of little fireworks, Bengal lights, and when they turned off the lights, a fountain of sparks rose up and created magical worlds in the darkness. Her mother began to sing a carol and Susanna joined in. In the end her father, too, did his uncertain best to sing with them.

At the beginning of March they came back from the hospital with Tadeusz. Her mother let his sister hold him. Susanna was astonished: she couldn't help feeling that this strange little creature, who didn't understand anything, recognized her. His eyes opened a bit wider, his mouth emitted a soft croak, and his body moved as if it wanted to cling to her. It was her little brother. Her little son.

Her father was ill. At first Susanna thought it was because he wasn't getting enough sleep, kept awake by the noise and commotion around Tadzio in the evenings, his crying and all the running about involved in dealing with it, and that this was why he was still in bed when she was already off to school. But soon she realized it was too frequent an occurrence to be just that. She recalled certain earlier signs that all was not well with him: that time he'd fallen asleep with his cigarette smouldering in the ashtray, or the way her mother looked at him—looks which had meant nothing to her at the time, but which in retrospect clearly expressed something more than ordinary concern. And then the gasping for breath, the fits of coughing, the long periods of time her father spent locked in the lavatory.

He was pale and getting thinner. At night she could hear her parents arguing. One day her father came home earlier than usual, in a gloomy mood. "I suppose you're happy now," he said to her mother, as if she were to blame for what had happened. "They gave me medical leave. I'll have to start everything from scratch. If I ever go back to my studies at all. If ...." He stopped and gave an irritated snort. Susanna had never seen him like this.

"But you know there was no way of keeping your studies up any longer, what with ...." Her mother trailed off, gazing at him sadly. Her father made no reply.

Spring was coming when her mother arrived at her school, carrying Tadzio. "Your father's in the hospital," she announced. "And I have to be with him. So you'll have to stay at home on your own and look after your brother for a few days." She evaded Susanna's questions. "I've told your teacher, it's all arranged."

Her father stayed in the hospital over a month. He smiled when she came to visit, tried to look carefree, and said the conventional phrases about how everything would be fine. But Susanna knew it wasn't fine. Suddenly she recalled her visits to the prison: His smile had been just the same. Now he gazed out of the window of the hospital ward as if it were barred.

It was summer by the time he came home. But he still wasn't well. He stopped going to work. He was very weak. He tried to look after his son, but it was hard. He had dizzy spells, and sometimes fell over for no apparent reason. More and more often he stayed in bed. He wanted to read, but found it hard to concentrate. And he was in pain. Susanna could tell by the way he would clench his jaw and shut his eyes, and sometimes bite his hand so as—she suspected—not to cry out. Sometimes she heard him moaning.

She spent the holidays in the country, with Tadzio and Aunt Gienia and her daughter. When they got back her father was more or less permanently in bed, getting up only for meals and to go to the bathroom. The radio was moved to his bedside table. It was on almost all the time, though sometimes he turned it down so that you could barely hear it. Occasionally he would talk to it, or—more often—just comment on what was being said. Sometimes Uncle Stach came to visit. At first her father insisted on getting up and sitting with him at the table, but the effort clearly exhausted him, and he soon resigned himself to staying in bed. Uncle Stach would sit by his bedside. They spent more time in silence than in talk. Sometimes they would have a cigarette together, though after a while Uncle Stach avoided this; Susanna's mother must have said something to him about it.

Susanna's father now left the house only for occasional tests at the hospital. Her mother always went with him; she had switched to working only the night shifts, so that she could be with him during the day. But it turned out it was the nights that were hardest for him. So she switched to day shifts. She would run home at lunchtime to bring him food from the hospital canteen, though it was hard to get him to eat anything.

"Will Daddy ... will Daddy get better?" Susanna finally got up the courage to ask this question one evening when her father fell into a restless, feverish sleep. His sleep was increasingly shallow and restless, and full of cries and moans.

"Of course he will, dear, of course he will," her mother said, in clipped tones. The conventional assurances, lightly, automatically thrown off.

"But I really want to know. I'm his daughter, after all, and I love him .... Surely I have the right to know. So you should tell me the truth," she insisted. Not quite able to express what she felt, she nevertheless plowed on: "I know it's not good. And that's why ... that's why I want to know."

Her mother looked at her as if seeing her for the first time. Something in her expression changed.

"You really want to know? You have the right to know? Well, I suppose you do .... Will your father get better? I don't know. He's very sick. He was sick when he came out of prison. The doctors can't fathom how he managed to stay in such good shape the whole of this past year. After the prison ... the things that they .... His internal organs are damaged. Liver, kidneys, lungs. And not just that. There's some damage to the brain, too. And in any case ... but ... if he was able to stay well ... to stay so well ... all last year ... then maybe ... maybe ...." She turned away and began to sob, covering her head with her arm. It was a silent sobbing; only the shaking of her shoulders revealed that anything was amiss. Susanna came up and hugged her, feeling more like a sister than a daughter. It occurred to her that she should take better care of her mother. And then she understood that her father was dying.

He went on dying for another year and a half. For the first time Susanna found herself wishing that school would last longer, so that she could get home later. Her father was slowly losing touch with reality. He moaned and cried out. Sometimes, overcome by nausea, he was unable to get up quickly enough and threw up in bed. Then it all had to be cleaned up. Sometimes he was incontinent. Her mother brought a bedpan and a bottle from the hospital. The smell of feces began to permeate the apartment. Susanna could stay silent no longer.

"Mummy, why don't you take daddy to the hospital?" she burst out. For the first time in her life she saw a look of real fury on her mother's face.

"Oh, yes? You want some peace and quiet, do you? You want him to go and die in hospital and not bother you? Well, there's one thing I have to say to you: As long as I live he'll stay here, at home. And if he's going to die, he'll die here, in his own bed. Under my care. And you … you can always go out, there's nothing stopping you."

Susanna was overcome with shame.

"No, I didn't mean …. That's not what I meant. I only… I only asked, because maybe in the hospital they could … they could take better care of him …."

"No one can take better care of him than I can!" she cut in. "And he can take his medicine at home. Even that month he spent in hospital was completely unnecessary!"

Susanna struggled with her feelings. She could no longer pretend that she wasn't thinking of her father's death with a measure of hope: Better for him to die, for him and for everyone else, something inside her whispered. She was ashamed of this thought and tried to suppress it, but it kept returning. It's not me, she repeated to herself silently; it's someone else inside me, talking to me.

Long before her father's death, the apartment was transformed into a house of mourning: the smell of dying flesh and its secretions, the moans of a mind losing touch with reality, imprisoned in its nightmares, and brief moments of deathly quiet as her father regained a measure of consciousness and in silence contemplated the approaching end.

Sometimes he asked her to read to him. He had asked her mother, who of course had assented with a smile, as always, but she was so tired that she fell asleep within a few minutes. She awoke with a start when the book fell from her hand, but Susanna's father told her not to go on: he was so tired, he said, that he no longer understood what was being read to him. A few days later he asked Susanna.

He handed her the book he wanted her to read to him—Benvenuto Cellini's *My Life*—and showed her where she should start reading. She remembered it still: page thirty-four. There was a bookmark with a picture on it of something vaguely plantlike, but unidentifiable as anything specific, and she used it to mark the place where she had stopped.

She read to him every few days, on average. There were periods when he asked for it almost every day, and others when more than a week might go by between readings. Their sessions did not last long; he could not concentrate for more than a quarter of an hour. But usually he tired much more quickly than that and signaled to her after a few minutes that it was time to stop. They got through less than half the book—especially as he sometimes asked her to read a passage a second time. She did not understand much of it. Something that had seemed clear suddenly became complex and obscure, hedged about with incomprehensible words and descriptions of bizarre situations. And yet the book drew her in, in its own way. It was like a mysterious, needlessly detailed and complicated fairly tale.

"I was always interested in that period most of all," her father said to her, explaining his choice of book. "The Renaissance. The birth of our world. Florence—it was just a small town then. Smaller than a single district of Warsaw. But all the great figures of the age met there—the people who shaped our imagination and made it what it is today." He talked like this several times, after she had stopped reading. He spoke in short sentences. It was only later that these brief fragments came together in her memory as one connected whole. "And then Cellini himself. Before the war I saw a photo of his statue of Perseus with the head of Medusa. It made a big impression on me. The sadness with which Perseus gazes at his trophy and Medusa's face: pain and horror. I'd so much like to see it in reality, to see whether it was just my imagination. It's in front of the Uffizi museum. I've read that it's one of the greatest museums in the world. You can see, when you go there, how the Middle Ages are gradually transformed into our world. The paintings acquire depth and perspective. It's not true that the medieval painters would have been incapable of painting perspective. It's just that they didn't need it. They concentrated on what was most important and didn't bother with any of the details that are part of how we see things. An art historian I met in prison explained it to me. He taught me a lot. I don't know what happened to him later, whether he's still alive. I wanted to see that statue so much. And others. By Michelangelo, by Verrocchi. And paintings. I promised myself I would take your mother there someday. Your mother and you. We'd follow in the footsteps of those people, look at what they saw. But now … I'll never take you now. When I found out about this book, Cellini's memoirs, I knew I had to read it. I started to look for it, but in the end it was your mother who found it for me. She asked all her friends, and finally she found it in an antiquarian bookstore. And she bought it. It was just before Tadzio was born.

One day he asked Susanna to come sit by his bed.

"I'm so sorry I made things so miserable after I came back," he said feverishly, seizing her hand.

"Daddy, don't be silly. What on Earth …."

"You know, I thought … I really thought I'd get better. When I saw your mother, and you … I felt so wonderful, better than I'd ever felt in my life. I thought I had all my life still ahead of me. That I could achieve everything I wanted. I felt so strong …. Even though I tired so easily. I felt almost no pain—the pain that had tormented me for years. From the interrogations. In a way I feel ashamed that I didn't manage to overcome it, that I didn't get better, that I won't be able take you to Florence …. Your mother deserves better. So do you. The only thing I can say is that I've loved you as best I could and will always love you."

He died in early spring. The coffin-bearers were Uncle Stach, Uncle Antek, Uncle Bronek, and one other person whose face Susanna recognized but couldn't identify. Her mother walked behind the coffin and leanded on Aunt Gienia's arm. Her face was gray and Susanna suddenly noticed that her hair was mostly white. It must have happened recently, and very quickly. When the funeral service was over and the coffin was lowered, her mother sank down on the edge of the grave. Susanna couldn't tell if she had knelt or fallen and broken the fall by propping herself up with her arms. But a few seconds later she straightened up and, still kneeling, threw a clod of earth down on to the coffin. Tadzio, his hand in Susanna's, began screaming and wouldn't calm down.

"Come," her mother said to her late at night, when everyone had gone and Tadzio was asleep. "Come. I'll tell you about your father."

Translated from the Polish by Christopher Adam Zakrzewski

Sheri Gabbert

What do I know?

Like Napalm Nam when I was ten,
I have seen life explode into death
so many times I forget I was never
there, only this time the ashes
in a zip-locked bag don't belong
to some other mother's son.

I slept unaware my boy was dead,
until officers, one in blue, one in brown,
came to our door.
I didn't sleep again for nine years
without seeing Dante's *Inferno*,
my son burning, like those sons

of Vietnam, caught forever trying
to grip life but finding death instead,
arms and hands charred but holding
firmly on to nothing.

The smells are as real to me as the sounds
I never heard except on CBS in the sixties.
How can we know, we mothers who were
not there, who will never be there to hold
our boys as they scream for us to save them?

My waking mind wonders if the cries
war mothers hear in their nightmares
are mine, too. What I do know is that

bombs and boys in Army fatigues,
eighteen-wheelers and boys in 1998
Monte Carlos, blaze in unearthly flames
and whatever it is that ignites the night.

Reba Rice

Atheism and Creation

I asked my father once what made us alive,
and he pointed out the sliver of moon, said
"There's God's thumbnail,"

took a swig of the same Mexican beer
that he complained made his back hurt.

But all I can see are craters, dust,
the way it confused me—
visible alongside the sun at 11 a.m.
when they lowered my brother's body
into the earth—

sweat dripping
down my thighs
under the heavy,
black cotton dress
that I never wore again.

Ian Woollen

Repeatable Sequence #2

Outlive the money, just as they warned. The implacable sun rises anyway. Summer nights sizzle into autumn, cicadas chirring. Filch a tomato from the community garden. Soft food helps the pain. Medicare does not cover dental. Jiggle the loose molar with a pair of pliers. Easy does it, like a baby tooth. Cancel the newspaper. Turn down the air conditioning and spend afternoons at the library.

Outlive the next-door neighbor and mother's cousin and the dog. Rediscover a forgotten secret: Freedom *is* just another word for nothing left to lose. Wave to strangers. Wade in the creek. More ancient song lyrics surface: *Sail on, silver girl*. Would they suspect a ninety-year-old in a ratty poncho of shoplifting? Of course, dearie, they suspect everyone. Drones and cameras hovering everywhere. Define *they*. The House Committee on Un-American Activities, who once sent an urgent letter which is now framed above the fireplace.

God love 'em. Study the want ads at the library and ponder employment again. Imagine working as an anonymous media darling. The representative impoverished nonagenarian quoted in magazine articles on public policy. "Social Security, my ass."

Outlive the cat. Eat cat food.

Replace the broken strings on daddy's fiddle. No rain in the forecast. No performance anxiety, either. Stake out the shady corner bench on the courthouse square. Busk for change. Humming and tapping a foot. Thirty bucks on a good day. Strangers stop to chat. Greet a group of university students, costumed as skeletal mimes, handing out flyers for a protest march in Washington, D.C., next week.

They've chartered a bus. Protesting what? It doesn't matter. Rise to the occasion. Answer the call again, however faint. Pack a satchel and climb aboard. Just like '64 and '68 and '71 and again for an anti-nuke rally in the eighties. Oh, and much earlier, the sixth-grade trip to the White House with Mrs. Riggins. Warm weather in the forecast. Mrs. Riggins loved the cherry blossoms.

"Is anybody sitting here?"

"All yours, lady, but you know where we're headed?"

"Straight to hell."

"That would be one way of putting it."

"Tell me about your costumes."

"We're theater students. We're in an improv class. Extra credit on our semester grade for performing at the march."

"I used to be an actress."

"No way."

Cough elegantly and circle a hand in the air.

"No way to live."

"It was tough finding work?"

"That went OK for a while. Something called the Blacklist."

The wide-eyed kid shrugs in commiseration and stares at his phone. He doesn't know anything about the Blacklist. Neither does the tattooed kid across the aisle. God love 'em. Share peaches and peanut butter sandwiches. Roll past familiar terrain on I-70. Dayton, Columbus, Zanesville. Study a guidebook. Free admission to the National Gallery. A dusty red curtain descends on West Virginia. Eventually, a few stars.

Share a jug of wine and, goodness, some whiskey. Read aloud from the guidebook about the Smithsonian exhibit on pinball machines. The students don't know from pinball. Be the shiny, silver orb, rolling left, rolling right, lighting up the dinosaur scoreboard with prehistoric smiles. Someone in charge taps on a microphone and gives a short talk about safely resisting arrest and other civil disobedience techniques. Speaking of tear gas. Raise a hand and mention the bandana-soaked -in-vinegar trick.

Singing starts up at the rear, flows forward, and soon includes the driver. Some things never change. All we are saying is give peace a chance.

"Would you like to borrow my pillow?"

"No, thanks, I won't be sleeping."

"How do you know?"

"Too many memories."

"I hope some of them are pleasant."

"Oh, yes. Lights, camera, action!"

"You were a movie actress?"

"Supporting roles, mostly. I did star in *Medusa From Moscow*."

"*Medusa from Moscow*?"

"Seen by the select few who stayed up for the last feature at the drive-in."

"What's a 'drive-in'?"

Really. Too tired to explain. Quiet on the set. Gentle rumble of midnight traffic. Kid's head curled on one shoulder. The boy across the aisle snoring. Reach down into the satchel for a vial of blood-pressure pills and find a rosary. *Dona nobis pacem*. A rosary? Way back when. The return of the native. Banished from the silver screen. A young thespian in a Midwestern burg trying to behave like she'd never left. Audition for the role of the doomed Nancy Hanks in the summer stock historical drama that plays weekends from April through November. Forever and ever. Attend sinners' mass at St. Charles. Play fiddle for the contra-dance. Pick up part-time work at the library. Volunteer to help Mrs. Riggins' field trips to the nation's capital. Rub the dusty beads again. Pray for no blisters and nobody gets hurt tomorrow.

The implacable sun squeezes under the curtain and shines briefly on the Lincoln Memorial.

"Are we there? I have to pee."

"Looks like we're aiming for the Union Station-end of downtown."

"Sorry about sleeping on your shoulder."

"That's what they're made for."

"Hey, those are frigging tanks on the corner!"

"The House Committee must have known we were coming."

"Nobody said anything about tanks."

"Don't worry. It's all a big theater piece. You'll get your extra credit."

Unload the bus, amid fifty others. Chants and cheers. And Styrofoam coffee. The students don their skeleton costumes. Horses. Whistles. Placard-waving masses. National Guard masses. A noisy production. Trying to corral everyone into designated protest areas.

A surge, another surge. Tear gas. Water cannons. The kids are scared. Their agitprop improv plan dissolves in the mayhem of crowd control.

Inch forward and inch backward. Spot a break in the line and lead the students up the slick steps of the Capitol Building. A confrontation that ought to provide a prompt or two. Daddy's view: Old age and treachery will always triumph over youth and enthusiasm. Grab the framed letter from the satchel. *Sail on, silver girl.*

"Ma'am, stop! No one is allowed in the building today!"

"I'm here to testify! I've been called by Congress. It says right here—."

"Ma'am, this letter is from 1954."

"I'm a little late. I'm ready to name names. I'm ready to reveal the evil-doers."

"Ma'am, please, all of you—go back or you'll be under arrest."

"Officers, behold the skeletons! The skeletons from your very own closets!"

The kids get the cue. God love 'em. Dance and play off "naming the names" and "revealing the evil-doers." Waving phones aloft to capture their ten minutes of notoriety. The cops do what cops do. Likewise, the people on the street below. Shouting in solidarity.

Go limp. Dead weight. Proud of the abrasions. The handcuffs and the dogs and the paddy wagon. The holding cell is a green room, literally. Backslaps. Embraces. Applause and a bow. Routine processing ensues. Deputies pass out tickets and summonses. Suitable for framing. Stumble back to the bus with a student on each elbow. Eventually find the right bus. Request a stop at National Gallery. The driver laughs and revs the engine. More singing and peaches and peanut butter sandwiches. Request some whiskey for the pain. Body-and-soul pain. A rumbling, groaning, sore night descends. Sleep finally. A final sleep.

"Is she all right?"

"I can't tell if she's breathing."

"Check out those big ear lobes."

"They keep growing, you know, along with the nose."

"Let's hope we have that much moxie when we're her age."

"What's 'moxie'?"

"Maybe we could get the department chair to hire her as an adjunct."

"Teach us about timing."

"Put this pillow under her head."

Goodness, dearies, not dead yet. Drop another quarter in the pinball machine. Back home in Indiana. Autumn leaves turning brown. The "Capitol Showdown" video goes viral. Over a million hits. Watch it at the public library with other afternoon patrons. A minor cult forms. Strangers nod on the street.

The tattooed student brings lunch on Tuesdays. He locates a print of *Medusa From Moscow*. Watch it at a special screening at the university cinema. Hair, nails, pedicure. Just like the old days. Eight thousand bucks for the adjunct job. Share basic secrets of the trade. Only actors with blue eyes should audition for sniper roles, because of the close-ups.

Grade benevolently, with justice and mercy for all. Students bring a pumpkin pie. Mrs. Riggins' daughter, now an archivist at the historical society, finds Super 8 footage of the Nancy Hanks performances. Another special screening and an interview with a reporter from an Indianapolis newspaper. Gatherings on the front porch. Practice a royal wave. Social Security, my ass. Receive admirers in a wicker rocking chair. Slowly moving forward and back, as if blown by the breeze. Play to the last row.

John Gifford

Power Seat

The pay was a tax bracket away from what he'd earned during his short term with the Burlington Northern Santa Fe. Still, it added a measure of purpose to his day, and it was a steady paycheck besides. Hauling hardened-criminal freight from the prison in Bidwell Springs to the county seat, and then back the other way, was its own challenge, especially when he was outnumbered, eight to one, and sometimes more. He saw the way these condemned men looked at him, and he could see the gears turning between their ears as they mumbled among themselves. A stray piece of wire, or a contraband key, was all it would take for them to bust loose and flee. Or try to strangle Roland with their shackles and chains. They had nothing to lose, their freedom to gain.

Things changed the first time Roland passed a long link of cars at ninety. Traffic was heavy that day, and he'd been running late. The men fell silent as he jerked the big prison van into the passing lane and stomped the gas, holding his breath until at last he had to swerve to miss the oncoming cars. Horns honked. Headlights blinked. His passengers' eyes flashed with fear, and he knew then that he would do it again, and that he'd still be here in a year.

Terry Minchow-Proffitt

Killdeer

Whether by caprice or comeuppance
the tornado arrived unseasonably,
rang in the New Year with a rare
St. Louis appearance
and skirted
away, left us well enough alone
before the ball dropped:
Homes piled into insulation and splintered pine,
an MRI Center twisted into toxic waste,
Growler's Pub missing its teeth.

We know what's left. See it. Pick
it through. We'll keep the pictures,
the prayer plant left untouched,
be consoled by neighbors we hardly know,
whose spared homes
make their faces all too glad
to comfort and take us in.

Years later, we still
don't know what was taken.
No abacus can do the subtraction.

A killdeer cries as I walk across
the old yard. She's far from shore.
She plays like she's wounded,
does her level best
broken-wing shtick, flaps in spurts

Killdeer

then looksings back in the hope
I'll be led away from the hedgerow
I once trimmed, in whose shade
lies the exposed nest
where her eggs pebble the ground.

Walter Bargen

A Different Prayer

1

I've watched so many hours, they've become indistinguishable,
yet I can't stop watching. The footage blurs into rain,
wind, darkness, fear, the fumbling amateur videographer
confronted by a mortal realization, the howling more real
than the real that has warmed his mind. There before the lens
the unframeable: path across the city marked by exploding
street lights, sparking Fourth-of-July transformers,
block after block of houses churning into debris,
cars parked on top of cars, then the silence
of the insufficient, the inadequate, the incomplete,
the incomprehensible, the welling-up in the disbelief
of flashlights skimming the unthinkable.
Morning a different lifetime, another country,
where each breath a prayer.

2

Once from the shoulder of a highway,
mid-afternoon on drought-riven plains,
I watched a squat mile-wide twisting
of the riddled and destitute, the swirl of pulverized dirt
and fence posts, barbed wire and tumbleweeds,
grinding eastward as the parked car I stood beside
pointed west. My daughter hanging out the window
shouting, "Dad, let's go! Let's go!" as I feigned
a leisurely photo session. The tail end of the front

swept past, trailing hundreds of foot-wide, hundred-foot-
long finely braided corkscrews of dirt, a beaded curtain
between rooms of dust devils leaving stunted corn fields
or the beaded curtain to a doorless room decades ago,
where the weather could change at a moment's entrance.

Walter Bargen

After the operation

everyone wants to know,
if I meet them on a street corner,
on the broken back of sidewalks,
at a benchless pocket park
where everyone wears a trench coat,
and if I meet them in a pictureless hallway,
in an elevator headed for the thirteenth floor,
at the water fountain where the Ark surfs
bubbles as it waits for landfall as the glass fills,
in the breakroom decorated with paper banners:
wishing us more birthdays, years of anniversaries,
flowered fields of retirement, in the closet
but don't tell, in offices with doors
opened and closed, again don't tell;
at the airport waiting in line to check in,
waiting in line to be checked out—
felt up, wanded, X-rayed—only to wait in line
to board, wait in line to be seated,
greeted, offered water, coffee, soda,
and a small packet of too-salty pretzels,
as we buckle ourselves in awkward seats,
ready or not to transcend all that we know—
and everyone wants to know anyway and I say
getting along, getting by, and just maybe getting down.

Thomas Shipp Burnett

The Anvil of the Sea

In Chile, I sat outside the Café del Mar with my coffee and watched the gulls pick intestines out of the sand. Big, stubborn birds that fought over coiled ribbons the color of unbleached silk. What struck me was the gulls' silence. They seldom screamed at each other, preferring to fight with closed beaks. In a few hours, the small fleet of trawlers and motorized skiffs, the lifeblood of the village, would return from the morning's work and bring a bevy of fish to be gutted in the tide. I thought the gulls understood that.

Caridad, who owned the Café del Mar, always smiled when I sat down at my table, always the same table on the edge of the Paseo Marítimo. She was in her late forties—twenty years older than me—but there was something grandmotherly in the way she moved: a conflict between the need to nurture and sadness. Each time, Caridad said, "*Buneos días, americano,*" as she brought me my cup of coffee and a little silver pitcher of milk, even after I'd introduced myself as Simon. I never used the milk, but every morning Caridad still brought the pitcher.

The Café del Mar was indistinguishable from the other restaurants that lined the Paseo, each with its half-dozen wrought-iron tables in the open air, but I preferred it. I lunched there the first day I emerged from the desert sick of traveling and bus rides and heavy things. From my table, I watched the Pacific unfurl over the western edge of the Atacama, convinced if I stared long enough I could collar that moment when the waves solidified. I lit a cigarette. My back was turned away from the sand dunes that stood hundreds of feet high on the outskirts of the village. Behind the dunes, the desert stretched to the horizon and the Andes hundreds of miles beyond it.

I had been in the village three days. Soon, I would have to leave and keep traveling south. I had only enough money to last another few weeks, and once I hit Santiago, two thousand kilometers down the narrow corridor of Chile, that anvil of the sea, I would fly back to the States. Back to the job search—to actually start it. Fluent in Spanish. That's what I'd planned to put on my résumé. Turned out my few classes at Ole Miss had hardly prepared me to converse. While I'd improved markedly over the month I'd been in South America, I still got confused. I could understand, but replying was still difficult.

On the second day I went to the Café del Mar, Caridad asked me why I came to the village. I didn't know what to say, so I said luck or fate or some horrible combination of both. She seemed amused, as if she'd heard a child accidentally say something profane, and brought me a pitcher of milk. The next day Caridad asked me again. I told her that all my life I had removed myself from situations too closely resembling mystery and then apologized for having created one. I explained that I had been traveling south toward San Pedro to see the salt flats but had decided to stop along the coast.

"If you do not like mystery, why come to Chile?" she asked.

"It's a start," I said.

Caridad then asked me why I hadn't gone to Iquique or Arica—someplace with something for me to do. I told her the slow pace was precisely why I had come to the village.

After I finished my coffee, followed by juice and toast smeared with avocado, I wandered the Paseo. Women with menus approached me from the other restaurants. A girl, no older than twelve, hawked the tangle of beaded bracelets around her wrist. Her smile was crooked in a way that made it beautiful, and I felt bad turning her away. When I reached the end of the Paseo, I walked back along the beach. The gulls took flight as I approached—a sort of reverse wake. A pack of mismatched dogs stalked the waterfront, led by a Rottweiler with mange down his black back like a five domino with the colors inverted. I took to following the dogs. They ate the guts the gulls had missed and the garbage left by the fishermen. Among the dogs, and constantly underfoot of the Rottweiler, was a small Peruvian hairless. The dog wasn't completely hairless; I had seen similar in Lima, where I'd flown into South America. A flaxen crest grew across the dome of the dog's head and between the eyes toward the snout, more tufts around the ears and tail. The rest of the dog was smooth, black skin punctuated only by rows of circular, white scars.

I followed the dogs some distance from the Paseo, toward the wharves that curved along with the bay, until the hairless got tangled up in the feet of the Rottweiler. The Rottweiler fell onto its forelegs and the hairless snapped at its neck. I was surprised by the sudden violence, but I knew what would happen. The hairless had picked a fight it couldn't win. The Rottweiler sprang to its feet, lunged, and pinned the hairless. The rest of the pack howled in anticipation.

I reached down and grabbed the top half of a glass bottle that had been discarded on the beach. I threw the shard and hoped it would strike with the jagged end; I didn't want to see the results of the fight. The bottle hit the Rottweiler on the flank and landed benignly in the sand. The dog turned its head, teeth bared, foamy, white spittle at the corners of its mouth. I saw the hairless writhe out from underneath the Rottweiler, but I didn't track the hairless in my peripheral vision. All my attention was on the Rottweiler.

Copper fur blossomed around its throat when it barked.

I thought maybe the other half of the bottle was still in the sand, but I didn't dare move. I just stared at the dog and its brown eyes constricted against a gray morning, listened as it snarled. I wondered what teeth puncturing my skin would feel like. Would it be like a needle, when you knew it was coming, or the careless slicing of an onion, that sudden slip of the knife and a crescent of skin peeled back? Either way there would be that moment when it was just a hole, before the blood pumped again to the extremities. I couldn't feel my feet. The Rottweiler crept forward.

I heard a man shout: "*¡Fuera, Grueso!*"

The Rottweiler froze and then a seashell caught it behind the ear. The dog yelped and slunk toward the wharves; the other members of the pack followed suit.

I turned and saw an old man cradling the hairless to his chest. He kissed its black skin and whispered into its ear. He wore a white linen shirt and black pants which were made all the more plain by the technicolor stocking cap on his head—bright bands of blue and pink and green, the words *La Paz* crocheted in white lettering. Something bulged near the hem of his shirt. At first, I thought it was fat, but the bulge was on only one side. I tried not to stare. The man smiled at me and I saw he was missing several teeth. He thanked me for what I'd done and introduced himself as Yaku Yana.

"Come have a pisco," he said.

I followed Yaku Yana to a single-story building on the Paseo, still contemplating the brown eyes of the Rottweiler—whom I learned the locals called Grueso. Two ceramic bulls stood astride the ridge of the roof, a wooden cross between the pair. Yaku Yana said he was Quechua and from Peru and that the bulls reminded him of home. I followed him inside. It wasn't a wide structure, but it was very deep. He led me through a room full of display cases whose metal edges were rusted by the Pacific air. The cases were full of silver jewelry: rings and pendants and necklaces set with green-and-blue stones and pieces of fused glass. In the next room was a pitted metal work bench cluttered with an array of tools that looked like they belonged in a dentist's office—both antiquated and modern. In the corner was a small octagonal kiln. I realized Yaku Yana made the jewelry himself. He walked through his work space and into the final room. Only then did Yaku Yana set the hairless down.

The dog immediately jumped onto a bed in the corner and dug into the sheets. On the walls hung a map of Peru—the kind a tourist would get from a kiosk—and a calendar from 2009 with glossy photographs of beautiful women. In the corner of the room was an exposed toilet. Yaku Yana plucked two glasses from the squat bookcase that served as his nightstand. Filling the shelves were a few bowls and plates—neatly stacked—a lockbox, and a dozen books in varying states of decay. On top was a hot plate, a handful of pesos and pill bottles, and a bottle of pisco.

"Últimas Noches," said Yaku Yana, as he handed me a glass. "Very old. They do not make it anymore, but it was the best in South America."

I thanked him and took a sip of the clear liquid. It smelled like dry grass and was surprisingly thick, yet the liquor hardly burned my throat.

"*Puro*," said Yaku Yana. "The best."

He disappeared into his work space and it was only then that I noticed how slowly he moved. The inundation of my body with adrenaline was over—maybe everything had slowed down. When I was nineteen, I had rolled my car when I'd lost control over a graveled turn and struck a culvert. As I stood outside the vehicle, time compressed and expanded so that the forty minutes I'd spent waiting for the sheriff seemed like an entire afternoon and yet just the opposite. I'd found myself with a cigarette constantly in hand. Those inerrant timekeepers—it took me six minutes to smoke—ran fast and slow. I felt like that again: thankful to have escaped grievous injury and desperately wanting another cigarette.

Yaku Yana returned with a folding chair. I took two leisurely sips of Últimas Noches before he finished propping up the chair. He sat down on the bed next to the hairless and adjusted the lump underneath his shirt. I heard the crinkle of plastic and the slosh of liquids.

Yaku Yana caught me looking.

He laughed and lifted up his shirt. Suctioned to his skin was an oval bag. Yaku Yana pulled the rest of the bag out of from the waist of his oversized pants. Through the opaque plastic, I could see the outlines of black masses and a waterline a third of the way up. A red, plastic clip cinched the bottom of the bag.

"Bowel cancer," he said. "It is not permanent."

I was surprised by Yaku Yana's openness. Here I had just met him—had hardly met him—and he had already exposed something hugely personal about himself. My first thought was to flee and take shelter at the Café del Mar, although I felt incapable of eating anything, but my revulsion shifted quickly to sympathy. I wondered how he still made the jewelry, if he could still use the torch, and if he ever thought what would happen if he dropped one of the sharp implements. I found myself asking him if it hurt. "*Cuando es de noche, y no hay sino la muerte, solamente la muerte, y nada más que el llanto,*" he said. I didn't know what to make of his words until Yaku Yana opened one of his crumbling books, pointed to the page, and said. "Neruda."

"I am well," he said.

Yaku Yana took a sip of pisco then pulled a pouch of tobacco from his pants and rolled a cigarette. He held it out to me.

"I have my own," I said.

"It will help with the smell. I apologize, but I must."

Yaku Yana squatted next to the toilet and detached the bag from his body. I started to stand up as he reached for the red clip at the bottom of the bag.

"Do you need a moment?" I asked.

"No," he said. "I am fast." And then he undid the clip. I sat back down and turned my head. I didn't want to see what was happening. The sound was over quickly, but the stench was unbearable.

I felt trapped: If I walked out it would be rude and I might see Yaku Yana cleaning the bag. Maybe he didn't trust me alone in his shop? But if I stayed I would have to put up with the stink. I didn't move from the chair. I thought I might vomit so I held my glass of Últimas Noches beneath my nose. The smell of reeds did little to cover that of human waste. Time expanded again: the air stagnant as if it, too, were decomposing. The hairless did not stir on the bed. I let my cigarette burn into the filter. What was taking him so long? It was one thing to go about one's business in front of a guest and another to do it so sedately. Again, I thought of the Café del Mar. I heard the pop of a match, smelled the chemical fumes, then the scrape of metal across skin. What on earth was he doing now? I turned my head and saw Yaku Yana smoking as he shaved the area around the blood moon stoma.

"It never rains here," he said. "It is a good place for me."

I thought I should leave. I wanted to leave. I stood up and Yaku Yana laughed and held out the bottle of Últimas Noches. He poured two fingers into my glass.

"It is early," said Yaku Yana. "Stay. Have a good time."

He reattached the bag and tucked it into his pants, then washed his hands in a bucket of water. He rolled another cigarette and handed it to me. I slid it into my pack, knowing I'd throw it away later, and asked him how business was.

"It is dead season," said Yaku Yana. "The tourists come to see the sea lions but they are not here yet. I do not sell much this month, but in two, three months the tourists will come and I will sell again. In meantime, I read and clean and walk with Pablito. I found him on the street and I take him in. I say business is very good."

He poured himself more pisco.

"But it is hard to clean shop with"—he gestured toward the bag. "There are many spiders. The spiders like it here, too, but I do not like them. Bad for business."

I looked around the back room and tried to imagine what Yaku Yana meant by clean. The coffee can next to the toilet overflowed with used paper. Dust coated the odds and ends in thick layers. Coils of wire and scrap metal covered the floor. Even the walls had begun to rust. He had no cleaning supplies that I could see—only a broom and dust pan. The pisco had warmed my belly and I realized I was sweating. The man sold nothing and had bowel cancer, yet he worried about spiders. Still, I'd heard the sadness in Yaku Yana's voice. Appearances were everything in a village where nothing distinguished itself. Caridad must have had the same concerns—why she always brought me the milk. I stood up and grabbed the broom from the corner.

"There is no need," said Yaku Yana. "It is early. Have a good time."

I ignored him and began to sweep the corners. It was something I could do for him. Cobwebs and hair and black grime stuck to the bristles of the broom. A few small-denomination pesos came loose from the shadows, the crown jewels of the mound of dust I piled in the center of the room. And there were spiders—but only a few. Their black bodies were perfectly camouflaged for the recesses of the shop, but they looked very common, like most spiders I'd seen back home. I noticed them only when they began to move.

The air crackled softly as Yaku Yana lit a match.

I swept in silence, not knowing what to say to the old Quechua man. I could sense that he too had run out of words. I felt strangely content to sweep the man's shop. It was the first thing I'd done since I'd come to South America that in any way resembled my normal life. No buses or crowded streets or tour guides at notable sites of antiquity. Just the satisfaction of seeing the floorboards better—although Yaku Yana's floor was concrete, no doubt to avoid the constant sea-rot. I had swept the remainder of the back room and had begun to move onto the work space when I felt Yaku Yana's hand on my shoulder.

"That is enough," he said.

I stopped sweeping and crouched down and gingerly picked up the few pesos in the pile of dust.

"Keep them," said Yaku Yana. "For your troubles."

I walked through the shop with the dust pan. Yaku Yana did not follow me. I emptied the pan on the street and, not knowing what else to do, walked back inside and set the pesos down on one of the rusty jewelry cases. Then I left.

That evening, I ate empanadas stuffed with fresh shrimp and cheese at the Café del Mar. Caridad asked if I wanted my coffee, but

I said no and ordered a beer instead. She brought me a brown liter bottle of Cuzqueña and two glasses.

"On the house," she said and sat down next to me. There was no one else in the restaurant.

The sun sank low on the horizon, mirrored by the Pacific—a mélange of reds and oranges, the slightest tinge of purple on the crests of the waves. The temperature fell quickly at night and I had brought the wool sweater I'd purchased in Lima: gray and black with white llamas parading across the front. I put it on.

"That is a lovely sweater," said Caridad. "But it has no color. I like the ones with lots of color." She gestured toward the sunset. "Like that."

We drank while the sun disappeared. The few streetlights on the Paseo came on, but they didn't illuminate far enough to see the beach. I could still hear the surf. We talked about business and the village and Caridad told me about her daughter, Rosa, who should have been back already. I asked Caridad if she was worried.

"Rosalita is off playing," said Caridad. "She will be home soon."

I supposed everyone knew each other in the village. There wasn't a sign as you came in, like back home, but I'd estimated the population to be only a few hundred by the number of buildings. Caridad wasn't afraid of what might happen to her daughter, or if she was she didn't show it. It was still dusk—the signal for all children to return home before the darkness swallowed them. It wasn't time to worry yet. Caridad refilled the glasses and I lit a cigarette. I told her about Yaku Yana.

"He is new here," said Caridad. "Maybe three or four years. He comes from the mountains. I do not know him well, only that he is very sick. I tried to bring him food once, leftover soup, but he refused. I think he is very proud and that he does not want help, even if he is very sick."

I thought about how I had swept Yaku Yana's back room. The whole thing suddenly seemed very selfish. I had done the one thing I could think of that was routine to me. I had swept as much to ignore Yaku Yana as to help him. I hadn't thought how he must have felt to have a stranger, who he'd invited into his home, clean for him. As if his home wasn't good enough or that he himself wasn't good enough. I told Caridad what I had done.

"That is very kind," said Caridad. "I do not think you should feel ashamed."

A trio of men walked into the café and sat down at a table on the far end. Caridad got up and greeted the men like friends—I assumed they were. Fishermen, skin puckered around their mouths and eyes, the cuffs of their sweaters permanently wrinkled from being rolled up to the elbow. They looked at me, alone at my table, and their beards did not conceal their distaste. I poured the rest of the beer into my glass and shuffled the deck of cards I'd carried with me across South America. I played a game of solitaire, but the columns got stuck. When I looked up again, I saw a girl walk into the restaurant. I recognized her as the girl I'd seen selling beads on the Paseo earlier; she still had that tangle around her wrist. Grueso and a few other stray dogs trailed behind her, but they did not enter the patio of the café. I stared at the girl and the dogs apprehensively.

"Buenas noches, Rosa," said one of the fishermen.

I watched Rosa turn around and pet Grueso. Her hand slid down his nape to the base of his neck, raised slightly over the ridge of his withers, crossed the slope of his spine—caressed the patches of exposed skin on his back—and then down his rump to the base of his tail and that last kiss of hair to fingertip. She repeated this motion several times. Grueso let out a short yip and put his paw on Rosa's forearm, nuzzled up against her. I could tell that he didn't want her to stop.

"*No más*, Grueso," said Rosa, and she pointed down the Paseo into the darkness.

Grueso wandered off and the rest of pack followed him, his dominance unchallenged. Rosa went into the kitchen and I heard her voice mix with Caridad's. I dealt a new hand of solitaire. I had just begun to rearrange the cards when I heard the clink of glassware and saw Rosa walking toward me with a cup of coffee on a white saucer. I noticed she no longer had her bracelets. Rosa set down the coffee, then returned with a pitcher of milk and sat down opposite me.

"What are you playing?" she asked.

I told her I was playing solitaire and explained the rules to her, but she didn't seem to understand.

"Do you want to play a game?" I asked.

The crooked smile I remembered from the Paseo appeared on Rosa's face. I put two cards facedown in between us, bookended them with two stacks of seven, and dealt out the remainder of the cards in two even piles.

"This game is called 'speed'," I told her and then tried to teach her how to play.

I beat her easily at first, so we played a game with the cards face up and I walked her through the rules again. After a few more rounds, Rosa took to it and she began to win. Caridad came over and asked me if Rosalita was bothering me. I said no, just the opposite. I noticed the trio of fishermen staring at Rosa and me as we laughed and competed to slap cards on the piles growing in the middle. One of the men—he was wearing a green, salt-stained cap—had repositioned himself so that he could see my table without having to turn his head. Every hand, I glanced over at the man in the green cap and saw him glaring at me; after a while, though, he seemed to lose interest and returned to the other fishermen and his beer. Probably just being protective. I must have played speed with Rosa for an hour before Caridad came by again and told Rosa it was time to go to bed. Rosa looked disappointed until Caridad said she could play one more hand. I dealt the cards out and thought about letting Rosa win.

I didn't have to let her.

After the game, I tucked the cards back into their box and handed them to Rosa. She rushed into the kitchen and came back with the tangle of bracelets. I saw Caridad smile as she brought a tray of food out for the fishermen and stopped to talk with them.

"Pick one," said Rosa.

I tried on several bracelets, but they were all too small. I imagined that Rosa used her own wrist, or maybe part of her forearm, to measure the string. I could see her dismay grow as each consecutive bracelet failed to wrap around my wrist. Finally, we found one that fit. The bracelet was made of tiny, black beads sequenced with brown ovals and round spheres of green, cream, and a shade of red approaching pink. I had to struggle to get the last bead through the loop, but it slid through—the bracelet tight against the hollow between my wrist and hand.

I asked Caridad for my bill, and she disappeared into the kitchen. The man in the green cap leered at me, made the subtle motions that prefigured standing up. He seemed to think better of it and mouthed a few words at me that I didn't catch, but whose meaning was clear enough.

☾

The next morning, I gathered up my things and set out with my backpack to have my final cup at the Café del Mar. As I walked along the Paseo, I saw Yaku Yana and Pablito—the hairless. Yaku Yana wished me good morning and asked me where I was going.

"No," he said. "Come with me."

"I don't feel like drinking today," I said.

"No. No," said Yaku Yana. "That is for guests. You are not guest. You are friend. I have coffee."

I still felt I had shamed him, and perhaps that was why I followed him back to his shop, but he had called me a friend. I immediately noticed how clean the showroom was; it must have taken Yaku Yana hours to sweep it—all day maybe. Yet he said nothing about it, as if it had always been that way, and walked at his slow pace into the back room. He boiled water on the hot plate and doled out spoonfuls of instant Nescafé.

"I hoped that I would find you, Simon," he said and handed me the pesos I'd left on the jewelry case the day before. "Keep them."

I put the coins in my pocket. Yaku Yana washed down some pills with his coffee. He pointed at the backpack by my feet.

"You are not staying here?" he asked.

"No," I said. "I'm leaving for Iquique."

"It is a nice city," he said. "They have surfers instead of only fishermen. There are tall apartments and the tourists come all year. Even Chileans go there to vacation. But you have missed the morning bus. It leaves very early. I take it to go to the hospital. The next bus is at noon."

"Do you have to go often?" I said.

"I am walking well again," said Yaku Yana. "Soon they will take the bag away."

"Are you in remission?" I asked.

"They have cut out what they can," he said. "I have no fear. It will be fine. God will take care of me." He grabbed a pamphlet he'd tucked between his books and handed it to me. The paper was heavily crinkled.

On the cover was a group of Chilean men standing in an awkward line. The man in front had his arms crossed and the heads of the other men peeked out from behind him. It was the same stock pose I might have seen in America. It would have been amusing if not for the words beneath the photo: "Colorectal cancer is the second leading cancer killer in Chile—but simple testing can change all of that."

"I do not think these men have cancer," said Yaku Yana. "It is fake." He laughed until it became a wheeze and then a series of coughs.

"Yes," I said and handed him the pamphlet back. "It's fake."

I sat there a while and smoked with Yaku Yana as he quoted Neruda and talked about the spiders breeding in the corners of his shop. "The spiders will always come back," he said. "I am like the spiders." I didn't want to contradict him so I played with Pablito instead. The dog nipped at my shirtsleeves and rolled around on the floor, allowed me to pin him momentarily before twisting from my hands. Yaku Yana made another round of coffee and I checked my watch. It was almost eleven. I told him that I would have to leave soon.

"Yes. Yes," he said. "The last bus is very late."

I thanked Yaku Yana for his hospitality and wished him good health.

He rolled two cigarettes.

"Do you want to know the real leading cause of death in Chile?" he asked me. "Death."

I purchased my bus ticket from the station at the edge of the village and walked back to the Café del Mar to buy some food for the ride. Rosa was seated at one of the tables. She was surrounded by a group of children and was teaching them how to play speed. Rosa saw me walk in and smiled, but then the boy she was playing with slapped a series of cards down and Rosa returned to the game. I sat at my usual table on the edge of the Paseo.

"I thought you'd already left, Simon," said Caridad.

"I'm going to," I said.

"There is not much to do here," she said. "I am not surprised."

"I like it," I said and ordered a few sandwiches.

"Sometimes I wish we could leave," said Caridad. "Rosalita and I. But this is our home."

She went into the kitchen and I watched the fishermen unload the morning's catch.

"Rosalita is going to miss you," said Caridad as she brought me the paper bag. "She has not stopped playing with your cards."

"She will," I said. I looked at my watch. "I'll have that coffee. But hold the milk."

Caridad laughed and brought me my cup and an empty pitcher.

All around me, the Paseo had come alive. The men carried baskets of silver fish and set up stalls on the beach. Women came out of the restaurants with pesos in their hands to buy food for the day. Children gathered around the largest fish and shouted. I couldn't tell if the catch had been good, but it didn't seem to matter. Another day had been provided for and that was enough. The fog that covered the ocean in the mornings had lifted and, for a few last minutes, I drank my coffee and smoked and watched the Pacific wash away the edge of the desert.

My seat was in the front of the bus, and I could stare out the windshield at a road stretched infinite to the vanishing point. The asphalt was nearly indistinguishable from the floor of the Atacama: The sun had baked it, too, to a uniform fallow. The occasional shrub or clump of tan grass grew in the ruts and clusters of rock. The only colors were discarded bottles and bits of plastic; red-and-white roadsigns indicated a wayside rest stop—just a semicircle of flattened sand. The scenery never changed. The mountains on the horizon, reflecting the sun in a way that made them appear blanketed in mist, never seemed to get any closer. I felt divorced from time, that in this place time didn't matter. I slept for an hour to the rattle of the window and everything was the same when I awoke. The desert was proof of how time broke down even the landscape. The prolonged death throes of rock as it split and crumbled to sand. Even the garbage on the side of the road, the cigarette butts and shreds of blue plastic tarp, would crumble, too—and be forgotten.

My wrist hurt from how I'd slept against the glass. The beads of Rosa's bracelet had pressed indentations into my skin. I undid the bead from the loop, twisted the bracelet in my hands, and spun the beads along the axis of the thread. It occurred to me that never once did Yaku Yana try to sell me any of his jewelry. *Business is very good*, he'd told me. What a fool. I would have bought something. I immediately regretted the thought. He might have been a fool in the way he smoked and drank pisco with his condition, but he was content. Better to be content and a fool than to be angry and wise. That was the only way to die.

Iquique reminded me of those towns on the Gulf Coast devoted to casinos and high-rise condominiums, or at least the beachfront did. White sand and outcroppings of black rock gave way to the Pacific. The water seemed more blue here than it had in the village. Everywhere, people tanned on the beach or swam out into the breakers with surfboards. A hut shaped like a pineapple sold fruit smoothies. Children followed mothers along the boardwalk, stopped to stare at an exhibition of black caimans in from the Amazon. I wondered if the tanks were permanent, if the dozen reptiles were a fixture of the beach or a passing moment of color, traveling from beach town to beach town along the Chilean coast. I watched the caimans for a while. They were docile, soaking in the sun the same as all those people on the beach. I listened to the line of children squeal as they brushed past me. The pace here was different, as if every last drop of sunlight had to be squeezed dry.

The buildings in Iquique proper were far different from the village: facades of yellow and green and red, doors engulfed by polychromatic murals. The city would have been beautiful save the snare of electrical wires connecting all the buildings. In a way, though, the wires made them even more beautiful: black lines cutting across a blue sky. In the Plaza de Armas, a Chilean flag—red and white fields, blue broken by a single white star—waved atop the campanile. I walked across a concrete path, surrounded by fountains and palm trees, and through the arches that opened up the bottom of the tower. Inside was a bust of Captain Arturo Prat, whose name I learned graced the plaza. A small plaque bore his words—*So long as I live, this flag will fly*—and the date: 21 May 1879. Prat's bust was balding and bearded, medals and epaulettes adorning his military dress. His eyes were blank hemispheres of bronze, but the way they fit into the sockets, the way the eyebrows arched over them, captured nothing less than pride.

I lit a cigarette and walked toward the harbor. Iquique was a full port, unlike the small wharves of the village. There were all manner of boats with names like *The Laura Isabel* and *The Popeye*, many of them painted the colors of the Chilean flag. Pelicans waited patiently in lines along the rooftops—no savagery of the gulls in them. They were almost like statues, strange gargoyles who came to life and flew clumsily away only to be replaced by an identical bird. A kiosk sold tickets for a boat ride and I bought one. I walked onto a boat with two rows of white benches and was handed an orange lifejacket. The benches filled with people. I wasn't sure where the boat would take me, but I wanted to see the ocean. I knew I would miss it. I knew that soon I would have to leave here and head back into the desert, that I had lingered in the village past schedule, that I already missed the Café del Mar and Caridad and Rosa and Yaku Yana, and that soon they would fade for me and I, too, for them.

When the boat disembarked, I realized everyone around me was Chilean. There was a solemnity to the group—men and women dressed in their best clothing. Even the children were quiet. I felt I had stumbled onto something sacred and I did not belong. The captain said few words, his voice nearly indecipherable coming through the tinny speakers. We passed a flotilla of gray vessels with gun turrets and radar towers. No one seemed to be aboard them. We passed fishing trawlers and cranes unloading shipping containers from barges, freighters anchored out at sea. A few hundred yards ahead, a small buoy bobbed up and down in the waves. It was red and white and blue, four grated half-circles extending from the frame, two interlocked circles on top and a flag pulled taut by the wind. All around me, the people began to weep as we neared the buoy dancing in the waves. I asked the man in wire glasses next to me why. He smiled, dark curls growing out of his head like an onion sprouting from the earth, and replied: "Below is *The Esmerelda*." Big, bouncing notes of trumpets rattled out of the metal speakers of the boat. And all around me they began to sing. I couldn't make out the words at first, but the boat circled the buoy and I began to comprehend them. *Que o la tumba serás de los libres*, they sang, as we circled the buoy again and again. The flag rippled in the wind; canvas pushed nearer and nearer to its shearing point, but the grommets held strong. And all around me they continued to weep and to sing, as we spiraled closer and closer to the buoy, singing about something I did not understand.

Contributors' Notes

Sayuri Ayers was raised in Columbus, Ohio. Her chapbook, *Radish Legs, Duck Feet*, was released in 2016 by Green Bottle Press. Visit her at sayuriayers.com.

Walter Bargen has published nineteen books of poetry, most recently *Trouble Behind Glass Doors* (BkMk Press, 2013). His awards include a National Endowment for the Arts Literature Fellowship and the William Rockhill Nelson Award. He was appointed the first Poet Laureate of Missouri in 2008-2009. He can be found online at www.walterbargen. com. His twentieth collection, *Too Quick for the Living*, will be published by Moon City Press in November as part of its Missouri Author Series.

Sarah Broderick grew up in the Ohio River Valley and now resides in northern California. Currently, she is at work on a novel as well as a nonfiction project based in her hometown. She can be found online at perfectsentences.org, on Twitter at @sebroderick. She edits *The Forge Literary Magazine*.

Thomas Shipp Burnett lives in Eau Claire, Wisconsin. He is currently working on a novel.

A former stringer for *The Boston Globe*, **Marty Carlock** is a contributing editor of *Sculpture* magazine. She also writes for *Landscape Architecture Magazine* and *The Internet Review of Books*. Her short fiction and poetry have been published in a dozen or so literary quarterlies.

Mallory Chesser has an MFA in fiction from Texas State University and lives in Houston, where she works for a nonprofit organization conducting medical mission trips to Guatemala. She serves as managing editor for *Story|Houston* and has work forthcoming in *Electric Literature*.

Steven Chung is a high-school student who currently lives in the San Francisco Bay Area. His poetry has appeared or is forthcoming in *Rattle, The Offing, Potomac Review, inter|rupture*, and elsewhere.

Pat Daneman's poems have appeared in many print and online journals, most recently *The Stonecoast Review, Smoky Blue Literary and Arts Magazine, South 85 Journal*, and *Escape Into Life*. Her chapbook, *Where the World Begins*, was published in 2015 by Finishing Line Press. This is her second appearance in *Moon City Review*.

John Paul Davis is a poet, musician, and programmer. His work has appeared in numerous journals and anthologies, including *Rattle, Muzzle, Word Riot, decomP*, and *Again I Wait For This To Pull Apart* (FreezeRay Press, 2015). Find out more about him at www.johnpauldavis.org.

Karen Donovan is the author of *Fugitive Red* (University of Massachusetts Press, 1999), which won the Juniper Prize for Poetry, and *Your Enzymes Are Calling the Ancients*, which won the Lexi Rudnitsky/Editor's Choice Award from Persea Books and was published in 2016.

Wendy Drexler's new collection, *Before There Was Before*, will be published by Iris Press this April. Her first book, *Western Motel*, from Turning Point, appeared in 2012. Her poems can be found in *Mid-American Review, Nimrod, Prairie Schooner, Salamander*, and other journals.

Matt Dube teaches American literature and creative writing in central Missouri. His stories have appeared in *Hartskill Review, Front Porch, Unbroken*, and elsewhere.

Sarah Freligh is the author of *Sad Math* (Moon City Press, 2015), winner of the 2014 Moon City Poetry Award and the 2015 Etchings Press Whirling Prize from the University of Indianapolis. Among her awards are a 2009 Literature Fellowship for poetry from the National Endowment for the Arts and a grant from the Constance Saltonstall Foundation for the Arts in 2006.

Kerri French was recently awarded the 2016 Moon City Poetry Award—her book, *Every Room in the Body*, is forthcoming from Moon City Press this fall. *Instruments of Summer* (2013), her chapbook of poems about Amy Winehouse, is available from dancing girl press. She lives and writes outside of Nashville.

Sheri Gabbert is a substitute teacher living in the Missouri Ozarks. Her work has been published in *Rat's Ass Review, new graffiti, 417 Magazine*, and *The Lawrence County Record*. She is the mother of Joe Brennan, deceased. "What do I know?" is dedicated to him.

John Gifford is the author of *Wish You Were Here* (Big Table Publishing Company, 2016), a collection of very short fiction. His work has appeared in *Harpur Palate, The Los Angeles Review, Cold Mountain Review, december*, and elsewhere. He lives in Oklahoma.

Katherine Gordon, a Midwesterner by birth, studied at the University of Glasgow, where she obtained a doctorate in Scottish literature. Her work has been widely published in the United States and the United Kingdom.

Benjamin Harnett is a poet, fiction writer, digital engineer, and historian. He holds a master's degree in classical studies from Columbia University and works for *The New York Times*. In 2005, he co-founded the fashion brand Hayden-Harnett. He lives in Brooklyn with his wife, Toni.

Dwight Hilson is a onetime businessman now writing through the midlife crisis with an MFA from the Vermont College of Fine Arts. His short fiction has appeared in numerous publications.

Andy Jameson lives in Greenwood, South Carolina, with his wife and daughter. His stories have appeared in *Harpur Palate, Sixfold, South Dakota Review*, and *Green Hills Literary Lantern*.

Erin Jones holds an MFA in poetry from the University of Florida. Her poems have appeared or are forthcoming in *Pleiades, Fourteen Hills, Passages North, The Journal*, and elsewhere.

Soon Jones is a recent graduate of Missouri State University and an assistant editor of *Moon City Review*. This is her first publication.

Sam Killmeyer is an MFA candidate at Colorado State University. Her chapbook, *Cups*, was a finalist for the Autumn House Press contest. Her poems can be found in *Chicago Quarterly Review*, *Coal Hill Review*, *Pith*, and elsewhere.

Tara Kipnees is a writer living in South Orange, New Jersey. Her work has appeared in *decomP*, *Serving House Journal*, *Tikkun*, and *Salon*, among other publications.

Angie Macri is the author of *Underwater Panther* (Southeast Missouri State University Press, 2015), winner of the Cowles Poetry Book Prize, and *Fear Nothing of the Future or the Past* (Finishing Line Press, 2014). Her recent work appears in *Arkana*, *Cimarron Review*, and *Redactions*. An Arkansas Arts Council fellow, she lives in Hot Springs.

Kim Magowan lives in San Francisco and teaches at Mills College. Her fiction has been published in *Atticus Review*, *The Gettysburg Review*, *Hobart*, *JMWW*, and other journals. She is working on a novel and a short-story collection.

John McNally is the author of several books, including *Lord of the Ralphs* (Lacewing Books, 2015), a young adult novel; *After the Workshop: A Novel* (Counterpoint, 2010); *Ghosts of Chicago* (Jefferson Press, 2008); and *Vivid and Continuous: Essays and Exercises for Writing Fiction* (University of Iowa Press, 2013). He divides his time between Lafayette, Louisiana, and Winston-Salem, North Carolina.

Michael Meyerhofer's fourth book, *What To Do If You're Buried Alive* (2015), was published by Split Lip Press. He is also the author of a fantasy series and the poetry editor for *Atticus Review*. Visit him at www.troublewithhammers.com.

Terry Minchow-Proffitt is a poet and pastor who lives in St. Louis. His poems have appeared in a variety of magazines and journals. He has published a chapbook, *Seven Last Words* (2015), and, most recently, his first full collection, *Chicken Train: Poems From the Arkansas Delta* (2016), both through Middle Island Press.

Travis Mossotti was awarded the 2011 May Swenson Poetry Award for his first collection of poems, *About the Dead* (Utah State University Press, 2011). His second collection, *Field Study*, won the 2013 Melissa Lanitis Gregory Poetry Prize (Bona Fide Books, 2014).

Jason Namey is a graduate student at the University of Alaska Fairbanks, where he edits prose for *Permafrost Magazine*. His stories appear or are forthcoming in *Hobart*, *FLAPPERHOUSE*, *Phantom Drift*, *NANO Fiction*, and elsewhere. He was also a finalist for the 2016 Subito Book Prize.

L.W. Nicholson is an English instructor, high school librarian, and homesteader in southeast Missouri. Her work has appeared in *Arkana* and *Sundog Lit*.

Daniel Paul received his MFA from Southern Illinois University. His fiction, nonfiction, and humor writing has appeared or is forthcoming in *Puerto del Sol*, *The Briar Cliff Review*, *New Delta Review*, and other magazines. He lives in Ohio, where he is currently pursuing a doctorate at the University of Cincinnati.

After receiving a master's degree in English literature from the University of Denver, **Alita Pirkopf** became increasingly interested in feminist interpretations of literature. Years later she enrolled in a poetry class, after which poetry became a long-term focus and necessity.

Ösel Jessica Plante's poetry and fiction have appeared or is forthcoming in *The Best Small Fictions 2016* anthology, *Mid-American Review*, *New Ohio Review*, *Puerto del Sol*, *Zone 3*, and other journals. She is pursuing a doctorate at Florida State University.

Reba Rice was raised in the mountains of Idaho and now lives in Los Angeles, working as an editorial assistant at Red Hen Press. Other work has been published by or is forthcoming from *The Lullwater Review* and *Rust + Moth*.

Staci R. Schoenfeld received a 2015 National Endowment for the Arts Literature Fellowship for Poetry. She is a doctoral student at the

University of South Dakota and the associate editor of poetry for *South Dakota Review*. Recent poems appear in *Rogue Agent*, *Rust + Moth*, and *Thrush*. Her chapbook, *The Patient Admits*, is forthcoming from dancing girl press in summer 2017.

Noel Sloboda is the author of the poetry collections *Our Rarer Monsters* (sunnyoutside, 2013) and *Shell Games* (sunnyoutside, 2008) as well as several chapbooks, most recently *Risk Management Studies* (Kattywompus Press, 2015). He has also published a book about Edith Wharton and Gertrude Stein (Peter Lang Inc., 2008).

Evelyn Somers is the associate editor of *The Missouri Review*. Her writing has appeared in *Southwest Review*, *The Florida Review*, *The Georgia Review*, and *Crazyhorse*, among other journals. She is finishing a second novel.

J. David Stevens teaches English and creative writing at the University of Richmond. His most recent work appears in *The Gettysburg Review*, *Meridian*, and *Denver Quarterly*.

Kendra Tanacea holds a BA in English from Wellesley College and an MFA in writing and literature from Bennington College. Her book, *A Filament Burns in Blue Degrees*, will be published by Lost Horse Press in 2017. Her poems have appeared in *5AM*, *Rattle*, *Stickman Review*, and *The Coachella Review*, among other journals. She can be found online at kendratanacea.com.

Laura Lee Washburn is Director of Creative Writing at Pittsburg State University and the author of *This Good Warm Place: 10th Anniversary Expanded Edition* (March Street, 2007) and *Watching the Contortionists* (Palanquin Press Chapbook Prize). Her poetry has appeared in such journals as *The Carolina Quarterly*, *Ninth Letter*, *The Sun*, and *Red Rock Review*.

Charles Harper Webb's latest book of poems, *Brain Camp*, was published by the University of Pittsburgh Press in 2015. *A Million MFAs Are Not Enough* (2016), essays on contemporary American poetry, is just out from Red Hen Press.

Bronisław Wildstein was born in Olsztyn, Poland. He is a writer, journalist, and columnist for the Polish weekly *W Sieci* and the host of *Poludnik Wildsteina* (*Wildstein's Meridian*), his own weekly program on Polish Public Television (TVP). He is the author of seventeen books and the recipient of numerous prestigious Polish prizes and awards. He was also a prominent member of the opposition movement in the 1970s and an activist in *Solidarność*.

Margot Wizansky's poems appear in many journals and anthologies. She won the Writers@Work Fellowship. The Patricia Dobler Poetry Award took her to the Isle of Innisfree, Ireland. She transcribed the oral history of her late friend, Emerson Stamps, the grandson of slaves: *Don't Look Them In The Eye: Love, Life, and Jim Crow* (Shell Beach Press, 2009).

Chad Woody is a writer, printmaker, scavenger, and building maintenance troubleshooter. He lives in Springfield, Missouri, with wife and daughter.

Ian Woollen lives in Bloomington, Indiana, with his musician wife. His day job is psychotherapy. Recent short fiction has surfaced in *Bartleby Snopes*, *SmokeLong Quarterly*, and *Fiction Southeast*. A new novel, *MUIR WOODS OR BUST*, is due out this summer from Coffeetown Press.

Christopher Adam Zakrzewski is the author of an award-winning English rendering of the Polish classic, *Pan Tadeusz*. Among the contemporary Polish writers he has translated are Kazimierz Braun, Maciej Patkowski, Krzysztof Koehler, Joanna Rostropowicz Clark, Aleksandra Ziółkowska-Boehm, Danuta Kostewicz, and Leszek Czuchajowski. He is an adjunct professor of languages and literature at Our Lady Seat of Wisdom in Ontario, Canada.

Tara Isabel Zambrano lives in Texas with her husband and two kids. Her fiction has appeared or is forthcoming in *Gargoyle*, *Lunch Ticket*, *Juked*, *Parcel*, and other journals. She is an electrical engineer by profession.

CPSIA information can be obtained
at www.ICGtesting.com
Printed in the USA
FFOW03n1025230917
40240FF